An ominous presence awakens in the small town of Gamin.

Fairies murdered by crazed monsters. Magic that makes immortals lose their minds and their heads (literally). Whispers of a vendetta against the fairy crime lords who own the infamous Kraken Club.

One ace siren detective, Lili, is dragged back into defending her turf...and hopefully, she doesn't die this time around.

WAKE THE DEAD

Gamin Immortals, Book Two

Sophie Whittemore

A NineStar Press Publication

www.ninestarpress.com

Wake the Dead

ISBN: 978-1-64890-654-1

First Edition, May, 2023

Also available in eBook, ISBN: 978-1-64890-653-4

WARNING:

This book contains depictions of murder and death.

To my grandmothers who left this world behind—Elizabeth and Katherine. Thank you for teaching me what love is.

And to my loved ones, I love you dearly.

Prologue

The Kraken Club

The Kuntilanak's name was Indah, at least, it was in the strip club. Her long, black hair wrapped like a shroud around her body as she circled the pole. When her hair coiled past her shoulders, it revealed the nail sticking out of the back of her neck, thick as a child's fist, the color of rust and blood. Black rope was tied around her legs, cuffing them to the soles of the boots she wore as heels. A tall and thin man, a fairy, with willow-emerald skin and eyes the color of lotus leaves, held out a wad of dollar bills. He placed them at her feet.

"Smile," he told her.

She did, baring her fangs.

The fairy grinned. "Ah." He traced his thumb against those fangs, still grinning as she sank them into skin that tasted of rotting leaves and nectar. The fangs retracted when he didn't flinch. "Like a vampire."

Indah laughed, bending over to pocket the bills in one smooth movement. "The vampires wish they were Kuntilanak like me."

As soon as she pressed the bills to the glittering zip-up pouch at her thigh, they disappeared. The fairy waggled his long, thin fingers. "Alakazam." He chuckled even though this wasn't a laughing matter. Being of fairy blood, he couldn't care less.

"Fae magic doesn't feed me. Money does. So, if you're not willing to pay with real cash, then get out." She spat at his eye, praying he went blind. "Setan."

She moved toward the bathroom, taking the long way around so she wouldn't run into the handsy Ljósálfar manning the bar with his light-blond hair and translucent skin. He thought he was handsome, and he took many a mortal woman to bed, but his overconfidence turned the Kuntilanak girl off him.

Overconfidence just made you all the more of an asshole, and she knew his type. Pelle was just another elf acting as a handler in this gods-forsaken place.

She slammed into the bathroom and took the sink covered in the least amount of glitter and wadded tissue paper. She splashed under her armpits and near her groin, counting the feeble bills she'd collected in the first hour of the night.

The blue bathroom door swung lazily open behind her, screeching against tile. "Fuck off, Pelle!" She screamed it out, hoping she could scare him off.

Instead, it was the green fairy. He stood in front of her with his legs splayed wide, his eyes focused on her face.

"You again? I'm not for free." She raised her middle finger, water trickling down the sides of her face. Smelling a sweet-smoky mix of nail polish and cigarettes in *the back.*

No reaction. His eyes stayed focused on her face.

"Hello? Fairy dude, you doing all right?"

His neck bent backward then slammed forward again. Something splintered: wood, blood, and bone. "They're coming," he said. "The ones who see all."

Then he struck.

His weight slammed into her, willow skin flaking off into the sink. She scratched at his arms, but he wouldn't stop, not even as the room erupted into the scent of over-due flowers and root rot. He went for her throat, taking her long wrap of hair and tugging backward. She choked and gasped, her hands against his chest, fingers digging into his skin.

Fluorescent lights flickered above her as she stared at the ceiling. One moment, then two.

Death called to the death in her blood.

She reached back to the nail behind her head, the one she promised not to remove if she wished to stay in Gamin. She'd heard what happened to the old Greek god-dess, the one who couldn't control her bloodthirst and went mad. She knew of the demon who played detective, the watchdog over all their sorry souls. Maybe Indah might look like a pretty jinn or guardian spirit, but she couldn't hold herself back any longer.

She couldn't hold back her true form.

She dug the nail out with a screech. Her long hair grew to her feet, her teeth extending past the pretty fangs. Blood dripped from her eyes and her tongue split into two as veins stood out against her skin, the muscles creaking and stretching to their full potential. Her feet and hands hooked like claws. She grew a head taller than the possessed green fairy.

"Setan," she spat.

It was the last thing that echoed in the green fairy's skull.

*

Moments later, Pelle, the bartending Ljósálfar, brought some of his pretty elf friends to see what was going on in the locked bathroom. When he brought the door down, Indah was sitting with the green man's contorted body resting on her lap. The nail was back in her neck.

"He attacked me," she explained, her gaze the glassy calm of shock. "I don't know what he was on. Something strong. Something that made him forget himself... Forgetting." She paused. "Do you think Lethe is at it again?"

"Call the detective," Pelle told his elf buddies. "Whatever this is, making everyone lose their heads"—he grimaced at the choice of words—"we don't want it in Gamin."

Chapter One

Welcome to Hotel Hell

THE WORLD IS a chrysalis waiting, desperately, for something to happen. And when things happen, that means chaos follows. And when chaos follows, someone inevitably writes something akin to the Book of Revelations.

The Book of Revelations is nestled between the thumb and forefinger of the wandering priest sitting with one leg crossed over the other in the lobby of the Sweeney Inn. A glass cup beads, crying condensation, at his side. He has stubble he probably dreams will, one day, become a beard.

He really shouldn't have a beard.

I shouldn't be thinking like that. There could be a mind reader in this very room. Gamin attracts those types more than most places. It attracts the magical like rats to disease. It's the magic river that does it, the magic hiding us from the human world. So, case in point, there very well might be a mind reader in this very room.

Hey, asshole, if you're reading my mind, and I smile

as I think this, *fuck off.*

The round-bellied, redheaded, and altogether-too-good-for-her-own-good witch beside me, Patty, scowls at the priest bearing the Book of Revelations. Specifically, she scowls at the mud caking his shoes. "He's dragging it all over the place." She watches the floor, how his legs swing across it. "I don't care if he's a priest. If he muddies the ground—" She ties her frizzy red hair back from her round face, making me wonder if she really will sock him. Her absolute kickass attitude never ceases to amaze me, and if fate took other chances, I would not hesitate to make her my dream girlfriend.

"He'll meet his Maker?" I finish for her.

She smirks, leaning her chubby, freckled arms against the front desk. She's about to answer when the man gets to his feet and crosses toward us. He's not too tall, about my height, with dark hair, thick brows, and skin that glows like a penny in the sun.

"Welcome to the Sweeney Inn," Patty declares, a little glint of pride in her eyes. A businesswoman growing comfortable in her power suit. Her brother, Jason Sweeney, keeps the books. Patty leads the running of this place, and she runs such a tight ship that her orders even make me weary at times.

Together, they run the (Evil) Eye Inc., your friendly neighborhood necromancy corporation and local coven business. Being younger, they've moved a lot of the business online with tech-wizard friend Erik Borden doing most of the magical for-your-eyes-only monster coding.

You heard me.

Witches are getting into the Silicon Valley big tech

startup business.

What's the world coming to?

I look around the lobby again and notice a tiny ghost rat scurry in one of the corners, still carrying the piece of poisoned cheese that ended its life.

It's a work in progress.

"Your name?" I ask the handsome stranger, my pen poised over the check-in book.

He points to the paper and pen. "Really, no computer?" He has crooked bottom teeth, but it doesn't detract from the glow in his smile.

I shrug. "I'm old, therefore, I'm old-fashioned."

He leans in a little closer at that statement. The Roman collar, a clerical collar, at his neck peeks out. "You look hardly twenty."

"Many people have told me that. Well, mostly people." Patty casts me a withering look at the inside joke. I point to the book. "Name?"

"One room." He falters at how far I've already skipped in the usual check-in process. "And my name is Adam. Adam Way." He pronounces it "*Aadom.*"

"Father Way?" I ask.

He nods. "As you say."

Oh, a poet. I hate poets.

"What brings you to Gamin?" Patty takes the crumpled bills he pulls from his wallet, watching him just as suspiciously as I do. This wouldn't be the first time a stranger tried to pull the wool over eyes. There was a ghūl just last week who tried to party with a selkie during a bachelors' party...ugh, the *teeth* on that one, I assure you it was—

"Training." He fixes his collar.

"For?" Patty shifts over, pressing his change into his open palm.

"The town's priest—" *I'm honestly surprised this town still has priests considering the string of murders that occurred a few months ago.* "—he asked me here for a very special reason. He wants me to become a purifier. No, that's not quite it. You will think it's silly, like the movies."

"I assure you"—and here Patty and I grin in unison—"we'll believe in anything."

"I am training to become an exorcist. I'm afraid my family back in Lebanon still hope I can become a lawyer or a scholar or something. Fight for justice. Get married again instead of chasing after some spiritual quest." He lowers his head and looks conspiratorially at me. "But I'm sure your parents act the same way."

I sign off on the rest of the book, checking off prepared rooms, and reach for a keycard for him from under the desk. "I don't have family back anywhere. I came from, well, I suppose it's..." *Ancient Mesopotamia. Now it's Iran, Iraq, Kuwait, Turkey, and Syria.* "But I left home a long time ago. My home, the home I knew...the people. That whole world is gone. It doesn't need me anymore."

"You left to go where?"

"Wandering the world. Traveling extensively." *Murdering. Thieving. Gathering an army of the damned, but who's counting? That was old Lili. Now, I'm changed. I've grown soft.*

Adam takes his keycard and nods at that. "I'm sorry. Without family, it must be hard."

I close my eyes and think of the strange little community I've recruited here in Gamin. Patty and Jason Sweeney, necromancer siblings. Byron the ghost and his boyfriend, Erik Borden, a techno-wizard (literally). Detective Ikiaq, a shapeshifter as old as I am.

And Jo. Jo Kim. My *gangshi,* soul devouring partner. Forever asleep because of a mistake I made, chasing after an oracle punk who turned out to be an angry Greek goddess with a murderous chip on her shoulder.

But instead of telling him all that, I say, "I found my family. Eventually."

He looks another moment into my eyes with his dark ones, his hand matching my complexion, the shade of the sun that made me when I wandered the world as a powerful goddess of Sumer, Lilitu. His hair's clipped back, perhaps a deterrent for his sex appeal as a priest, but it does a poor job of it. A gathering of ladies at a bachelorette party nearby whisper about how they'd "want the priest to come to the party *before* the wedding and not after."

Even the slight case of sideburns only serves to accentuate his tense jaw, his teeth gritted in nervousness. Everything about him is tightly wound, a watch ticking in a gentleman's pocket, waiting to spring.

Those are always the most fun to break.

"Of course." He nods. The gaggle of ladies behind him giggle as he turns around and raises his hand in what could be a wave, a blessing, or both. "We all need family in these trying times. The world seems to be on fire, if you've read anything of the news or heard the gossip lately."

"We didn't start the fire!" Patty quips, already launching into a half-hearted humming of Billy Joel.

"You act older than me sometimes," I gripe at her, biting my tongue back as I note Adam's curiosity. Patty and I may both look twenty-one, but I've seen empires fall eons before she even learned they existed. Or before she existed, for that matter.

Adam, smiling, clutches his room key and his Bible in hand, his simple faux leather soles shuffling against the lobby floors as he turns toward his room. "Funny. My room number is 177. One more seven, and I might be considered blessed." He bows a little toward me, the movement stiff, his eyes a little too curious for my comfort. "But it was a blessing to meet you, *Lili.*"

As he turns around, I'm cursing beneath my breath. *What is he, a mind reader?*

"How in the nine Hells did he know my—?"

Patty stops me by pointing at my lapel, where my nametag reads my printed name, "Lili," alongside "concierge" beneath. "Cool it, Sherlock. Not everything has to be the start of some mystical case file with you. What is this, a TV show?"

She picks up a stack of newly printed Gamin town maps from beneath the desk and goes to restock the sad little pile next to the magazines by the door. Funnily enough, the maps mention town destinations like the riverfront, historic town hall, and hiking in the woods.

The pamphlets say nothing about the dead bodies of sirens, the cursed waters that make you forget your memory, or the string of serial killer murders that, somehow, flew under the radar thanks to a fair bit of magic.

Monsters make great bedtime stories but horrible

advertising.

Adam goes off to his room. The bachelorette party goes to get drunk in our brown bar. And us? We shuffle out from behind the desk, wanting to stretch our legs after standing in the same, listless position for so long. Putting maps at the front of the lobby just to give us an excuse to do something. *Anything.*

"*Three,*" I say, breaking the silence finally.

Patty glances over, curious. "Three what?"

"Three months, Patty. It's only been three months since we caught Lethe." I pick up a map from the pile and leaf through it. I stop at a cheery mention of some no-name diner with fraying booths and too-thick pancakes, too-thin bacon. "And suddenly, everything's just back to normal again? There could be a copycat killer out there following in Lethe's footsteps. And Detective Ikiaq might remember how well I did on the last case—"

"You're not a detective," Patty tells me.

"But I could be," I reply.

"You were at the right place at the right time," Patty huffs, fixing my nametag and pointing to the empty cups that need replenishing by the water coolers. "Don't consider yourself Gamin's private eye after happening to catch one killer. You don't have a license."

"Not everyone who's skilled in a profession has a license."

"No, but they sure make you feel better when the dentist is performing your root canal." She glances at me with an intense side-eye, a habit she's adopted from her twin brother, both with the same red-blonde hair, freckles, flushed pale skin, and pesky habit of ignoring their self-preservation instinct. "What's with the rant, Lil? Have you been dreaming again?"

"Immortals don't dream. We have memories that we fall back into, uncontrollable visions." I examine my fingernails, just regular mortal length, clipped and harmless. No talons that could skewer three grown men. No growing to the size of city buildings in my true form. No unleashing of power.

No terrorizing, there's just fear that I'll do it again. Lose control.

"Tell me, Lili. I'll try to understand. What's been going on?" Her honey-hued eyes bore into mine, trying to find some semblance of my soul, I suppose.

I exhale, thinking of the memories that hurt so much to remember. "I miss her, Pats." I think on the last vision I had, a week ago, the one I wanted to fall into so badly that I banged my head against a wall for an hour afterward, only stopping when I worried about freaking my neighbors out. "I remember everything about what it was like to see her conscious. Her eyes dancing as they stayed on mine. Holding her in my arms, smelling like hair dye and cigarettes in the bathroom where we first confessed our feelings to each other. Hell, I'd even have her put a hole in me again with that shotgun of hers just to see her living. I'd do it again and again just so I could say, 'I love you' and ruffle her short-cropped blue-black hair and drink Bloody Marys with her with the actual blood intact and..."

"Shit!" Patty leans over to pick up a fallen magazine with a sprig of lavender in it to promote household harmony and curses as her phone slips out of her pocket.

Beneath the table holding the magazines, Patty's carved out a small ward to keep guests in good spirits while waiting in line. "Sorry, love, keep telling me about your vision." Patty's gaze is filled with—and this hurts to think about—*pity*, as her eyes stare into mine. "At least... I mean, at least you had Jo Kim while she was..."

"Awake? *Alive*?" I sigh, digging my thumbs against my eyes, wondering if tearing them out would hurt less. "What is living anymore for a true immortal or reanimated? Existing is hard enough."

"Better than dying. I'm perfectly content *not* fearing for my life, thank you very much." Patty blows a loose curl out of her eyes as I slowly return her smile. "I'm set on wild, crazy adventures for a good, *long* time. Thank you."

Patty's cell phone screen lights up as the ringtone blares, something from that indie college crooner she likes, the one with the androgynous stage persona and the lip-biting habit. The contact reads, "DETECTIVE IKIAQ" with a small smiley face symbol beside it. I pluck the cell phone out of her hand before she can pick it up.

"Hey, don't you have your own?" Patty grumbles.

I wave my smartphone at her. "The AI thing always cusses me out in Italian. We're fighting right now." I angrily switch my own phone off as I steal Patty's. "Hello?"

A heavy sigh from the other end of the line. "Lili, did it ever occur to you that I might be actually trying to reach Patty?"

I laugh extra loudly, "Ah, detective, you're so funny."

"You're on speaker phone, dumbass." Patty flips me off as she goes to fetch more maps from the front desk.

I switch the speaker phone off as the detective tunes

back in. "Well, you're lucky that I'm going to need all of you back for this case. We have a murder involving quite a few Gamin reanimated and immortals. The mythical underbelly of this town might talk more freely to you than to me if we need to interrogate them."

"You mean I'm more intimidating than you." I gloat.

"You're reckless and violent, yes," the detective gripes. "But word travels fast in Gamin, especially about the hotshot demon who tracked down a killer of monsters. The legendary townsfolk respect a legend even more powerful than them."

"And Patty?"

"The Sweeney siblings have a way of...controlling you, to put it nicely. Last time you went full-on and skewered Lethe with a giant talon, you'd left the Sweeneys behind entirely."

"A dog without a leash?" I offer. "And my friends are the leash."

"Precisely. Why do you keep interrogating me like this?" The detective pauses, sipping from his favorite mug of hot chocolate, I'd presume.

"I just wanted to hear you admit that I'm *bigger* than you, at least in my true form." I try to contain the smile in my voice, the sick morbid fascination that would get my mind off this sense of ennui. This nothingness of pining over a broken heart, trying to wake someone whose soul was even more lost than mine. "Show me the body."

Chapter Two

But I'm a detective!

THE KRAKEN CLUB sits at the edge of Gamin, a few miles left from the gas station where Lethe murdered the monster hunter, Dakari Borden, in her sick fantasy quest to get to me. The strip club is hidden behind a billboard where a half-naked selkie with her furs draped dramatically around her neck poses with her hands on her knees, deep-set eyes staring out at the world like they're trapped in the advertisement. Wanting to be set free. The headline over her shoulders reads:

GIRLS OUT OF THIS WORLD!

(Only at the Kraken Club 18+)

"Out of this world." I smirk, shaking my head as Patty's lips draw into a thin line at the advertisement. "Don't they know it."

Patty rolls her eyes. "Chill with the one-liners, Top Gun."

We get out of Patty's bumblebee-yellow car, parked

beside Detective Ikiaq's shorter-framed vehicle with thick, dramatic plumes of exhaust. The detective sports a new peacoat that drapes dramatically from his large, stout frame. He brought Toothpick as his partner, the scrawny half-werewolf rookie with acne and a squeaky voice. The native Inuk *Ijiraq* shapeshifter towers over the "fearsome" barely-out-of-college werewolf, really acting more as Toothpick's elder brother than anything else.

Detective Ikiaq looks every inch the fearsome true immortal that he is. Not just a human who has some magic or a human who died and became one of the *reanimated*. Anyone who is of immortal stock was created at the beginning of time and will roam the world, most likely, until its end. They are the ones mortal mythology placed as its gods, its creation, and its heroes or worst of its demons. The reanimated are the bratty upstarts who were once human, but now believe they are of the gods. And the mortals with a little bit of power, necromancers, witches, etc., they're still human. Just with a little flavor mixed in.

I place my hands in the pockets of my peacoat, nodding at the detective's new style. "Copying my look, detective?" I stick my tongue out at him.

He laughs, the sound deep from his belly, calming with an edge of old danger, and does a little twirl, his aviator glasses sliding down his nose. He reaches into his pocket and hands me a matching set. "Wondered when you'd show up, Nancy Drew." His mortal façade flickers out of existence for a moment. If you see him from the edge of your vision, he turns into a skeletal figure from your nightmares, hunched and humanoid. Jaw dislocated and slavering, with bone antlers sprouting from his skull.

But from the front, he's just amiable Detective Ikiaq, law of Gamin.

That is, only if you don't know any better.

I put on the glasses and check myself out in the reflection of his car. Hair plaited into raven braids; eyes turned vibrant silver. Everything looks sharper about me, like I'm bursting out of my skin.

Literally, if I lose my mind and transform into that...that beast again.

Lili, the god that time forgot and mortals misremembered.

Yup, that's me.

Mother of monsters.

Best remember it. You'll need it for later.

I snatch Detective Ikiaq's telltale hot chocolate out of his hands, take all the cream and chocolate off it, then hand it back to him. "Call me Nancy Drew again, I dare you. Next time, you lose your head."

The detective just laughs at me. "Ah, Lili. Same as you ever were."

"What happened here?" I ask, but the mood noticeably falls at that.

The detective and Toothpick, the acne-possessing werewolf, exchange an uneasy look, then glance back at the cracked glass door of the Kraken Club, gaudy neon lights disguising the hole in the front. Waves of energy radiate off it. Desperation. Fear. And the power, magic repressed. Magic unleashed with lethal results. Patty shudders beside me, retreating within her burgundy hoodie, hands hidden beneath her armpits.

"The report you sent me said decapitation. This

monster's got a dramatic streak, huh?" I pause for a moment before going for the front door. I can see a mix of mortal, reanimated, and magical human clientele through the windows. No immortals, not unless they're in hiding or trying to be discreet.

Too bad I'm not.

*

Questionably having a good time

(But not a long time)

I STEP INSIDE, hit with a wave of sweat and dried liquor, some of it regular, some tinged with magic. Ambrosia, mead, and cheap beer and wine. Vodka splashed with nectar of the gods, chasers mixed with sake, amaranth, and blood. A runway where eternally youthful men, women, and those in between or not at all strutted. Dressed in little, showing much. Except for the scars that didn't quite fit, puzzle pieces glamoured to appear something akin to mortal.

The floor's beaten in with glitter and varnish. The walls are frosted mirrors that seem to reflect off into a disorienting infinity. The ceiling boasts a low hanging, lazily spinning disco ball flashing in iridescent sparks that ultimately lead to nothing. The bar is populated by a host of green-tinged skin, tattoos like scales, and piercings that glint like wings. You wouldn't be able to tell mortal apart from monster. Not unless you had a monster-hunter Seer on you or didn't belong entirely to this realm.

Patty flinches, pressing her thumb and forefinger to

the bridge of her nose to clear her vision.

"Are you all right?" I hold out my arm as she takes it, trying to regain her balance.

Toothpick even looks a little queasy, his teeth elongating slightly and the hair on his forearms prickly. The werewolf in him called upon as his adrenaline flight-or-fight instinct kicks in.

Detective Ikiaq kicks a couple of chairs over with his boot. A red-faced human with a kitsune young man on his knee shouts at us. He goes instantly silent when I snarl at him. The detective reaches into his jacket, pulls out tiny bottles of water, and tosses them to Patty and Toothpick.

"Be careful of the glamours. The Fae syndicate runs this joint, and it gets disorienting fast for those of mortal stock," the detective rumbles.

The red-faced human beside us takes up pomegranate seeds by the fistful. The kitsune, fox ears and tail flicking, looks relieved as his client distracts himself with the ever-replenishing red plastic cup of beer.

"The faster they fall, the quicker their wallets empty out," I murmur, and the words are thick as the pomegranate seed juice spilling on the floor. Bodyguards stand at the front. They look reanimated or mixed with some kind of immortal blood. I can't see into their eyes, deep wells. Their skin is cracked clay. "Golem guards just boot the broke ones out of here once they're finished and have no more money to give. Like so much trash."

"Not that different from a politician," Patty quips, shaking her head clear and passing the water bottle back for me to tuck away.

"Where's Jason?" the detective asks, looking at the

door as though Patty's twin will waltz through at any moment.

Patty shrugs. "He spends a lot of time in New York lately. He doesn't like staying in Gamin for long. Ever since..."

There's a lot of ways to finish that sentence. Ever since he lost his arm in the Dead Realms. Ever since me and him got in a fight and he accused me of murder. Ever since he had to recover from the traumatic, not-of-this-world experiences chasing after a serial killer three months ago...

I wouldn't say we were ever best friends, but now, the most I could hope Jason would have with me is a little bit of tolerance.

Patty pointedly avoids my gaze. "But he carries on his work remotely. For the inn and the coven and such. And he comes back. He always comes back."

Detective Ikiaq looks as though he's about to say something when a man walks toward us, his skin so pale it's see-through, with long platinum-blond hair and a couple of choice piercings.

"We got company..." the detective warns with a rumble.

The newcomer looks like that kind of walking, model-like sex appeal you see in big cities, the perfect amount of wannabe Mr. Right mixed with a generous dash of wrong and faux designer.

A light elf. I don't like how he keeps staring at Patty and me, like conquests. When his gaze lingers on me, I take great care to flip him off.

"Oh look," Patty grumbles, getting shakily to her feet.

"Legolas got an undercut."

Excellent hearing, wonderful. We love eavesdropping elves.

He smirks, nodding. "Ah, a full frame and gorgeous curves. I like a woman who's unapologetically herself."

Patty shakes his hand, brief as possible. "Thanks, I like women too."

"Ah." He shakes the detective's hand and Toothpick's next, leaving me for last. "And you are?"

"I'm not giving my name in a Fae establishment." My voice is so cold, it should be a carrier for frostbite.

"I'm *Ljósálfar*, not Fae. Nordic mythology, I'm afraid, darling." He nods. "And we all know who you are, Lili, after you...*unleashed*, as it were. Though you have *many* names, don't you? Too many to count. Tsk, tsk..." He smiles, though it doesn't reach his eyes. "Clever way to avoid the Fae. But they're so petty, they might just try to find another way to get to you." The warning dissipates as he focuses on a flourishing, courtly bow like I saw back in the Elizabethan courts. "I just run the bar here at this wonderful establishment. Babysit the working pretty young things, tasks like that. You may call me Pelle"—he smiles wider at me—"or anything you'd like."

"Demisexual, and I'm taken," I bite back, turning away from him. "You can try Toothpick, if you'd like, though. He's single."

"Hey now!" Toothpick squeaks. "I'm on the job."

Pelle's eyes widen at that, his eyebrows raising in a wrinkle-free forehead. "On the job?" He looks to Ikiaq and his demeanor instantly snaps to all-business. "Ah, not customers then, but here as detectives. Wondrous, I loved reading about Sherlock. He was asexual too, you know." He winks at me. "So, I suppose you'll want to see the body."

"We'll need to see the girl who was found with him too," the detective says as we follow him down a dank hallway to where the bathrooms are located, most of the stall doors missing from their hinges.

"Woman, not girl," Patty interjects. "I'm assuming she's over eighteen. Or eighteen thousand with how immortals are."

"Yes, my bad. The woman," the detective remarks.

Pelle still faces front and away from us, fixing his brows in the mirror. "Oh, is she guilty until proven innocent?"

"We're immortals, but we don't work that way," Detective Ikiaq informs him.

"Don't get me wrong, the *Ljósálfar* are of your stock, detective. We began since mortal imagination could fathom us. But the Fae, on the other hand..." He laughs, pressing his hand to the silver chain at his neck. "My employers run by Fae rules. Fae time. They will want revenge for the murder. Besides, I can't help you there. She skipped town as soon as we found her with the body." He glances down at his faux-leather shoes, tapping his toe against the sink's edge. "The Fae will bring her to justice soon enough."

We look around the bathroom, empty, if a little grungy. "And where is the body?" My words echo off the walls, bouncing off words and graffiti with anti-mortal sentiment. Sigils and renditions of sexual anatomy, human and otherwise.

He pauses for a moment before going into the only stall with a locked door. He opens this with a skeleton key. He pinches the air over the toilet, revealing a shimmering curtain so thin that it reflects all light around it. A decapitated Fae man with his head sewn clumsily back on his shoulders sits on the closed porcelain seat, skin the sickly gray-green of a willow tree. Blood like rot and damp dirt of the forest. His eyes are tinged with gold veins, starkly standing out against the lotus color. "Not good for business," Pelle tells us.

"So, you just put glamour over a corpse."

Pelle shrugs. "The Fae have hidden worse."

"But you're not Fae," I reply.

He raises an eyebrow at me, irritated now, voice short and snappy. "Wondrous memory recall."

"You aren't one of the Fae. Which means you can *lie*." I stand in front of him, hands balled into fists.

He swallows as I hold my finger at his throat. "Will you skewer me too then, just like you did to that Greek goddess?" He laughs, the sound high-strung, his golden hair pulled back over skinny shoulders. "Come now, I'm too pretty for that."

I ram his body into the stall. Ikiaq steps forward, his voice a rumble low in his throat. "Lili..."

"I'm fine!" I snarl, but I pull back a little. *The detective only cares that you don't lose yourself again, idiot. Despite it all, he still damn well cares. Your friends care.*

I lower him a little, so his feet touch the floor. But Pelle is still firmly in my grasp. No escaping for him. "Where is the woman who removed this man's head from his shoulders?"

"Gone!" he shrieks.

"*Lili!*" It's Patty this time, arms crossed over her chest, staring me down with the fury of a vengeful deity. "We don't torture people. He hasn't done anything wrong aside from being a bit of an asshole, but then we'd have to beat on every person in this place." She points to the ground. "Drop him."

I do so. He grunts as he hits the ground, hard. "Toothpick! Watch him," I bark. The rookie pulls a taser out and points it at him.

"Mortal's pet," Pelle mutters. I kick him.

Pat glares at me. "Sorry." I shuffle my feet against the ground. "My foot slipped."

"Can't you see?" Patty throws her hands up in the air. "He's protecting the woman who ripped this guy's head off. Shouldn't we be asking why?"

Detective Ikiaq leans forward, squatting to the guy's level, his large hands propped on his knees as he still towers over the guy. "You said it yourself. Fae Court doesn't operate by our rules. You're risking a lot for the Fae not to have dragged your ass to Summerland by now. After all, I've been informed that you were the second one to stumble upon this Fae lord's body."

"And who told you that?" Pelle shoots back. "Who leaked this info to you?"

The detective purses his lips into a thin line. But the scrawny *Ljósálfar* makes a good point. "Yeah, detective, who *did* call us onto this case?"

The detective gets to his feet again, a heavy sigh as he tosses his empty hot cocoa into the trash. Crumpling the cup with one fist. "The Fae did. They were concerned that one of their own had been taken out."

"You should know better than to make deals with Fae, Ikiaq." Pelle's words rumble out, clear as can be, ringing in the small room, echoing in our ears.

"*Any man can lose his hat in a fairy wind,*" Patty mumbles. "Our parents even warned us about trusting Fae kind when they were alive. The Fae are beyond our control. Neither reanimated, nor immortal."

"You heard the witch," I snap at the detective. "You *know* that, ever since the Fae line began, the Fae Court play by their own rules."

The detective cracks his knuckles, glaring at me with dark eyes beating with intensity. "The Fae exiled themselves to Summerland because they were run out of their forests, out of their lands by the immortals and reanimated and humans and witches who overtook them back in Europe." He chuckles bitterly at that. "*Aqaa!* Trust is hard for those whose trust has been broken one too many times."

"Listen to your master, Lili, like a good dog." Pelle smirks.

I'm going to kill him.

"Lili." Pat again, stepping forward and glaring at me till I'm convinced she might actually shoot lasers from her eyes. "I said it once, but I won't say it again. Drop him."

"Good girl," Pelle grunts as he hits the floor.

I rear back and punch him, satisfied to hear my fist connect with his nose. The crunch of bone. The elf howls, his pretty face askew as he bleeds all over the bathroom tile.

"You bitch!" He forms spit bubbles out of blood as he

clutches his nose and wails. "You snapped my nose."

"Keep calling me dog, you really will find the true bitch in me." I wince. *Too corny, reel it in, hotshot. You've been streaming too many of those true crime shows.* "It's not us you should be afraid of. I don't know why you're protecting this woman, but last time I checked, none of us here are actually Fae. We're what passes as magical law enforcement in Gamin, buddy. We don't work for any one person. All we know is this guy"—I point to the stall where the green-tinged corpse is slumped over—"was decapitated. Why one of your workers decapitated him, we don't know. But this isn't Fae court, not guilty until proven innocent. We just want the whole picture to ensure this doesn't happen again, understand?"

Pelle laughs, spitting out blood and wincing when his nose wrinkles the wrong way. "I don't even know why I'm protecting her. I...I know I come off as an asshole. But against my best judgment, I fell for her. She doesn't like me back, and how can I blame her? I'm a mess."

"You got that right..." I mutter, only getting elbowed in the ribs by Patty for my trouble.

"I don't deserve her. I shouldn't get to play the shining knight in armor chivalry card bullshit and try to protect her like this. She even told me to call the detectives, shocked by what she did. But I don't want the Fae finding her. Getting their revenge when...when it wasn't her..."

"We aren't your therapists." I soften as he turns to me, his face all messed up with blood. His eyes *sad* in that asshole douche way, thinking they were on top of the world until they got a harsh reality check. "And you've got a lot of issues, clearly. But you said it yourself. You don't get to try to protect her. She makes her own choices, so you should let her talk to us. Besides, you falling for her? You're in a position of authority as her supervisor. Falling for her is just taking advantage of her situation. It's wrong, Pelle."

"No, no, it wasn't like that!" he moans. But he's gone from being a pitiful thing to a selfish, grasping thing instead. He shakes his head, likely trying to play the sufferer when he's just using us. Probably like he used his worker too.

"She's innocent until proven guilty. That's how the law works here in Gamin. We won't have vigilantes killing her outright." Detective Ikiaq nods at Toothpick, who pockets the taser. "Check on the car. It's got enough iron in it that the Fae should leave it alone, but it doesn't hurt to check. Use your human form though, can't risk touching silver."

Toothpick goes to leave. Pelle shoots a dirty look up at me. Sighing, I get behind Patty. "There, now it'll take me more time to get to you if I'm going to beat you up," I say, ignoring Patty's glower at me, "but I *won't* beat you up because you're going to cooperate now. Isn't that right, pretty boy?"

Pelle tries to look pleadingly to Patty, but I glare at him until he turns back to me. "Your business is with me, pretty one," I reiterate, my scowl only deepening despite Patty's heavy sigh.

I swear, even his silence makes my skin crawl.

"Fine," Pelle spits out after another long, agonizing moment of hesitation. "Indah couldn't stay here. She was the last one to see our headless friend, the green Fae man, after all. She was the last one to see him in this state we long-lifers dare to call living, before unfortunate circumstances separated his head from his body. But his power still lingers, even in his un-death, when the Fae plan to take him off to Summerland for a proper burial." He lowers his head, his eyes still locked on me, the hatred and confusion swirling within them as blood trickles down his split lip.

"That's all well and all, but we'll wait to deal with the Fae another day," I begin, bringing my index fingers up toward my knuckles, cracking the bone there, willing my heart to stop racing, to keep the beast from losing all control within me. *Remember what happened with Lethe. You mustn't lose yourself again...even if this bathroom could do with a remodeling.* "Tell me where Indah is now, pretty boy. It's crucial we get her story..."

I want to say, *"it's crucial we get her story before the Fae get her,"* but that seems too negative. I'd like to think positivity is my newest virtue. "It's crucial we get her story as soon as possible for the sake of this case."

I spot movement from the corner of my eye. Patty is waving her thumb, whispering words past her barely parted, cherry-lip-gloss-scented lips.

A truth hex. Clever witch, Patty.

"Interrogation magic can be dangerous with elves," Detective Ikiaq mumbles. "Magic mixing with magic blood, like mixing two different chemicals, you don't know how they'll react."

"What could go wrong when everything's already wrong?" I reply, but I keep the detective's warning in my mind as I step closer to Pelle.

Spurred on by Patty's quiet incantation, Pelle relaxes a little when he speaks. "She lies in hiding with the Snake Woman. That's all I got out of Indah before she fled. She was in shock, even terrifying herself." His eyes glaze over further, a haze of sleep rumbling in his voice as he rambles on. "Imagine, the whole mess scaring the shit out of a *Kuntilanak,* a flesh-eater. So, you know whatever's involved in this case must be from, well, if I was a believer in the Abrahamic religions, I'd call it hell."

I nod and Patty, satisfied, stops chanting. Thus ends our witch's truth hex.

Pelle gurgles, a strangled cry.

"Ah..." Detective Ikiaq warns. "And there's the withdrawal symptoms."

I brace myself, knees bent and gaze steadying on Pelle.

"W-what—?" he sputters, eyes aglow with a bronze flame. "What did you do to me?"

"Withdrawal symptoms," the detective says, squatting in a defensive position. "Magic can be a hell of a drug sometimes. And it seems Patty's truth spell has reached a limit with you, light elf."

Pelle spasms, throwing his head back and rolling his head around, stretching his neck out. He lurches to all fours, pushing his torso up higher so his arms tense, every tendon visible. The flashy designer clothing is rumpled and stained from the toilets and his own blood. His platinum hair plasters to his cheeks and neck as his eyes sharpen to a feline structure, narrowing in on Patty.

He reaches for his leg, and a thin bone dagger is strapped there, bleached the color of ivory, stained with rust.

It's then I let go of some of my power.

And I ever so slightly lose control.

I grow half a foot taller in a crack of bone and sinew. My nails sharpen to points, teeth curving too. The faint outline of tattoos marks my skin, my names. Lili. Lilit. Lilītu. ki-sikil-lil-la-ke. Lamia. The First. The Dark Maid. Maiden of Desolation. Mother of Anathema, amongst others.

In the bathroom mirror, the whites of my eyes disappear, giving way entirely to black.

Pelle, even in this crazed, instinctive state that Patty's magical withdrawal has driven him to, falters. He holds his pitiful bone dagger between us, pointing the blade still at Patty.

"Do it." My voice is a crackle of ancient energy. *"Give me an excuse to feast on your bones, little elf."*

Pelle trembles, sense returning to him as he sobers up from whatever magic Patty had him under. He takes in my new height, claws, and teeth, and he spins around and raises his bone knife. The murky ivory color gives way to a clear reflection...

Not a knife.

A mirror.

The light flashes from Pelle's fingertips, magnified by the mirror blade, blinding us all with the radiance of a miniature sun as the room goes unbearably white. Closest to the energy blast, I'm knocked back, unable to continue the transformation from the interruption to my powers. The return to my normal, weaker form costs me as I crack my skull against an exposed pipe. Patty, luckily, slides into the flat, safer wall. Detective Ikiaq braces against the closed toilet stall.

When the room returns to normal, there is no trace of the *Ljósálfar*. Even his blood has turned to ash, like the debris a phoenix leaves behind as it is violently reborn.

Chapter Three

One down, nowhere to go

DETECTIVE IKIAQ DRIVES me back with Toothpick in the passenger seat, listening to music through his headphones. Patty follows with her own car behind us, wise to avoid the chaos. The volume's so loud, I can hear the beat of a generic pop song from all the way back here.

"There's a town where I cannot see...
The monsters that come out of me."

"Turn it off!" I tell Toothpick. The young werewolf smiles at me and gives me a thumbs-up, then proceeds to turn the volume up louder.

The nerves of steel in this jellyfish of a kid...it must be the werewolf in him.

I press my forehead against the glass as the beat goes into some strange rock-techno house mixed with too much synth and reverb.

"How the hell can you proceed?
When the devil herself can't sign the deed?"

Ikiaq, thankfully, is sharper than his assistant and shuts the radio off just as it goes into its duetted chorus.

We stop real quick at a chain restaurant called Grid's Griddle. The joint is owned by a half-giant, most likely named Grid.

"I went to school with Grid," Toothpick says, all smiley. "She's amazing."

"Oh, so you went to school, did you? That's a surprise," the detective snarks, ruffling his head when Toothpick pouts. "Ah, I'm just messing with you, kid. Let's get some fries."

So, the detective and I get a good deal on raw hamburger meat and blood packets. Toothpick grabs some chicken nuggets and Patty gets a milkshake and fries.

The smells of blood and fast food should never mingle, let me be the first to tell you. Even as the mother of demons. I don't approve of whatever monstrosity makes up that scent. It breaks my unbreakable heart.

When we finally make it back to the Sweeney Inn, the parking lot's quiet. Some straggling guests walk into the lobby, but they file quickly into their rooms when they spot us.

I guess some humans have a knack for sensing when trouble's coming.

The detective waves me back from the inn's entrance. I jog over as he leans one arm on the car door, his other large hand on the wheel.

"Detective, about losing Pelle, I'm so sorry—"

But he holds up a hand to stop me.

"What happened back there..." He sighs, looking up at me with intense eyes. His entire form shimmers, part of the consequences of being a shapeshifter. "Look. I know you're struggling with keeping this form. It's a lot of work, and I don't blame you for losing Pelle. We got information out of him. We'll be able to locate the *Kuntilanak* woman and keep her safe from those who might seek retaliation for the green man's murder."

"Indah," I murmur. "First we find Indah, and then we can deal with the Fae."

I close my eyes, thinking of Pelle's wild eyes as the truth magic urged him on to violence, the mirrored blade that exploded into a shimmer of light. The portal that brought the *Ljósálfar* somewhere safe from us—hopefully also safe from the Fae who lorded over both Pelle and Indah back at the Kraken Club.

She lies...with the Snake Woman. That's what Pelle said.

Hopefully she isn't lying there as a corpse.

"We'll keep Gamin safe," the detective says. Toothpick is drooling a little, sleeping with the passenger seat cranked back a bit. "Rest up, Lili. Or rather, get some unrest. Whatever you do."

"Same to you." I wave, but he's already driven too far to see me.

When I turn back to the Sweeney Inn lobby, Patty's sitting on one of the sofas. A stack of luggage and a duffel bag crowd the entryway. At one end of the entryway stands Patty's prodigal twin brother, Jason. Strawberry-blond hair, broad shoulders, and wearing a denim jacket. One arm is replaced by a prosthetic. One might assume it's just an advanced system of tech, but the metal casing hides Jason's secret. His prosthetic is powered by the energy of the Dead Realms, the same place that tore off his arm in the first place.

Perks of being a young necromancer, I suppose.

At the other end of the entryway stands a figure I've never seen before. But whoever they are, they exude the sort of quiet, powerful confidence only the very strong possess. It's the kind of confidence that knows firsthand they can overpower most people they come across. It's the kind of confidence warriors and world-class fighters wield. It's the kind that looks death in the eye continuously and spits in its face before walking calmly down a cement sidewalk, hands in their pockets as they smile at the nice old lady, confused, down the way.

The new figure stands at medium height with muscular shoulders and compression gloves, flexing their fingers and bobbing a little in place. Their whole body is thick and muscular with a soft, round stomach peering out with a belly ring. They move like a fighter, shifting a little like they're going into another stance, just seconds away from ducking into a finishing blow. They've got a backpack strapped over their shoulder, the logo of a training gym on the back, souvenir pins from other countries. Dark skin, brown eyes, and black hair dyed purple on the ends of their curls. On their arm, a tattoo of vines snaking up their wrists, ending in a blue moon.

Patty and I exchange a glance. *Who the heck is this?*

Jason nods to the stranger and kisses them on the cheek by way of introduction. The calculating fighter façade melts in an instant and they lean into Jason's touch.

Patty and I exchange yet another glance. *Ah, there's about to be a new addition to our informal Scooby gang.*

"Patty, my twin sister. And Lili, our..." He pauses, still fumbling over the words as he turns to me. Fun fact, Jason thought I was a murderer when we first met, or at the very least, an asshole. So do most people. I equate that to my unusually receptive charm. "Lili works here at the inn. I think we're friends." Jason swivels to his amorous engagement, nodding to us. "Patty, Lili, meet Stace Casey. They're my wonderful partner." He smiles shyly when Stace kisses him back on the cheek. "Somehow after two months, they aren't sick of me."

"Oh, no. Quite sick. Positively *infected*. But that's love." Stace winks at us as they come in to hug Patty first, who's beaming at the surly Jason's obvious happiness. They have the good sense to see how uncomfortable I am with the prospect of free hugs, and instead opt for a firm handshake.

Patty gestures to all the luggage. "So, what's all this then?" Some of the cases, on further inspection, are labeled with various names, like scientific specimens, followed by dashed numbers. Others are filled with, when half-zipped, what appears to be a pair of thick gloves and tape.

"Guess," Stace challenges.

Patty and I exchange another look.

"Botany equipment," replies Patty.

"Boxes," I guess. You know, like an idiot. "Bodies?" I venture, further cementing my demise.

"Close, and...weird." Stace luckily cuts us some slack. "I'm sort of a boxing botanist. Which goes to say I'm in graduate school for botany, a study on rates of floral decomposition. Boring really."

"And the boxing, babe?" Jason points to the gloves.

Stace throws a few jabs into the air, but even joking,

I can tell those would absolutely *murder* on impact. "I teach self-defense courses. I used to box back in high school and a little in college." They point to their tattoo, the curling vines ending in the lunar glow. "I was a little too into Poison Ivy as a kid. The plant and the comic book character. I guess it rubbed off in my choice of life decision. I always wanted to be a badass super who got into scrapes, but I guess instead, I'm fighting rogue fungi."

Jason points to himself. "Am I a fun guy?"

Stace rolls their eyes and fake punches Jason's shoulder. "Never do that again."

I look between the two of them. Stace and Jason seem happy enough, but not trusting much of anything that arrives in Gamin, I interrogate further. "So, how did you two meet?"

"Well, I went to check out Stace's university in NYC. I was thinking of enrolling. Ended up staying to take extra courses they were offering. You know, between-terms stuff."

That piques my interest. *I wonder what Jason was up to while he was away.* Despite hating his goody-two-shoes attitude, I do have to admit, I miss this idiot sometimes. "What sort of courses? Chemistry, the occult, maybe cut up a few cadavers? This guy, he really likes that sort of thing." I know full well that Jason's been eyeing me nervously ever since introducing his new lover. *Stace should know what you dragged them into, necromancer boy.*

Jason gives me a withering glare, rubbing the back of his neck sheepishly. "No, just boring stuff. Coding, not cadavers. I signed up for one of their self-defense classes too, thinking I was hot shit, and had bruises on my butt for weeks after."

Stace looks around the inn, examining the lobby, the quiet hum of the new elevator we just installed. "I don't know what he'd need to defend himself from in Gamin," they say, one hand resting on their hip. "It seems like a really chill town."

Jason glances at me; it's only for a second, and there's less malice in it. At least, I think there is. *Mortals don't forget danger so easily. It's like sheep watching the dog that herds them. Even your friends can have fangs.* "You'd be surprised what this town has to hide."

"And Stace is...?" Patty again, but I can see what she's trying to get at this time.

Not botany, not boxing.

No, Patty wants to know...

Is Stace messed up like us?

"No," Jason replies, his lips thinning out a tense line. "No, Stace didn't grow up in a town like Gamin."

Which is code for: *No, Stace is just a regular mortal. No magic required.*

"I'm from just outside New York," Stace chimes in.

The room goes quiet, and Stace's smile falters as they glance between our little band.

Jason takes this opportunity to snag Stace by the hand and move to the door.

"So, we'll take that as our cue to go..."

Patty steps in front of his way, smiling her customer service smile that doesn't reach her eyes. "Afraid not." She nods her apologies to Stace as she pulls her brother aside. "Stace, do you mind if I borrow him quick? We have

Gamin-related business to discuss."

"Business?" Jason asks, nibbling nervously on his lower lip. His eyes cloud over as he notes the tone in Patty's voice, the high strain hinting that, per usual, nothing is normal in Gamin.

Hopefully not as bad as that business of serial killers and ancient deities like last time...but nothing's off limits in this godforsaken town.

I'd know. I was one of the godforsaken.

"Yeah, yeah, sure. I'll head back to our rooms, babe." Stace kisses Jason on the cheek before heading out. They lift a couple of the boxes in one arm and hoist a taped-together suitcase in the other like it weighs as much as Byron does—which is to say, nothing.

Gods, they could crush my skull with their pinky finger. How the hell are they just a regular human?

"Are you sure they aren't descended from Hercules or Hannibal of Carthage or some other superpowered figure or something?" Patty's staring at Stace in wonderment, as well.

Jason has his head in his hands, partially out of embarrassment and partially because he looks like he'd love nothing more than to bundle himself into one of the suitcases Stace is so casually carrying off. "Look, don't make me regret not staying in New York for longer..."

Patty and I exchange a look.

Oh, boy, is he in for a treat.

Jason sighs heavily, and even with his hands covering his eyes, he says, "Somehow, I sensed that neither of you are going to give me good news."

"Someone's been murdered. Robbed too, if you count

that his head's been robbed from his body." I tell him, point-blank. "The victim was a green-skinned lord from the Summerland. The main suspect is a *Kuntilanak*, an Indonesian blood-sucking demon who went by Indah and worked as a stripper. I can send you what we've found of her pictures. The fairy was patronizing the club she worked at, and there might have been an...unfortunate altercation. Detective Ikiaq called me and Patty in to sort it out."

"Well...?" Jason ventures hopefully.

"Yes?" I phrase it like a question, much less hopefully.

"Did you solve it?"

Oh, to be a hopeful necromancer standing in front of an immortal demon, asking her to—

"Attack him." Words really aren't coming out of me so easily tonight. I blame Jason, mostly because I don't want to blame myself. "I *maybe* attacked one of the suspects. Indah had a handler of sorts, a light elf. Pelle from the Kraken Club."

"Maybe?" Jason's eyes look bloodshot. College life doesn't suit him. Or maybe it's us.

"*Did*. I *did* attack him," I amend. "And he disappeared in a flurry of light."

"Stace can't be dragged into this," Jason tells me.

"I know," I reply.

"They have to go back to the city, return to New York," he continues.

I nod my agreement again. *Good, send them away from all this.*

"I have to go back with them." He finishes his train of thought.

And oh, how that train of thought crashed faster than the Andrew Lloyd Webber musical based on anthropomorphic train sets...

"No." Patty speaks up before I can. That's probably more fitting anyways. Jason is her twin brother, after all. "You can't go back. Mom and Dad left the Eye for both of us to run. The necromancers in this town look up to us. The company isn't just a business; it's our coven, and we need to protect it!"

Jason stares deep into his twin sister's eyes, to the point that I start believing they're using some weird, necromancer telepathy.

Or maybe that's just how twins are.

"Patty," he says, "we only survived what happened three months ago because of a stupid amount of luck. I was hoping to tell you during peaceful times, but perhaps it's for the best it happens now and proves my point." He inhales deeply, pausing to chew on the words before he speaks them. "We have to leave Gamin together. It's far too dangerous for us to live here."

"But..." Patty's brows draw low over her eyes. She can't seem to tear her gaze away. "This is our home."

"It doesn't have to be," he replies. "We can sell the inn and the necromancy business. You can start school or a job in the city with me and Stace. Somewhere without magic." He glances at me for the briefest moment, looking away again when I return his gaze. "Somewhere without monsters."

Patty stands still within the silence, staring at her feet with an unmatched intensity. I can feel the dread, the simmering rage, rolling off her. Jason, for all his stupidity, isn't too stupid to keep talking just then. Instead, he finishes with, "I'll be in my room with Stace. Let me know when you're ready to talk further."

Jason waits another moment, holding Patty's hands in his, before giving them a quick squeeze and going to pick up the leftover packages in the lobby. They're scattered like so many puzzle pieces, and unfortunately, none of them seem to fit.

Especially not in Gamin.

Chapter Four

Midnight hours bring me flowers (I hate flowers)

PATTY'S AT THE front desk for the late night/early morning shift at the inn, freckled arms splayed underneath a tangled mess of strawberry hair. Her pretty eyes blink blearily up at me, circles deep beneath them. Usually, I just take this oddly timed shift. It's not like immortals sleep anyways; no room for dreams when one has centuries of guilty thoughts to battle. But the fact that Patty's working this early, and knowing how she sleeps later than vampire bats do...

She must be absolutely exhausted. And then. *I hope she doesn't accidentally zap me with her witch powers out of irritation.* This is more in self-preservation, you understand. Just because I'm immortal, doesn't mean I'm immune to pain. *Which is both a blessing and a curse, depending on what sort of person you are...*

"It's for you," Patty tells me, pointing at a package.

"Thanks." I hesitate, seeing the surprise bouquet of squat flowers in a little vase with a gilded piece of paper tucked away inside the blooms. The card is circular, painted delicately with a small boat that's shepherding tiny figures across a vast, watery expanse. Staring at the image too long makes my vision swim.

I duck my head closer to the blooms for a whiff...

"I wouldn't do that if I were you," a voice booms from behind us.

Patty and I turn toward the figure.

It's none other than the incomparable Stace Casey, wearing a lavender tank that matches their hair, a binder, and joggers, a towel slung casually over one muscular shoulder.

The lobby is otherwise empty. Nobody in their right mind would be up this early, and any guests who come here wouldn't have any form of nightlife as a treat. I mean, not unless you count the vampire orgies. And nobody ever counts the vampire orgies.

"Where'd you come from?" Patty asks. Her words are clipped. Her eyes are bloodshot.

Stace shrugs. "Training. Y'all have a nice gym."

I turn to Patty. "We have a gym?"

"We have a pool too." Patty shrugs. "You never looked."

I mean. I guess Patty has a point. Sometimes, I forget the Sweeney Inn isn't just a convenient gathering place to center the story's plot. I mean...for us to plot what we're going to do. Yeah, that's it.

Stace comes closer, examining the card. They smirk at the image. "Cute." Then they examine the blooms. I notice they put contacts in today, shining pink-lemonade-colored eyes, and their ears are modified to look like elf ears with the clever snipping and stitching human surgeons can do.

I'm not jealous that a human looks more other-worldly than me. I'm not jealous that a human can shapeshift like that without magic required. I'm not... I'm really, really jealous. Damn, Stace would make a way better immortal than I would. They could probably still kick my ass even without any magic.

But then Stace turns their brilliant smile on me, and I forget I ever thought a bad word against them. "Yes, just as I thought. Look at that, they even got the berries." Again, Stace glances at the circular card with the strange little boat on it. "How cute."

Patty and I exchange another confused expression. *Damn, every time Stace speaks, it's like they're in on a joke... And I want to be in on it too. Damn their easygoing charm!*

"What's...cute?" Patty asks, backing away slightly from the flowers.

"Foxglove and bluebells. Aside from being wildly poisonous, their berries seem to have been pierced with either needles or thorns so the juice will drip down their stem. It makes all these lovelies poisonous to the touch." Stace laughs at this delightful little tidbit. "Cute."

"Oh," I snort, "is that all?"

Stace shakes their head. "Bluebells are also *incredibly* unlucky to bring inside. In Ireland, picking bluebells means you're picking a one-on-one fight with the Fae. Foxglove also invites the Fae to pick on you...or witches. Foxglove helps witches' magic. Crazy to think of, isn't it?" Patty picks up a little when she hears that foxgloves help witch magic. She discreetly takes one of the blooms for herself.

Stace reaches for the towel around their neck and gingerly plucks one of the bluebells. They lift its gentle, seemingly harmless petals to their face. "If you hear a bluebell ringing, it either means a Fae is near or death is."

"Why not both?" I mutter in response.

"What was that?" Stace asks, turning away for a second to look at me.

"Oh, ignore Lili. Her sarcasm precedes her brain sometimes," Patty responds.

Hey! Unfair...

But you make a good point.

Stace peeks over the edge of the vase. "There's root rot in these flowers. You can tell how the stems are bloated and the rancid smell coming out of them. And I think I see a dead slug at the bottom of this vase, which bodes poorly for a couple of reasons. Slugs engage in mycophagy or eating mushrooms. And mushrooms, as you well know, feed on rot."

A dead slug feeding on a mushroom that devours corpses. The dead feeding on the dead feeding on the dead... How sweet.

Finally, Stace lifts the circular card with a boat on it. They point to the boat first. "Ferry boat." Then they point to the card itself, running a chrome-polished fingernail around its circumference. "Circle." They smile, giggling a bit at that. "It's a pun, a fairy circle! What a prankster!" Stace's sensible chuckle builds up a little more.

Patty and I smile, but our smiles are weaker than waning moons in a darkened sky.

"Sorry"—Stace wipes away some post-workout

sweat—"the botanist nerd in me jumps out occasionally. Must be a full moon."

"Oh no," I tell them. "Trust me when I say that we'd know if it was a full moon."

Stace raises a brow at that. "Are there that many weirdoes in this town?"

"You have no idea." My false smile drops entirely.

Stace, pleasant as they are, takes this foreboding answer in stride. I should remember that human or no, they are from New York, after all. "Do you know who sent this prank bouquet?"

I go behind the desk, pluck out a trash can, and shove the whole mess in there with my nose curled up at the smell. "I don't make many friends in my line of work."

"At the hotel?" Stace peers around, scratching their head. "It looks nice enough."

I sigh, wondering just how much I could tell Stace and get away with. Might as well come clean. It might save their life later. "This is just my day job. I moonlight as a detective. And Patty here owns a...well, how about we call it a separate recreational facility?"

Patty catches Stace's look of surprise.

"No, no, not drugs!" Patty waves her hands emphatically at that. "More like homemade remedies, herbs and stuff. And we're attached to, well, it's like a spiritual retreat kind of thing. With group members who practice...unconventional convictions."

Bravo, Patty. You just made it sound like a cult. A coven. You could just call it a coven. For necromancers. They reanimate dead people. Or re-kill them. Yeah, it sounds crazier the more I explain it.

I grin. "She brews up potions that can alter your entire state of existence."

Patty casts me a withering glare at that. *Ah, just like her brother.*

"That's really cool! You both are such awesome people. You're out here doing *Law and Order: SVU* and *Sherlock* stuff." Stace nods at me, then swivels over to Patty. "And you're all independent business tycoons running two businesses like it's nothing." Stace's lemonade-pink-contact-wearing eyes widen in sincere interest. "I can't believe Jason wants to move to NYC when you're doing such cool things here."

"Neither can I..." Patty looks down, wringing her hands nervously. "But I can see why Jason's concerned for me. This town gets dangerous at times." She blushes, placing her head in her hands. "Damn, I'm sorry. I shouldn't be unloading this on all of you."

"This place, dangerous? Like what, occasionally a few kids hang around the gas station late at night?" Stace chuckles a little at that.

They don't believe that Gamin is anything other than a sleepy little town when, in reality, it's more like Sleepy Hollow. "Patty isn't exaggerating when she says it's dangerous here." I sigh, shuddering at the recollection of the horror of it all, what made Gamin so cruel despite it being our home. "There was a string of killings three months ago. This town might be just a blip compared to the population of NYC, but when things happen, they're just as big as in any large city. Larger, if you consider the inhabitants here."

That killer took so many lives. Our friend. And my

partner, Jo...

Gods, Jo...

Stace's brows furrow, and they lean in close. "Did you find the killer?"

I nod. "Her name was Alethea Styx. She was my, I suppose, you could call her my stalker." I pause, thinking it over. *She was the Greek goddess of memory, of forgetting. And her river, the river of Lethe, gathered all the power of Hades to cloak this town in shadow, in eternal mist so that the mortals wouldn't rise up and kill the monsters, and the monsters would be placated by their strange circumstances.*

And she was madly in love with me, to the point she slaughtered multiple innocents as sacrifices to turn me back into the merciless, demonic killer she thought I was.

But I'm not that anymore... I'm better. Aren't I?

I steady myself before going on, "She's been institutionalized. But Jason, understandably, doesn't want any of you around this sort of thing."

"That's not fair, Lili." Patty slams her hand against the counter, and the action even causes levelheaded Stace to jump. "That's not fair. The only reason you caught the killer was because we worked together. You had friends to keep you in check along the way. And I understand if Jason doesn't want to do this anymore, but I want to. And it's about to happen again so—"

That's when Stace snaps back into sharp-eyed focus. "It's about to happen again?"

Patty looks to the ground and takes a deep breath. When she exhales, she's staring into Stace's face like one of the stock-photo figures on the "welcome to Gamin" pamphlets.

I match her energy with a placid, shit-eating grin. "No. No need to worry. This is an *entirely different* case. A woman who worked in a local strip club was involved in a fight with a customer there. He died, she fled, and his kin... His buddies aren't too happy about it." I point to the trash can with the rotten, venomous bouquet.

"Huh." Stace crosses their arms, the Poison Ivy tattoo with the vines standing out along the path of their skin. They tilt their head to the side, as though the whole messy history of Gamin is appearing before them and they're trying to make it out. "I've worked with former sex workers before whose clients asked too much of them. They show up at my self-defense courses, to learn how to protect themselves and for closure." Stace chews on their lower lip, a habit they've picked up from Jason, most likely. "And the dead man's family seem prone to intimidation tactics, so it'll be dangerous for her to be on the run. Do you know if there's a safe house or a domestic violence shelter around these parts?"

It's my turn to chuckle. *Oh, innocent Stace. They waltz in here with those cool body mods, impeccable boxing strength, botany knowledge, and deductive reasoning and just think...* "Oh, hold up there." I smile, buffing my nails on my shirt. "I appreciate the help, but we've got this..."

"Lili." Patty's typing something into that devil box of a computer of hers. She swivels the screen around to face me. I resist the urge to hiss at that blasted technology. I'm no fan of it. Machines that talk back to you. I remember back when the camera was first invented, when people thought those unwieldly lenses took their souls. Now we just willingly give these machines our names like they won't turn on us. *Hah!*

Patty snaps her fingers at me to get my attention, which as always, is remarkably fleeting considering how many years I've lived. "Lili, you have to look at this."

I lean in closer, and the words come into reluctant focus against the too-bright flash of the computer screen. There's an image of a serpent in a rainbow flurry of colors, and a middle-aged Black woman with deep circles beneath smiling brown eyes. She has a cloud of natural-worn brown-black hair around her head, curls touched with a soft, downy shine. She wears an emerald dress with a white doctor's coat on her, and her fingernails are painted in colors of the rainbow as she folds her hand gently over her other arm.

I feel an instant sensation of calm, which is rare for me on any given day, but especially rare from simply looking at someone's image.

THE RAINBOW SERPENT SHELTER FOR SURVIVORS.

And beneath the woman's picture.

DR. WEDDO.

I close my eyes, remembering what Pelle, that silver-tongued light elf, told us.

"She lies in hiding with the Snake Woman."

"Imagine, the whole mess scaring the shit out of a Kuntilanak, a flesh-eater."

"...if I was a believer in the Abrahamic religions, I'd

call it hell."

I cough gently into my hand. "Well, it um…it looks like we found a suitable lead." I hold out my hand for a high five, which Stace politely obliges. "Good job then."

"All right." Stace smiles. "I'll shower, change my clothes quick, then come with you."

Gods, look at their face. How can anyone say no to their face?

"Oh, that's…" Patty, even exhausted as she is, clearly struggles to come up with the words to tell Stace no. "That's perfectly all right, we can handle…"

"Don't worry about it. I'd love to help. Besides, I've had training dealing with survivors, and I might be able to help get your runaway to cooperate." Stace smiles and Patty and I can't help but melt and smile back. "Be back in a few."

They glide away and Patty and I, yet again, are left with the conundrum of truly accepting that Stace Casey, somehow, is entirely human.

I sigh and Patty just hugs me briefly. "It'll be all right, Lil. Maybe an extra pair of eyes would be good for us. And besides, Stace can take care of themselves. And if not"— Patty grins, holding up the foxgloves she took earlier—"I got an extra boost here. Witches' magic, and it might've been good for Fae once, but it'll be their bane if I have anything to say about it!"

"You seem awfully chipper considering your lack of sleep."

Patty pats me on the head. I growl at her in reply. "Of course I'm chipper," she says. "If we wrap this case up quickly, Jason might be persuaded to stay in this town for longer. And besides, there's nothing like dusting off the old broomstick and taking a ride."

"You have a car, and you only rode on a broomstick once, purely for aesthetic purposes," I reply bluntly.

She sticks her tongue out at me.

Patty, ever the resourceful young witch, bustles off to make a quick breakfast in the break room: a turkey, bacon, and egg sandwich for her and a thick cow's blood pudding for me. I look over to the trash where the sickly-sweet smell of rot and wilted blooms greets me. Staring into the mess there, I can't help but feel the feather-light touch of dangerous Fae at my throat.

The green man's friends run quickly to his aid. I've only dealt with lone wolves before. Rogue deities and overconfident humans. But to have an entire group like the Fae at our backs... Maybe a little extra help is needed. I pluck the circular card with the boat up. Fairy circles, how quaint. I flip the paper over, and a feeling of deep, profound dread hits me.

> *TICK-TOCK. WE'LL FIND THE SCARED LITTLE INDAH, CLUTCHING HER FROCK.*

The paper mocks with the smiling, eerie face of a clock with holes in it like a block of cheese.

> *TICK TOCK, MOTHER OF DEMONS. TICK. FIND YOUR RUNAWAY GIRL BEFORE US. TICK. TOCK. TICK TOCK!*

> *BETTER YOU FIND HER THAN OUR MERRY CREW.*

BETTER YOU FIND HER BEFORE WE DO!

The sound of a grandfather clock ticking down echoes within my skull. No matter if I plug my ears, the sound just goes on and on. It sounds like the gnashing of gears and the dreaded pounding of a heart beating in fear and all the things the terrified person shoves to the deepest, darkest recesses of their mind to avoid.

I rip the page in two and crumple it with my talons, impaling the card on my claws.

The words and the ticking vanish just as quickly as my hope for normalcy.

Patty comes back with our breakfast. She sets aside two glasses of water and places a corked vial the size of my thumb into my palm.

"I made the latest batch with more rat tail. It should help with your symptoms."

I look to the murky red-black liquid and uncork the vial as I place it at my lips. "Cheers," I say before downing the beverage, thick and warm. "Demonic antidepressants. A witch working as my part-time pharmacist. What a world we live in, huh?" I laugh.

"To getting better," Patty replies. "And getting the hell out of here."

I wait for the vial's contents to work their magic. My mind clears, edges of fog breaking through the constant fatigue, the thoughts of inadequacy like slugs worming through the pit of my stomach.

But something else happens. The clearness comes with an edge, a blade inside my body. My stomach twists, not just regular flutters.

"Hey, Patty, did you change this dosage?" I squint at the vial, trying to make sense of the residue left on the bottom.

"No, why?" She presses the back of her palm to my forehead. "You feel as cool as a corpse, just like usual."

I laugh, trying to shake off the weird feeling. *Side effects. No, that's impossible. Immortals can't feel side effects, can they?* Patty's gaze lingers, her brows furrowing lower. *Don't cause trouble. She's doing so much for you already.* I paste a smile onto my face and snag some turkey from her breakfast sandwich. I force myself to chew the warm, cooked meat. *Yuck, how do humans eat this stuff?*

"Come on, that's enough worrying about me." I pretend to go for another slice of turkey, and she dodges, laughing, out of my way. "Let's go catch a killer."

Chapter Five

Lifehack cooking tips (hacking lives too...)

PATTY DRUMS HER fingernails against the slightly dull wheel of her new yellow car. She's named it, quaintly enough, Bee Bumble. (Maybe Patty was a big fan of the famous robot franchise, if not the copyright laws).

Stace hops into the car, wearing a plaid skirt, button-down, and tie. They have crescent moons clipped to their elf-mod ears. When they sit, the vine tattoo along their arm gleams a little. I smell the scent of tattoo aftercare oil on it, the too-sharp tang like citrus. The oil gives it a 3D quality, as if the vines will crawl out of their skin at any second.

Seriously? Even Pelle would be jealous of their casual glamour.

Stace sees me eyeing the crescent moon clips. They unfasten one from their ears and hand me the smooth piece of jewelry. "It's all cool. Take one. I got them for cheap from my cousin who does jewels and stuff."

"No, I..." I stare into the surface, how it's polished clean as a mirror.

They cast me a sterner look than that, chin tilted down and lemonade-pink contacts somewhat off-kilter now as they twist around their pupils.

"Well"—I obediently grab the jewelry—"if you insist."

I fasten the new accessory to my ear, and Patty's smirking to see me warm up to someone so quickly. A regular human, nonetheless.

Yes, my dear, that's character development for you.

Patty reaches back with her cell phone, showing me the destination address. "You're sure we should go here, right?" I read the title over again, the Rainbow Serpent Shelter for Survivors. I take another look at Dr. Weddo.

There's something about her.

Her eyes...

Victorians were onto something when they said cameras capture part of someone's soul. Sometimes, they can reveal the true essence of someone. You just need the patience, and the power, to look for it.

"Patty." I type in something, picking at the virtual keyboard with one finger. This, for some reason, seems to amuse Patty greatly. "I have a feeling about this Dr. Weddo. I've met her before."

Stace and Patty look at me with surprise, though Patty's gaze is apprehensive whereas Stace's is a look of mild interest. "How?" Patty ventures, nervous.

"Let's say my Satan senses are tingling," I tell her. "One quick stop, I promise."

*

Old MacDonald had a farm. Ee-i-ee-i-oh!

PATTY IS ENTIRELY unimpressed as I now sit in the backseat of her precious Bee Bumble car with a black-haired, fuzzy piglet under one arm, a new carton of farm-fresh eggs under the other, a small jug of fresh cream between my knees, and the finest rum we could find at the 24/7 liquor store down the street balancing on my lap.

Stace reaches for the liquor, and I move to smack their hand away. They dodge my halfhearted swipe easily.

Damn, they really are a professional boxer, huh? I wish I could be Stace when I grow up someday. Although, that would be hard, considering I'm an immortal.

"Look, I'm all for farmer's markets, but why did we stop here?" Stace asks. They still haven't taken their eyes off the rum. Patty gives them some of her blueberry muffin we picked up as consolation.

"Yeah, Lili, why did we pick up Wilbur from *Charlotte's Web* in the backseat?" Patty wrinkles her nose at the baby pig. Her tortoiseshell glasses slide down the frame of her nose.

Patty's still glaring at me as I cradle Wilbur in my arms and rock the poor thing to sleep. I hold one finger to my lips and whisper, "Please, Patty..." I close my eyes, thinking on our next destination. Those gleaming eyes hidden beneath pixels within the picture.

I have a sneaking suspicion I know Dr. Weddo's true form.

And gods, is it a powerful one.

I grin sheepishly at Patty, waving at her while trying to keep Wilbur tucked still beneath my arm. "Trust me when I say you don't want to show up to Dr. Weddo's house empty-handed."

Or face the consequences.

*

Knock-knock, we're here!

IMAGINE OUR SURPRISE as we knock on the door of the Rainbow Serpent Shelter for Survivors, only to see a beautiful young woman's face greet us.

And she looks dreadfully familiar.

The woman who answers the door has eyebrows that have been shaved off halfway at the arch, leaving them square points crossing half her eyes. She has smudged circles beneath her eyes indicating a failed attempt at washing off heavy eye makeup. Long black hair pinned up beneath a batik scarf, a pattern like fire flowers against a backdrop of sand. She's wearing soft slippers and a towel robe with gray shorts, both a bit big for her. She's a skinny thing, dark skin and a pretty pout to her lips. She has a scarf wrapped five times around her neck, and her hands are warmed up by thick fingerless gloves.

Stace and Patty behind me seem too stunned to respond. I'm barely able to form words myself, not knowing we'd actually find her.

The runaway.

"Indah?" I step forward first, whispering, like a fool, "Indah, we just want to talk."

She moves to close the shelter door again, the chain lock swinging from the edge.

"Non, pitit mwen." A kitten-heeled shoe blocks the entryway. Slowly, gently, the lock is removed. The chain scratches against the wood, swinging against the lock. A figure steps forward, head shaved so their blue-dyed hair is tight to their dark skin. They wear a pink pantsuit with a gold-trimmed blazer and spectacles in white. The newcomer places their body smoothly between us and Indah. "Ah, and what can we do for you folks today?"

Patty this time. "We didn't wish to inconvenience you, but we're here on behalf of Detective Ikiaq..."

The figure steps forward. They smell like orchids and drip in delicate cords of jewelry that slide down their wrists. They're tall, leaving Patty craning up to their beautiful face with a squeak. "I...I...um..." Patty seems to have forgotten how to use her words, entirely entranced by the heavenly being in front of us.

Only Stace can manage to push past us. They're leading Wilbur on a makeshift leash the farmers gave to us, alongside carrying a wooden crate filled with all our goods. The cream is still fresh and stoppered, the eggs resting in straw, and the rum is good and golden-hued in color.

"We brought gifts," Stace says, straight to the point. Then, they address the blue-haired figure. "Are you Erzulie Fréda by any chance?"

How the heck do they know this person's name?

"I searched you on Google before we came here," Stace amends. "One of the counselors here, right?"

Ah. That was smart of them.

The blue-haired figure nods, the tension in their shoulders easing as they open the door fully. "Ah, I see my reputation precedes me." Erzulie Fréda's eyes linger over the gifts, especially Wilbur and the rum. "You lot come in peace, I suppose. Detective Ikiaq's never steered me wrong before. We used to have fun occasionally. He isn't always as tough as he seems." Erzulie Fréda smiles as Patty's blush deepens. "Oh, aren't you the cutest? I think I tried to seduce your mother once too, darling. I had a different body at the time. I'm always switching it up, so to speak. For now, I'm like this. But who knows who I'll be in a decade or two?"

Stace again, a curious gleam in their eyes, "And your pronouns are...?"

"She, her, hers are fine today," Erzulie Fréda replies. "Thank you, love."

Stace probably thinks Erzulie Fréda is genderqueer. This isn't exactly this loa's situation. No, the ineffable Erzulie Fréda possesses and leaves pretty bodies like new flesh-suits.

No wonder I didn't recognize her right away. She's changed bodies again.

A sneaking suspicion tickles the back of my head. *I wonder why Dr. Weddo didn't move to greet us first.*

Patty laughs awkwardly and stares at the floor. Then, alarmed, her head snaps up again. "Wait, did you say you dated my mother?"

Erzulie Fréda avoids that question until, finally, her attention alights on me. "Oh, you"—she trails one fingernail beneath her chin in thought—"you're immune to my charms, aren't you?"

I smirk, holding up one hand slightly. "It's all aces in here, I'm afraid."

She nods at that, and then, in a fluid motion, she pulls Indah to her, a mother bird hiding her chick beneath her wing. The scarf draws away a bit, and I see the thick, rusted hardware nail, the size of a small fist, embedded into Indah's neck beneath her long black hair. Indah nuzzles in closer behind Erzulie Fréda, but there's something in her stance. She might be hiding now but bringing the *Kuntilanak* in would be no easy task.

Indah's more dangerous than she looks, so I can't fall for her stray kitten act.

Just look what she did to the green man...

"Will you eat and drink with us, *zanmi'm yo*?" Erzulie Fréda asks, already heading back into the shelter. The hall stretches out. The building itself is falling apart at the seams. Though the home's original architecture is fancy with expensive carvings on the banister, a spiral staircase, and statues out front, the place itself and its materials are in disrepair. Moth-eaten curtains, rotting front steps, and holes where there shouldn't be.

Immortality doesn't always immediately lend itself to luxuries.

"It's been a while since we've received such a generous donation, or donations of any sort you see."

"We weren't here to stay." I finally regain my composure enough to move closer to Indah. Again, Erzulie Fréda puts herself between us and the hidden *Kuntilanak* woman. "I'm afraid Indah has had serious charges placed against her by a very prominent organization. It'd be safer for her if she came in with us."

"Oh, I'm sorry. I can see the confusion. When I said, 'will you eat with us?' that was my mistake." Erzulie Fréda smiles as she turns back around, swiveling on one kitten heel. "I meant, darling, you all *will* eat with us. It's not a question, my loves. It's a demand."

Erzulie Fréda, the *loa*, one of the powerful intermediary spirits of Haitian Vodou, strikes a power pose. Her long legs stand shoulders' width apart. She balls her hands up into fists.

The *loa* isn't entirely alone. Even Indah reaches for the nail at the back of her neck. I'm afraid to see what tearing out the device would do to her.

And consequently, to me.

I hunker down, falling to one knee. A sprinter about to take off.

It's been a while since I fought. This could be fun.

Patty holds a warning hand to my shoulder. "Lili, please, not with Stace here."

I turn back, seeing Stace look at me with confusion in those lemonade-pink, cosplay contacts eyes of theirs. The *loa* catches my moment of hesitation. When Erzulie Fréda relaxes from the fighting stance, Indah follows suit.

"I see we're all peace-lovers here." Erzulie Fréda again, hands spread out in a calming motion. "And you've brought honored guests just as we have ours." The *loa* points to Stace when mentioning honored guests, then to Indah, a tension at her violet-tinged lips.

I see we both have our weaknesses in this fight.

"Come." Erzulie Fréda turns around again. I bristle to see her tall, elegant back turned on me. It's like I'm just a rabble-rouser at her doorstep. *I suppose, in some ways, I am.* "Dr. Weddo has been waiting for you three."

Patty and I exchange a glance, but Stace pushes on,

once more, in front of us. Wilbur trots along. *It seems even the pig's taken a shine to Stace.*

Well, I can't go ahead and let a human outdo me. Mustering some semblance of bravado, I square my shoulders back and step into the *loas'* lair. Patty's at my back. The door swings shut behind us as Indah kicks it closed.

In the darkness, her eyes glimmer; her pupils are tinged a dark red like stars trapped in seas incarnadine. Long, dark hair drinks up the shadow. And though she's swallowed up by her borrowed clothing, the shadows suit her well.

Hard to forget Indah isn't just some lost young woman.

I close my eyes, thinking once more to the green man back at the Kraken Club, just how cleanly his neck was cut. I think on how his head was robbed from his body. I wonder at how much those now prettily human-passing nails of Indah's could take once they carved into flesh.

No, she's just as much monster as any of us. She's me without the control. Though, luckily, she's not half so powerful.

Indah nods, waiting for Patty and me to go before her.

I oblige, following Erzulie Fréda up that long, endless spiral staircase. They might look pretty, but the spiral pattern makes you dizzy in seconds. Every step causes you to question where to next place your foot, like each movement upward is just skirting the edge of a cliff's face. Or, maybe, that's just the scent emanating from the hidden alcove above.

We enter a space with the yellow-daisy curtains

drawn back from the windowsills. In the kitchen is Dr. Weddo from the photographs, natural hair tucked under a headscarf. She wears a full green skirt with a white jacket, decked out in brass buttons. Her slippers make a *hush-hush* sound against the hardwood as she samples a spoonful of stew.

The pot on the stovetop hisses and burbles. It smells rich with red beans, dried corn, spices layered with bits of fatty meat. The oil glistens at the top, popping every so often. On the side of the oven, cooling in a pan, are fresh puff pastries. Indah snags one, watching us warily from the corner of her eye. She takes her prize and retreats to a far window, the one letting in all that sunshine. As soon as the sun hits her, she becomes a regular human-seeming woman again. In fact, she becomes strikingly beautiful, unearthly so, save for the nail stabbed into her neck that keeps her other form at bay. Her long, raven hair gleams as it pours past her shoulders.

She winks when Patty catches her eye. Patty looks away quickly, blushing.

Indah smirks and finishes the last of her puff pastry. I glance at Patty, raising an eyebrow.

The young, red-faced witch shakes her head in warning. She presses her thoughts into my mind using her favorite witchy power of telepathy. It tires her at times, so she only does it when I'm really being a brat. *Drop it, Lili.*

I grin. *Oh? But it just got interesting.*

"Well, if it isn't Lilītu!" I bristle as Dr. Weddo calls upon one of my old names. Stace, luckily enough, is too preoccupied with some puff pastry to notice. Dr. Weddo laughs, and when she laughs, she brings her rainbow-painted nails to her lips. The nails gleam so brightly that, when the light catches them, they look like rainbow-painted scales, brilliant as gemstones. "It's been so long since we've seen each other again, old friend."

Embarrassed, I bunch my shoulders up. "I'm not the same as when I wielded that name, Dr. Weddo."

She examines me closer, bringing her hand to rest at the air beneath my chin. "Yes, that's right, isn't it?" She moves her hand, and though she doesn't make contact with my skin, a force pulls me to look the other way. She drops her voice to a whisper, so no one overhears. "You're different now. Just like when Erzulie Fréda takes a new body, but still, you're different from that too, *manman monstr*."

"I'm tame," I reply.

Dr. Weddo tilts her head, still staring curiously into my face. "Perhaps."

Stace leans over the pot, their hand still holding onto Wilbur's leash.

"Ah, ah, ah! Don't touch it, *cheri*." With a gentle touch, Dr. Weddo steers Stace away from the stew just as the pot hisses and spits hot steam up into the air.

"What are you making, doctor?" I inhale the savory aromas, tasting the salt and spices on the air.

"Do you like cooking?" She raises her brow at me as I inhale the aromas.

Not enough flesh and blood in it for my taste. I like things a little more...raw.

I laugh. "The only cooking show I watch is that funny one, the one with those aesthetically pleasing cooking se-quences named... Oh, it rhymes with cannibal..."

"*Hannibal*?" Patty's voice goes higher in register when she's shocked or disgusted by me. It never fails to amuse my immortal, jaded self. "Lili. That's a *horror* show, not a cooking channel."

I shrug. *Honest mistake for someone who also used to eat humans.*

Stace nods. "Aside from devouring human flesh, it *does* have pretty cool cooking sequences."

See, Stace gets me.

"We're making *tchaka*." Dr. Weddo goes to stir the overflowing soup pot, throwing in a dash of something from a lidded jar in the shape of a coiled, clay-cast snake. "It's a house favorite lately. My husband Damballa carries it in a thermos sometimes when he goes to work and makes those creations of his."

"He claims it makes him a better lover too," Erzulie Fréda pipes up. "Should have more of it with two partners to please."

Dr. Weddo smiles. "He'd need more hands to please you, *cheri*."

"A blessing and a curse." Erzulie Fréda drapes one hand dramatically over her forehead, leading to some chuckles from all of us. Even Indah, nervous of us as she is, lightens up as the kitchen smells warmly of fried foods and stews.

Erzulie Fréda picks up the slack on the makeshift leash that Stace, in their shock at nearly being burned by the pot, dropped. Poor Wilbur squeals when taken from Stace's care. "You even brought the meat." The *loa* of love and seduction laughs, staring at the poor pig. The beast, terrified as it is, calms a bit at her touch. *Ah, so Erzulie*

Freda also possesses an aphrodisiac, eh? "You're too kind to bring such a plump offering as this." She licks her lips.

Stace, in alarm, rushes to pick up Wilbur. Patty blocks them, shaking her head.

Stace's lower lip trembles in panic as Erzulie Fréda picks up a long, flat butcher's knife from the chopping block that's stained red with old blood.

"No!" Stace shouts. "Wait, you're really going to kill it?"

Erzulie Fréda shrugs. "And eat it too, *bèl.*"

Nobody takes a gift back from a loa.

Dr. Weddo stops Erzulie Fréda at the last second. She cradles Wilbur in her arms for a bit, soothing the pig, before giving the little one back to Stace. "Nonsense, *cheri.* We don't have to use a fresh pig when *tchaka* calls for salted and cured pork anyways." She claps her hands together, rainbow-colored nails gleaming. The light reflects off the walls. Faintly, I can hear the sliding of the scales of a serpent. "Besides, our lovely guests brought more gifts."

Here, Dr. Weddo's gaze shifts a little. In her eyes, I see the vast rainbow serpent who held up the heavens and the skies. I see her, the one whose spiritual nectar formed life itself. She is within everything, the earth and the waters beyond it. She is the one who carried life on her back and in her belly and in her hands and in her eyes with the aid of the Sky Father.

And this, *this,* with the rainbow glinting off her nails and the power inherent, deep within her eyes, this is just the façade that hides her.

The mighty *loa*, Ayida-Weddo.

She peers at us closer, tapping her fingernails against

her thigh.

"You *did* bring more gifts?" she asks with a smile that feels harsher than it should, like cold fingernails tapping down warm skin. "Didn't you?"

I meet her gaze for a moment before nodding, posting a courteous, too-tight smile on my face. "Of course, doctor. I'm old enough to know my manners." I pick up the crate and place it near the table, where it rests at the feet of the two *loa* women. They stare down at it with what I hope is calculation instead of distaste. "Please, this is the finest we could buy in the small town of Gamin. Fresh cream, honeyed rum, and eggs laid just this morning."

Erzulie Fréda, still a bit sore and glaring over at the escaped Wilbur, plucks up the rum and takes the stopper off. She inhales deep of the liquor's scent. For a moment, her eyes flash a brilliant gold.

"Mm." Dr. Weddo looks over the farm-fresh offerings, an unknowable expression on her face. "You bring good gifts. But..."

But?

Uh-oh.

Dr. Weddo steps up, moving closer to me. She isn't a particularly tall woman, but the way she carries herself, you know she's got power. She drums her fingernails again, and once more, I hear the sliding of serpent scales cutting through night. There's a golden necklace in the shape of a sleeping serpent around her neck. When I blink, I think I see it slither around. "My darling, for what you seek, you'd best have more than this."

Patty bites her lip nervously. Stace watches the scene play out from their spot half-kneeling on the floor, still clutching the dazed Wilbur tight. "Please, Dr. Weddo, we had Detective Ikiaq call ahead—"

"You called the detective without me?" I snap around. *This is news to me.*

Patty nods. "This isn't like last time, Lil." She shakes her head. The young witch's amber fire eyes glow against her round face. There's something new in them. A wisdom to my impulsivity. "We have to do things right this time. Remember what happened when we went all *V for Vendetta* last time. People got hurt."

Ah yes. Remember the friend we lost, when the killer murdered Dakari Borden because of my stupid foolishness in running off alone. The loss of Jason's arm. And of course, the coma Jo Kim was put under...

"Yes, I know you're here for the case of the green man. His kin want revenge for his...untimely end, and you think Indah over here has the answers you seek." Dr. Weddo nods, her eyes flicking over to Indah. The *Kuntilanak* has her knees drawn tight to her chest. Erzulie Fréda smiles, drinking more of the rum. "But that's not the price I'm talking about, is it, Lili?"

Erzulie Fréda leans closer, grinning. "Ah yes, I see her, the one you want to bring back from the brink of eternal sleep. I see her in your heart."

I cross my arms over my chest. "Stop looking there. I didn't think I even had one."

Erzulie Fréda shrugs, leaning back in her chair with the rum in her hands. "My bad, love, my bad. It comes with the job description. I see people's desires, love and sex. Though, for you, it's more just the former and not so much the latter, eh?"

Dr. Weddo moves her hand through the air, and again, I feel my face compelled to turn toward her. *Damn, her power's strong. We are in her home, after all. Her castle.*

"This isn't about Jo Kim; this is about Indah."

"When you deal in death," Dr. Weddo replies, "the murdered and the murderers are one and the same. They all end up with our kin who walks the Dead Realms, Baron Samedi. It's Baron Samedi you'll be wanting to talk to."

Stace sighs in frustration at that.

Fear grasps my spine as Erzulie Fréda and Dr. Weddo turn as one to face the impetuous mortal. They're just holding on to Wilbur with that damning look of disbelief on their face. "I'm sorry, I'm sorry." Stace looks up, nervous about being caught. "I don't mean to offend, but we are trying to solve a murder here. This investigation is time sensitive. We have to look at the facts of the case, and that, unfortunately, doesn't involve talk about the Dead Realms when we should keep firmly grounded in the land of the living. We should talk of facts and observation, not beliefs."

Dr. Weddo looms taller if possible, and her shadow drapes over Stace as she moves toward the oh-so-clueless mortal. "You do not believe in the powers that be, young one?"

Patty steps forward, attempting to shield Stace. "Please, they just arrived in Gamin recently. They don't..."

But Stace plows ahead, steamrolling on, as confident as only mortals can be. *They touch the moon once and think they know all. But they scream when the moon reaches down from the heavens and touches them back.*

"I respect other's beliefs, but I'm a scientist. I harbor none myself," Stace says.

And with those words, Erzulie Fréda and Ayida-Weddo glance at each other and laugh and laugh and laugh. Their laughter rings in the cramped space for so long that I can feel it, the power thrumming beneath my skin, the energy in the room calling for a transformation, for a potential fight. I'm already calculating how long it would take me to reach one of the chairs and break it over somebody's head…

Not as long as it would take for Ayida-Weddo to pick up the knife tucked on the counter and stab Stace, or worse, Erzulie Fréda to smash a glass bottle and stab it through their heart.

Dr. Weddo snaps her fingers and, all at once, her and her partner's laughter stops. Indah stares out over her bony kneecaps, her eyes wide as she watches in that eerie silence.

"Okay, young friend," Dr. Weddo says, lowering herself to Stace's seated level, "I'll stick to the *facts* of the case." Here, she points to Indah. "This girl was targeted by a very powerful crime family, the kinfolk who own the Kraken Club."

Erzulie Fréda puts one arm around her, pulling Indah into her like she's a shield between us. "Indah came to our shelter seeking help, seeking protection from those bastards. We'd be remiss to give her up so easily to people who call themselves detectives but hold no badges themselves."

Stace glances uneasily to me and Patty. "I thought you said you lot were detectives."

I shrug. "It's really more of an honorary certificate."

Stace shakes their head at that and takes Wilbur to go off to the edges of the room, putting a generous amount of space between us.

I look at Indah, now in her glamoured mortal form in the kitchen. She doesn't seem like the type to murder in cold blood. She's not what the Fae made her out to be. And thinking back on Stace's analysis that Indah was acting out in self-defense...

We're working for the wrong side. No, not us. Not exactly.

"There's one benefit to not working under a badge." I step forward then. Dr. Weddo steps back, one hand, I note uneasily, on a kitchen knife she's slipped into her waist-band. *Though her true powers could do far worse than a simple blade.* "We aren't working for Detective Ikiaq, not technically."

Patty's eyes widen. "Lili..."

"So that means"—I wink at Indah before turning back to Dr. Weddo—"we aren't working for the detective's cli-ents." I drop my voice to a whisper. "No Fae involved."

Erzulie Fréda grins, licking puff pastry crumbs and rum off her lips. She bares her teeth at us. "That means nobody knows you are here either, eh? Nobody to hear you scream?"

Patty glares at me. *Now look at what you've done, you stupid idiot.*

I shrug. *I know.*

"That's right," I go on. "That's right because...be-cause..."

Erzulie Fréda and Dr. Weddo watch me, leaving me

feeling uncomfortably bare in front of them.

Damn, I hate being exposed like this. Unless that can be a positive thing.

"We come here completely vulnerable. We even brought a regular..." I look to Stace, who glances at me with sheer confusion mapped on their face. "A regular botanist here. We did that to show you we mean no harm. We just want to help solve this case."

Dr. Weddo crosses her arms over her chest, not leaving her knife. "Why?"

"We're good people." At the room's incredulous reaction, I plow on. "Well, at least, Patty's a good person. And she makes sure I do good...or at least, better."

Patty nods, going to stand by my side. She's a bit shorter than me, and she slips her freckled hand in mine and gives it a squeeze for support. "Look, I know Lili isn't perfect. But surely, you've heard rumors of what Lili did three months ago, how she singlehandedly apprehended the last killer. I know you two are extremely powerful, but Lili..." Patty glances over at Stace nervously. Stace, luckily, is preoccupied with brushing Wilbur's hair. "You know that Lili is intimidating. If the murdered man's kin don't fear her yet, they will. It can't hurt to have extra protection on your side while Indah's hiding out here."

"Okay, but *why* help us? Forgive me for saying it, but I don't know of the Sweeneys being particularly charitable." Erzulie Fréda cleans a bit of dirt from her nails, buffing her sharpened manicure on her blazer, leaving no visible mark.

My tongue feels dreadfully heavy in my mouth.

I'd get angry that they don't trust me, but they have

every reason not to. Hell, there are many days I don't even trust myself. I'm the reason Jason lost his arm. I'm the reason Dakari Borden was murdered by that last serial killer. I'm the reason my partner Jo Kim still sleeps, unable to wake up, unable to live or die. I'm...I'm the reason this terror will end.

"I believe Indah deserves to be found innocent until she's proven guilty." It feels strange to say this out loud. It's a wild guess, what mortals would call a feeling of intuition, deep in your gut. It has no rhyme or reason to it, yet... "I've been called a monster before, even a killer. I was lucky to be able to prove myself innocent. I want to prove Indah innocent, but we cannot do that without hearing her side of the story." I raise my head, beaming widely, baring my own teeth for all to see. "And, as Patty said, it couldn't hurt to have some extra muscle on your side."

Stace glances curiously at me. "You don't look particularly fearsome..."

Ouch, all right, human. This is just my glamoured form, take it easy now. We can't all live in the gym and be pro boxers, now can we?

Erzulie Fréda chuckles, pointing at Stace. "You know, I'm starting to like you. You stole my pig from me. You insulted our beliefs, but I'm starting to like you, if only because you make Lili angry. And that entertains me."

I shoot the blue-haired *loa* a dirty look.

Dr. Weddo sits in an empty chair besides Indah. She folds her hands in her lap. Indah shrinks further into her chair as Dr. Weddo leans down, lowering her voice to a gentle hum that feels like a massage across your scalp just to hear it. "What about it, *cheri*. Are you ready to talk about what happened at the Kraken Club?"

Indah takes in a deep breath and lowers her legs to the floor. She looks up, pushing her long, dark hair past her shoulders.

And then, she speaks, and images bloom in our heads like the venomous foxgloves. Every word threads another line in a tapestry woven of a bloody sort of magic.

*

Indah speaks (if this can be called speaking)

THE GREEN MAN had a princely son, one whom he neither loved nor spurned. But the prince was a scoundrel, a ruffian who often accosted the women of the Kraken Club. For that, I was not sad when the Green Man lost his son.

And they have hated me ever since they learned my name. For names hold power, especially for the Fae.

But I felt something the night I tore his head from his shoulders. I felt something pushing inside me, pushing inside him. It turned us to the Before state, back to the times before we were just dying, gasping shells of ourselves, begging for one last taste of true power. It made us forget that we had ever been forgotten at all.

His eyes were dead already when he attacked me, and I felt that I was dead too. (If we could die, then this was it. To walk without knowing what my body was doing.)

It was only when it was all over, when his golden,

royal blood stained my fingers and claws, when the nail was firmly lodged back in my neck. It was only then that I came down from the high I was on. The feeling of power left me, and instead, I just felt utterly lost. I had lost...if I were human, I would've called it my humanity. I would've called it my soul. But, as you lot know, I don't have one.

Instead, I lost something else that night I was forced to kill the prince who tried to kill me.

When I looked in the mirrors, I still recognized myself. Same ashes over my skin that could never be scrubbed out, the taste of mourning on my tongue. The long, black hair, the earth-brown skin. I still recognized myself. But, at the same time, I didn't. The being in the mirror was a farce, a puppet who had been violated. My strings had been pulled, dangled, and cut in one foul swoop.

But the Green Man did not know any of this. The rush of power. The dead eyes set in both our faces. Some cruel puppeteer had us both in their grasp that night. The Green Man could not know this. He only knew that he had lost his son. And I was the unlucky pawn who cut off his head.

*

What in the Nine Circles was that?

WHEN INDAH STOPPED speaking, the tapestry of images fell. Only Stace remained unaffected, perturbed slightly that the rest of us had all gone silent at once. The air is thick with magic. All Indah did was rearrange it with her words.

And her pain.

Stace gets up while the rest of us are still in a magically onset fugue state, attempting desperately to separate the vaporous wisps of magic from the mundanities of our daily existence.

No, don't do it, human.

I want to hold them back as Indah is huddled with the nail poking out of the back of her neck. There are deep circles underneath her not-quite-human eyes. I can see the faint, wiped-away tears of blood underneath her left eye.

But I cannot move as Stace, still with Wilbur trailing out behind them like a strange sort of puppy, I cannot move as Stace kneels in front of Indah and just...

Waits.

They place their fingerless-gloved hands on their thighs and wait for Indah to take notice of them. Slowly, cautiously, Indah glares up from the ground and stares at the bold human before them like they're the greatest fool in the world.

Stace licks their lips, pauses a bit, and stares back with an unnerving sort of calm. One of their contact lenses has slipped, leaving the pink-toned lenses turning more violet in the odd light of the *loas'* home. Indah takes this in stride. If anything, it probably helps the botany-loving boxer mortal to blend into an environment that would otherwise eat them alive, literally.

"Please," Stace begins, "I don't blame you for not trusting us. You've been through a lot and just want to rest, I can see that. We aren't going to tear you away from this place if you feel safe here. We aren't asking you to trust us, but just…try us out for a little bit, okay? At least give us a chance." Their expression darkens for a moment, storm clouds hovering in their eyes. "We will protect you from the monsters who did this to you. Do you understand?"

I want to interject. *We're all monsters here.* But then, my snide self realizes that Stace, despite not knowing they are literally in the midst of actual monsters, isn't talking about that sort of monstrosity. *The Green Man. Pelle. The entire outfit at the Kraken Club. The kitsune boy getting leered over by that creepy older human man…*

I look to Indah. A fearsome entity in her own right. I can see the muscles corded underneath her human physique. I can sense the power lashed up tight inside her. Having seen her visions, the handiwork of the remnants of that green prince in the bathroom stalls, she's nothing to scoff at.

But the monsters… Stace isn't talking about the kind that sleep under your bed at night. No, they're talking about the rotten fruit of a society that does not respect a person's body as being their own. Stace is talking about the monsters who believe no means anything other than no.

Indah accepts Stace's open palm and, together, they get to their feet. They stand, sizing each other up in the middle of the shelter kitchen. The room smells like spices and meat and just a hint of rum. The floor beneath us, the tiles, shifts ever so slightly as the sun moves outside. Flickers of silvery sunlight vanish just as quickly behind the clouds.

Stace stands like the boxer they are, but their touch is anything but rough. They cradle Indah's palm in theirs as delicately as a butterfly.

And Indah, despite the ease with which she could simply remove the nail in her neck and assume her true form... She holds Stace's hand in return. And, for the moment, she even smiles slightly. "Okay," Indah tells Stace. "Consider this your chance granted." Then, she turns to Patty and me with a far less friendly expression. She bares the tips of her teeth at us, eyebrows drawn tight over her dark eyes. "And to you lot...you'd best prove me innocent. Or, if the Green Man's people get to me first, I swear I will curse your names as they tear me apart. And I will pray they do the same, and much worse, to you."

Patty, amber eyes shining with determination, makes two fists. Her hair gleams more auburn as the kitchen light strikes it. "I won't rest until you're safe."

Indah's face shifts suddenly as her eyes linger over Patty, taking the redheaded witch in. "Hmm, aren't you my knight in shining armor? Will you save me, knight in shining armor?" She sticks her tongue out at the last moment, a forked tongue if you had the sight to see it.

Patty pulls nervously at the ends of her hair. "I...um, I mean...I...if you wanted me to..."

"Okay, Romeo." I pull Patty away from where she and Indah are staring holes into each other. "Nice talk." I bow my head as I grab a puff pastry before we make for the door. I crunch into the dough, wishing desperately that the insides were raw. Perhaps we can even persuade Stace to donate Wilbur after all. Nothing tastes quite so good as fresh pig's blood. Well, except for revenge. But that's rarely delicious these days. *Damn my having something resembling a moral compass.*

"Uh-uh, Lilītu, not so fast." Dr. Weddo moves to block my path. "We all know you came here for more than a puff pastry and a chat. You want to talk to your lover, Jo Kim, right?"

I bristle. The skin on my arms suddenly seems to burn and itch. I think it's just spite grabbing hold of me like the devil it is. "Hard to do that." I swallow and the puff pastry goes down my throat like a chunk of cardboard. "Considering my girlfriend, Jo, is dead. Or might as well be."

Both my and Dr. Weddo's voices drop again, to keep this away from prying ears.

"Those who are undead don't die properly," Dr. Weddo admonishes. "You of all beings should know that, Lilītu." The doctor picks up a cardboard box seeping with oil and unmentionable liquids. The insides look normal enough, more puff pastry and some bundles that are too tightly wound to move otherwise. If I hazarded a guess, the contents of this case are anything but innocent. "If you want to see her again, you're going to need a necro-mancer."

My gaze slides to Patty, who quickly looks away. "But the Sweeneys aren't really taking commissions anymore after what happened three months ago..."

"No, not their kind of magic. *Our kind.*" Dr. Weddo closes the box lid with a snap. The oils at the bottom of the box disappear and the surfaces appear newer, brighter. There's a geometric pattern inlaid on the lid. I can't even see through the transparent casing anymore. "I have a young man who's been studying under our wing. His name is Erik Borden. He has old power in his blood, traces from the priestess of vodun in New Orleans. He can take you to the place where your sweetheart's waiting for you, the place where our kin Baron Samedi walks. There, you'll also find the Green Prince to tell you his side of the story." Dr. Weddo brings the box closer to me. The air tastes of bittersweet flowers and unsaid words. "Just take this bundle to Erik. He'll know the rest."

Erik Borden... Oh, gods above, is there anyone in this town who doesn't hate me...? Including myself?

I paste the sweetest smile on my face as I swallow the bitterest of pills.

"Of course, I'll deliver this to him." I take the package in my arms. "We're friends," I say, lying through my newly sharpened teeth.

Chapter Six

Wise men say only fools rush in

(Thank the gods we aren't wise)

Oh, by the way, we're at a farm.

Ee-i-ee-i-oh

WE'RE BACK AT the farm where we got Wilbur. Stace cradles the piglet in their muscular arms. The poor thing nestles in, occasionally whimpers, then relaxes again.

"It's staring at me. It's like its eyes *see* inside me or something," I whisper to Patty, noticing how the pig squeals whenever it looks at me for too long.

"Well, of course," Patty replies, smirking, "it knows you want to eat it."

I shrug. "Me? No..." The pig looks at me sideways again. I lick my lips. *I can hear its heart beating. The fear in its eyes. It smells so fresh.* "Okay, maybe."

Stace kisses Wilbur on the top of its head. "It's okay, buddy. You're safe now."

Patty and I exchange a glance.

Stace, unfortunately, catches it.

Scientists, always into being observant. Voyeurs, the lot of them.

"Wilbur will be safe, won't he?" Stace asks, hugging the pig tighter.

Dammit, I don't want to reenact Charlotte's Web *here.*

"Yes," I lie, unflinching.

"Well..." drawls Patty, avoiding Stace's gaze entirely.

Stace is about to respond when someone walks down the long path to the farmhouse. It's a rustic red building, except the red paint that was intended to make it look homey is all flaking off and looks more *Chainsaw Massacre* than anything. There's a porch out front and various yards for the animals to reside in. I doubt Wilbur has any memory of this place, but if he has, it's probably best not to remember it in the end.

And that pig is too smart for its own good.

The person walking from the farmhouse looks normal enough, except there's something to their gait. And not just their gait, but their shoes. The bottom of the soles, they look like...

"Evening," the figure drones. An upturned collar covers their neck up past their nose and thick sunglasses. "What brings you folk here?"

Stace holds Wilbur up to the heavens above like it's a reenactment of *The Lion King*. "We're here to return Wilbur."

"Wilbur?" The figure examines Wilbur for the briefest moment, then swivels to look at Patty then back at me.

It lingers for a while on me, and I shift my stance a little in the disquieting anticipation. "Who are you?"

Patty steps forward, pulling out a thin, flimsy receipt from her wallet. "Here, we bought a bunch of products earlier today. Turns out, our friends didn't want the pig. So, we're here to just...return him."

"His name is Wilbur," Stace adds, stroking the piglet's back for comfort.

The stranger nods, but not just their head. They move their entire chest section so it's really more of a bowing motion. "Okay. And your names are?"

But I'm not watching the figure anymore. I inhale deeply and smell something... *Odd*. No, not just odd. *Familiar*.

I look to the buttonholes of their jacket, a flannel tucked beneath a stereotypical set of farmer's overalls that are stained red at the knee. And beneath the oddly creased boots, like shoes that don't fit right, a set of bluebells are wilting.

And there's not just the scent of bluebells in the air. No, there's this odd humming in my ear, like bees or flies buzzing too close to my skin. No, not humming. *Ringing*.

And I remember Stace's words from earlier today, back with the fairies' bouquet in the inn. I remember how they held those flowers to their face and said... *"If you hear a bluebell ringing, it either means a Fae is near or death is."*

So, when the figure dressed in the ill-fitting guise of a farmer again asks, "What are your names?" I know I cannot keep silent any longer.

I answer their question with a command. "Tell us

your name first." Luckily, my words catch the imposter off their guard.

"My name...?" they ask.

And it's then I strike. Before Patty can scream or Stace can drop Wilbur, I tug the farmer's flannel so hard that the buttons pop open. And the creature inside the farmer's getup hisses and melts right out of their disguise. They kick off the boots and their toes grow into thick talons like a bird. Its hands are gloved by what appear to be large bluebells and its eyes and skin are dark blue. It wears crushed powder beneath its lids and over its eyes and has a human-enough seeming face except for teeth sharpened to razor points and a body comprised of wisps of flower petals held together by some invisible force. The petals unfurl into wings on its back, tattered slightly at the edge.

Around its neck is a locket, the charm made of sealed walnut shells.

"You're an *ellyl*," I whisper, "an elf of the *Tylwyth Teg* of the kind Queen Mab was a part of." I snicker at a sudden memory that pops into my head. "Aren't you supposed to be no bigger than an agate stone as Shakespeare wrote?"

"I got an upgrade because some of us have taste." The *ellyl* spits, gesturing to its walnut charm. It has a piercing at the bottom of its lower lip, and this catches on its sharpened teeth occasionally with a resounding *clack*. It turns to Stace first. "Why does that pixie hold onto that pig so closely? Are they bespelled?"

"A pixie?" *Oh, they mean Stace.* "Do you mean the boxer over there with the lemonade-pink contacts holding the pig?" Stace is staring at us all, slack jawed when their eyes catch the *ellyl's* piercing blue gaze. Wilbur is squealing to high heaven for the god of pigs to save him. "Nah, they're just a human, I'm afraid." I'm extra careful to avoid mentioning any names.

Fairy rules, after all. Names spell trouble in bespelling.

The *ellyl* does a double take, squinting its neon-blue eyes at them. "Are you sure?

The *ellyl* looks between me and Stace. "Seems an awful waste for *you* to be the immortal one and them the human. They're just so much stronger and more capable looking than you are."

I bristle.

Dear gods, the insults just keep coming. What an inopportune sort of day. My name isn't Narcissus, but damn if I'm not taking a big hit to my ego right around now.

"All right, joker." I try to grab on to the being's body, but the flower petals don't consolidate enough for me to get a proper grip. I unleash some of my power from my true form and my eyes go black. I can see it in my reflection in the fairy's crystal eyes. My power flows to my hands, allowing me to break past whatever fairy's cant allows the *ellyl* to fade in and out of existence like this. I feel its knobby body hidden beneath the flower petals, feel the cords of tension tighten. "Who sent you?"

The *ellyl* laughs, giving me a first-row seat to its sharpened teeth. "Up yours." And it spits in my eye. It smells like spoiled honey.

I lose my grip on the creature. It slips away and rushes toward Stace. They've dropped a frightened

Wilbur, who sprints back to Patty's vehicle. It hides beneath the car, behind one of the wheels.

The little traitor.

Stace is still in shock from seeing the magical creature before us. "This..." they mutter incredulously. They take a single step back. "Reality...impossible..." They scream when they finally take in my quarter-transformation. The eyes of pure black and the outgrown claws on my hands. "Lili? What the hell are you?"

Hell, how ironic.

"Yes, magic's real!" I shout. "Now duck!"

As the *ellyl* is still barreling toward Stace, their boxer's instinct finally takes over as they dodge at the last second. The fairy groans as it passes Stace without so much as a scratch and runs, instead, into a parked beige truck.

Probably owned by the farmers of this place...assuming the ellyl hasn't eaten them.

The *ellyl* spits into the grass. Tiny bluebells sprout from the place where it dribbles.

I stretch out my hand and my nails lengthen to talons. The ancient ink hidden beneath my skin comes into view, listing the unsaid names of power. The names shrieked out by the humans whose homes I decimated for time immemorial. My blood thrums this selfsame ink. I was cast out of clay, the villainized creation of the one called "Iam." I was made of the same clay that Adam was, the firstborn.

But they never gave me a chance.

They called me many names when they cursed me to the heavens, Hell, and back again.

But the most common one was...

Lilith.

"Oh no," Patty sees it on my face, sees my change about to begin. "You aren't going Super Saiyan here, Lil." She steps in front of me and the symbol of the Eye, called Evil Eye by some, the symbol of the Sweeneys' disgraced coven, appears on her forehead. It drips in dark blood, more for show than any real damage, and the power flows to her fingertips. Her nails gleam in bright-orange hues, as though fashioned out of molten glass.

Ah, there's the badass witch I know and love.

"Distract the enemy for me." She hisses the orders at me sidelong.

"Oh"—I crack my knuckles—"gladly."

You don't get to be this annoying in a single century, you know.

"Hey, Elly!"

The *ellyl* grimaces at me. "I'm an *ellyl,* you fool." It crouches down, its knees bending the wrong way despite its humanoid appearance, making it look like some spider in the dirt. "Prepare to die."

I raise an eyebrow at that. "What? No grand sweep of a sword? The whole 'my name is Inigo Montoya, you killed my father, prepare to die' speech…"

Dammit. Detective Ikiaq's nerdiness is really rubbing off on me. Speaking of which, we really should do another movie marathon once this whole murderous revenge plot case is over. Oh right. Someone's trying to kill me.

The *ellyl* tilts its head to the side, its face remaining eerily impassive. "You're protecting a murderer. And that *Kuntilanak* did kill my father, you fool." The *ellyl* shakes its whole upper body, digging its talons into the dirt. "Sam Hain, the Green Prince, son of the Green Man. Your lot beheaded him. Killers of a mighty prince." It opens its mouth and reveals its gaping maw once more. "Time to die!"

It rushes at me and digs its talons into my shoulder.

"Lili!" Stace reaches to the ground and picks up a discarded tree branch the width of two of their fists and the length of over half their body. I take up the branch, huffing a little.

Stace made lifting that thing look so easy.

"Patty, a little help here!" I can barely squeak the words out as the *ellyl* gnashes its teeth at me and I wedge Stace's branch between its teeth. A crown of bluebells sprouts up around my head, tugging at my skin. Its spit catches on my cheek and the flowers attempt to dig their roots into my skin. The ink wards barely keep them from settling in.

Parasitic bluebells. They really do think of everything, don't they?

Patty whispers something and an intricate design appears in front of her in light. She mouths another word, and a blast of dark-violet energy bounces forward and accidentally hits her bumblebee-yellow vehicle. The energy scatters through the air, bouncing with beams of light like stray bullets.

Something squeals as the car shakes.

"Wilbur!" Stace army-crawls toward the vehicle and cradles Wilbur in their arms.

But the pig...it's moving.

Or rather, it's transforming.

From its back, steel-gray feathers poke out. At first, they're hair-thin, but then, more feathers emerge en masse from the little pig's back. Soon, the gray feathers grow until they span twice the pig's body. Wilbur also grows stronger, more muscular, like he's suddenly become a proper hunting boar or something.

The wings spread, and I realize that Wilbur's wing structures are fashioned entirely of bone. Wilbur also has an encasing of armor, made of bone. A skeletal grim reaper sort of battle boar. I'd expect nothing less from a necromancer's magic.

The pig... Now... Pigs fly. And then. *Gods help me, this is absolutely ridiculous.*

I clasp one hand over my mouth, stifling laughter and simultaneous screams as the *ellyl's* talons sink further into me with the action. Skin tears in bright-hot heat as the creature's teeth sink into my exposed collar.

"Why are you laughing?" the *ellyl* shrieks.

"Because I've never seen something so ugly in my life," I reply, sneering at it.

It digs its talons in further, prying apart muscle and bone, sinew and blood. I can't hold my scream in any longer as one of its teeth catches my fingers and crunches at a nail.

Oh, that'll take a while to heal.

Patty screams and aims the spray of magical energy at the *ellyl*. The creature roars as it takes the full force of Patty's blast. The bluebells beneath me wilt and die. The flower petals on the creature's body blacken and rot. Its teeth yellow, and I turn my face away before I can see the *ellyl* grasping at what's left of its gums.

"Enough, *trócaire*. Mercy!" the creature cries, cradling its fallen teeth and bluebells. "Mercy, I beg of you. Stop the vile magic. The putrid magic from the rot-witch. Death, death, we cannot die. We do not die."

Patty raises an eyebrow, sweating profusely from her forehead, a sheen mingling with the black that drips from her coven's Evil Eye symbol. "Would you like to test that theory?" she asks the *ellyl*. "See if fairies die...just like your precious Sam Hain."

The *ellyl* snarls, pain and something akin to sorrow in its eyes. Patty's finger twitches and the *ellyl* goes silent, the pain replaced by an emotion I know all too well.

Fear.

"All right, Pats, that's enough." *Can't let the witch have all the fun.*

I lurch to my feet, my eyes dimming to regular, the tattoos fading on my skin. It's never comfortable, like stuffing oneself into fancy clothes after eating a large meal. Groaning and bleeding all over the place from my wounds, I place my boot on the fallen *ellyl's* knobby chest.

I hold the fairy's locket fashioned of walnut shells and tear the bit of cord. I gloat, holding it up over the *ellyl's* undulating body as its cantrip wears off and it begins to shrink to the size of an agate stone, just like Queen Mab.

"Mercy!" it screams.

Amidst its howls, watching it writhe in rotting bluebells in the dirt, I whisper with a smile on my face, my blood staining my shoulders. "Don't expect mercy from a demon, fool."

Once it shrinks to its proper size, I cup it in one hand and clench the walnut charm in my other fist. I go to the vehicle and take an empty fast-food cup from Grid's Griddle when we stopped to eat with Toothpick and Ikiaq.

"Enjoy your new home," I say, plopping the now miniature *ellyl* amongst the melted ice-cube and soda pop residue mixture. I fasten the lid firmly on top.

I examine the creature's angry silhouette as I hand the cup to Patty. "I think we'll call this little murderer Bluebell. Is that a good name for a pet?"

"I'm not a pet!" the enraged *ellyl* squeaks.

Patty tuts at it. "Quiet, Bluebell, or I'll accidentally charm you to have no tongue. I get cranky when I'm hungry." She closes her eyes to concentrate, dipping her fingertip quickly in the blood at my shoulder.

"Hey!" I hiss, clasping my hand protectively to the wound Patty had clawed into. "What was that for?"

Patty draws a script in my blood over the plastic drink cup's striped lid. The entire cup glows for a moment before settling once more. "Brief containment spell." The lid's sealed on the edges now with a thin band of light. "But, just in case..." Patty rummages in the front seat of her car compartment and plucks out a bag of cereal.

I raise an eyebrow as she shakes some of the flakes into the container through the straw opening, also glowing with a faint light. The *ellyl*, newly dubbed Bluebell, whimpers miserably.

Patty points the cover of the baggie to me, and I read "Iron-Fortified Flakes" next to a strangely anthropomorphized cartoon mascot rooster. "Fairies hate iron."

I nod. "Not the most conventional way of keeping fairies contained, but I give you high marks for creativity."

We turn around to the former battleground, little

more than a patch of dirt, some trees, and bluebell flower petals and blood. I kick dirt over the most suspect bits and turn to search for Stace. They're still, petting Wilbur's tiny skeleton tusks and snout with a dazed expression on their face.

I crouch down besides Stace, one hand hesitantly stretched out to them.

They glance at it with distaste. No, not distaste. *Distrust.*

"You're supposed to take it or…" I hold my hand out again, waving it a little. "Clasp it or something. It's meant to be a mortal gesture of comfort."

Stace gets to their feet and leans slightly against an ecstatic-looking giant enchanted boar with folded wings and unnerving looking eyes that I'm almost certain glow in the dark. "Magic and power and all these things exist." They fold their arms over their stomach, staring at a tree with a fresh battle indent in it. "Were you lot ever going to tell me or…?"

I pause, lowering my awkwardly outstretched hand. I open my mouth, close it, open it again, then finally settle on a hapless shrug. "Would you have believed us?"

Patty joins me at my side, mouth agape at Wilbur. "I didn't know my magic could do that. That's so cool! I made a whole ass battle pig." She's so absorbed in her handiwork, flushed with pride, when I elbow her. She coughs, flushing as she turns her attention back to Stace. "Ah, yes. Magic existing. We're sorry we didn't tell you about this. We didn't think you'd have to deal with it, but trouble follows us wherever we go."

Stace looks between me and Patty, their eyes searching for something.

If they're looking for a soul, they'll be distinctly disappointed in me.

"Jason knows?" Stace asks.

We nod.

"And..." Stace swallows. "It's why he was trying to leave for New York. And the murders you were talking about that happened a while ago. And...even Dr. Weddo and Indah and Erzulie Fréda, they were real *loas*?"

Again, we nod. Just like bobbleheads at this point.

"Well, Indah was a *Kuntilanak*. A flesh-eating spirit, but yes." When Patty mentions Indah, her flush only deepens further. "A really pretty flesh-eating spirit. With soulful eyes. And her voice sounded like daisies."

Stace doesn't notice the embarrassment and Patty's crush. They've still got that thousand-yard stare, and I almost miss their regular cockiness.

What is this feeling, guilt for lying to them? Damn my new conscience. It was for their own good... I think.

They scratch nervously at their ear, their piercings glinting in the sun. They reach into their pocket and pull out an inhaler, use a puff or two of albuterol, and hold their breath a moment. We wait in the quiet until Stace is ready to speak again, standing taller and breathing a bit easier. When they look to me again, their gaze is back to normal.

With that same cocky self-assurance I've grown fond of.

"Then I'll stay. If magic exists, it's my duty as a scientist to study it." Stace grins with a little wink. "This is the most fun vacation I've had since my sophomore spring break."

Patty and I exchange a look. Confusion, worry, and everything in between.

"Fun?" I wave one hand out, meekly grasping at the air. "This isn't..."

"Meet you in the car." Stace goes off, humming a merry tune, making for the passenger seat.

"I...they can't..." Patty's about to finish that thought when I point to the farmhouse.

We spy humans moving about the farmhouse windows. The owners, most likely the ones the *ellyl* charmed, are getting up and moving about the tiny space, tripping over their own feet and half-dressed in underwear and undershirts. I make out details of mussed hair and thoroughly confused expressions, eyes locked in an enchanted haze.

Time to go.

Patty points helplessly to Wilbur.

I lean into the boar and whisper at it. "It's your lucky day, bacon bits. Welcome to the family, kid."

I don't know if Wilbur understands me in his newly magicked status, but he looks happy enough. He trots along to the car, trying to keep close to Stace.

Patty nods, and we make our way to the car with a hissing *ellyl* called Bluebell in Patty's hand and a winged boar who takes up far too much of the backseat for comfort. He crushes me beneath his weight, squeezed in the back as I am.

We drive off from the farmhouse, the scent of rotting bluebells following us as we go.

I think back to the fairies' rhyme, back to their surprise poison bouquet.

Better you find her than our merry crew.

Better you find her before we do!

Well, we found Indah. She's protected by two of the strongest beings in Gamin.

The Fae. And we have one of their assassins in a sippy cup. *Your move, Tinkerbell. Your move.*

*

In the backseat of a bumblebee-yellow vehicle called Bee Bumble (for absolutely no reason whatsoever)

AS WE DRIVE along the road, Stace seems to have been lulled into a passive slumber with all the excitement. Patty's drumming her fingers along the wheel and fiddling with the radio when the silences go on too long. The speakers hum in a low talk show voice. I didn't realize Gamin had a talk show until the names start rolling in. They're talking about a different Minnesotan town not too far from here. I should've known.

Interesting things happen in Gamin, but none so interesting as having our own radio station, outdated as that may seem. What would our radio station talk about? The weather dragon stormfronts bring in? The top five nagas to visit or avoid? The murders being carried out by a potentially vengeful fairy-led organization?

Preposterous.

Patty doesn't seem to take much notice of the talk

show or the shadows flitting past the vehicle as we drive on in silence. She doesn't notice until I clear my throat to ask one heart-stopper of a question.

"Um, Patty, can I be dropped off somewhere?"

She startles and wriggles uncomfortably in her seat like I've mentioned that Wilbur grew zebra stripes alongside his skeletal wings or something. She sneaks her fingers toward the radio dial, as though wanting to turn it up higher. At the last second, she reconsiders and leaves us in that staticky limbo. "Should you be left alone after all that?"

I shrug. "I don't want to be a bother and take up any extra beds." I nod to Stace and Bluebell and Wilbur, all snoring away their troubles except for Bluebell, who chirps angrily. I shift slightly to avoid the fairy's burning gaze. "Besides, it seems there's no room at the inn with all the new magical misfits we've somehow gathered."

"There's *always* room for you, Lil. Always." Patty glances at me in the mirror. It's funny, how human eyes shift like that. They always search your gaze for something. Perhaps your heart, maybe your intention.

I'm used to how immortals look at you, like you're their next meal.

But Patty's searching for something, so I have to tell her something of the truth. No, not have to tell her. I want to. *Because she deserves at least that for being my friend.*

I lick my lips and dig a little deeper. "I want to be dropped off at Jo's house. It's been a couple days now. She'd kill me if I forgot to water the mandrakes. Well...*feed* the mandrakes." I notice how Patty's amber eyes shift ever so slightly away at the mention of Jo. We don't pass any vehicles on the road. It's eerie how there never seem to be any cars when we're driving. Just another perk of living in a place enchanted to be hidden from most nosy humans, I suppose. If the monstrous residents of Gamin didn't want to be found, then magic and the help of a willing coven would do the trick.

Mysterious murders don't help the tourism industry. Well, not except for the treasure hunters and the freaks and weirdoes, I suppose.

"Should I really drop you off at Jo's house? You were telling me all about those nightmare things you've been having. Those horrible visions."

I lean back, grinning a bit at that. "Aw, Pats. When you get to be as ancient as I am, every waking moment you continue to exist becomes a horrible vision. You get used to it." A fold between her brow creases, and she gnaws on her inner cheek until her freckles disappear. I soften my tone at that. I hate it when she worries. She's the only friend I'd made and managed to keep in over a millennium. I'm not going to lose her now because of some misplaced bravado. "I need to see her again, Pats. Even if she's a shadow. I need to remember Jo's voice, what she looked like." I curl my fingers up and straighten them again, marveling at how they've returned to something resembling a mortal's pretty flesh. Brown skin. Soft, curved nails. Not the talons of a demon walking around in a siren's body like a pinstripe flesh suit.

The hands of a person, not a monster.

I think back to Dr. Weddo's words.

"I have a young man who's been studying under our wing...Erik Borden."

"He can take you to the place where your sweetheart's waiting for you, the place where...Baron Samedi walks."

"There, you'll also find the Green Prince to tell you his side of the story."

"It's like Dr. Weddo said," I tell her, putting my thoughts to my lips, speaking the truths that haunt me. "If I have to face Erik Borden and atone for my sins, pledge my guilt—" I want to swallow my words, but too late, they've squirmed past my treacherous tongue. "—then I need to see Jo again, even if she's just a memory or a vision inside my head." I catch Pat's amber gaze in the mirror. For once, she can hardly look away. "Even if Jo isn't real, I need to see her. I need to see her, so I know what I'm fighting for...*who* I'm fighting for."

The vehicle, thankfully, rolls to a hesitant stop at the lone light. The red light blinks against a road that's half cement and half dirt with how it's paved. Construction projects seem to quit in this town just as soon as they start up again. I wonder if a golem's on the town council. They like open patches of dirt. Reminds them of the clay they were born from.

Just like me and Adam.

Patty turns around, twisting in the car seat, her bandaged and pastel-painted fingernails chipped from our recent fight with the *ellyl*. She holds out her hand for me to take, a firm handshake. A none-too-gentle reminder and a subtle threat.

Ever the resourceful witch, this one.

When Patty speaks, she sounds ten years older. I wonder, for a moment, whether that much time slipped away from me again. But no, she hasn't physically aged all that much for a mortal. She's just grown wiser. Indubitably stronger. "I'll take you to Jo's house," she tells me, voice firmer than her car's current rumbling ignition, "but you need to come back to us afterwards. No sinking into that other place. No letting *anything* get the best of you, not memories, not nightmares, not even yourself." She nods, her round face set and determined. "Promise?"

I take her hand and shake it, a smile tugging at my lips despite my best efforts to appear serious. "If I didn't know any better, I'd say you cared about me, Patricia Sweeney."

She smacks my forearm lightly, tutting at me as she turns back around in her seat. Bee Bumble rumbles slowly onward with its strange passengers occupying its seats. "You know I care, Lili." She laughs. "That's why I'll always keep coming back for you. And I'll do whatever is best to help you, no matter how much trouble it gets me into."

"No way I can persuade you I'm hopeless?" I ask. "Almost certain death, for example?"

Her giggles only grow as we drive on, the giddy, uncontainable kind. "If you think death will stop me, remember"—she winks in the mirror's glassy reflection—"you're talking to a necromancer."

Chapter Seven

Jo Kim's house

I'm not okay, but that's why you read about me

IT HURTS, HAVING to see the person you love over and over again in your memory, but not being able to interact with them. It hurts doubly when you might never interact with them again.

But I'm not doing this just to torture myself, no. I'm doing this for a reason. I need to talk to her memory. Even if she's just a shadow, I need to tell her our plans. At least then, I'd feel like she's with me still. I can feel like I'm actually capable of bringing her back to us.

She looks like I remember her during the first time we kissed. The first time I confessed romantic feelings. The first time I confessed it all. She looks like the first time we held each other, in a bathroom of all places. Feet against the tile. Arms all tangled up. She looks like the last time I remember being completely untroubled, blissfully, stupidly happy. She looks like how I remember her. Undead, with a little side of reborn just to keep things interesting.

I'm so busy staring at her that the rest of the world sort of fades away. I'm back in her house, where I return at the end of the day to ensure it's taken care of while she's...gone.

Yes, gone, that's the word. That short, ugly word.

Gone.

I'm at her house that smells like her, like lavender and gunpowder, smoke and cinnamon. I've stripped the covers off her bed and folded them neatly on a chair beside it. It's not like I need sleep anyways. Most nights, I just stare at the ceiling or do as immortals have done. We don't sleep, not really.

If humans and immortals are to be compared to computers, then humans sleep by shutting the computer off entirely. Entities and the magically infused variety of immortals don't need sleep. We're the ironic "sleep" function on an overheated laptop. The machine still whirs, everything still left on by all accounts. We cannot dream. No, at best, we enter this realm between sleeping and waking. We just wander our own memories like princesses caught in labyrinths. Minus the singing goblins, of course.

Sleep becomes a routine of resting within the darkness. We enter the space no mortals can enter without cursed magic. We roam a plane of endless wandering, the space wherein the horizon stretches for infinity. These are our Dead Realms. The curse to walk on and on forever until what counts as our bodies return to the dust that bore us. Never allowed to rest. Never allowed to die unless we are destroyed until the point that we fall into this plane for good.

If you get good enough at it, you can play old memories out as you wander. You can rearrange your memories to play out how you wish. You can't change that much about it. If you killed somebody in a memory, you can't pretend it didn't happen. But you can maybe make the sky purple. Or you can insert words you never said. Words you wish you had.

It's like filters over photographs. Dubs over bad audio. *Wishful thinking.*

I've re-entered the memory of the last time we stayed on a bed together. I'd already confessed my demisexuality to her, of navigating an intimacy inextricably tied to my emotions, of not feeling sexual attraction even to strangers I found aesthetically pleasing. I'd explained how it felt, of feeling sex-repulsed without love present, of having to seduce as a siren just to eat.

She'd understood. She'd understood better than most what it was like to be called a monster by others. She had died and been turned into a *gangshi,* a reanimated corpse according to the legends her Korean family had told her growing up. A fair bit of magic ill-begotten from crooked necromancers had turned the clock back. She's in her twenties now, half her head shaved and the other half falling in wisps dyed silver and blue. A tattoo of wings decorates the shaved part of her head.

I want to reach out, but I can't.

That's not how the memory goes.

"You're not here right now, Jo. As much as I wish you were. No, you're gone right now. They won't tell me where they have you. They're afraid it might set me off again." I tell her all this, venting, knowing this won't change how the memory goes. I know I'm speaking to a goddamn marionette for all it's worth, though the feel of her, even just the ghost of feeling, is enough to make me simultaneously love and miss her more.

"I'm sitting on this bed alone, Jo." The confession comes out unbidden, like a goddamn hiccup. "I'm sitting here, not sleeping, just remembering."

She says something. It's the same script as my memory holds, but it has nothing to do with what I'm telling her now. I might as well be speaking to ghosts. At least ghosts can talk back if you can see them. I've befriended a few in my own time.

She sips at ginger ale; I sip at the Bloody Mary with real blood. It tastes like a mere echo of actual Bloody Mary, a sour taste like the kind at the bottom of a can.

"People are trying to kill us again," I say, feeling better for telling her all this even if she can't hear me, can't respond. "But everyone tries to kill us. You know this." I chuckle at that. "You tried to kill me when we first met. I accused you of murder, being the hothead I was. Am. You used a shotgun to try and kill me, remember?"

I rub circles into her shoulder, and she leans into my touch. Pain stings at the memory. She feels so soft. Her hair touches feather-light against my skin. Lavender. Cinnamon. Smoke.

"It's all happening again." She's staring at the wall, contemplating a different conversation. A different time long past. I continue filling the air with my words, talking to memories. Talking to shadows. "Last time, it was forgotten gods trying to murder people in sacrifice and be less forgotten. This time, it's fairies trying to kill us. Two powerful *loa* are involved too. Ayida-Weddo and Erzulie Fréda." I pause, wondering how to go about this. I feel guilty just telling Jo's memory this. "I don't want to hope that what the *loas* said is true, that I can reach you. Because...because if I hope, and it doesn't come true..."

I laugh.

"Gods, Jo. I'll want to stop existing all over again."

She fidgets with the edge of her shirt, the shirt covering scars from past medical history. I see it. Crescent silver and gold. I squeeze her hand, just like in the memory. She looks to me, eyes caught and frightened, lower lip trembling. "What do I do without you, Jo? I know it's unhealthy to need someone so badly, but I'm so afraid I can't learn to love myself alone. How can you love someone who can't love themselves?" The words catch in my throat like folded sheets of paper. "Patty's been helping me manage my mental health. Witches can experiment and make medicine that actually affects ageless immortals like me, you know? She's been trying it all. Trying to brew potions for depression. Trying hexes for anxiety... And they've *worked.* I've been feeling it all again. Or...they worked until they didn't anymore. Maybe I am hopeless."

This part's hard to get out. To confess it all, even to a shadow, seems silly. "It's like opening your eyes and realizing the monster's been breathing down the front of your neck the whole time and you just couldn't see it, couldn't *feel it.* But now, I can feel again. And it's been so long that I forgot what it was like...to not feel like everything is dull and gray all the time. But feelings, dammit, they fucking *hurt.*"

I hug my arms around her, lower my head into her

hair. The shaved part of her head, the bristles, they poke into my upper cheek. "You were the only person," I tell her. "You were the only person who didn't look at me like a monster. An asshole, sure, but never a monster. And when you spoke to me, you felt safe, like I could be safe wherever you were. You didn't want me for my body, you didn't want to hurt me. You just wanted me. Messy, conceptual me." Her body cradles so neatly into mine as we cuddle it's a wonder we were ever separate at all. "And I wanted to save you, Jo..." I can't manage the next words.

But I couldn't.

A few moments pass, and I continue my one-sided speech to a shadow of memory, repeating words from a conversation long past.

"What if I don't do it?" I ask Jo's shadow. "What if the *loas* lied and I can't bring you back from whatever cursed place you ended up in?" I want to hold her tighter, but I can't. The memory doesn't play out that way. "You're sleeping now, trapped in the building of the Sweeneys' coven. They're trying to wake you up, Jo. You've been sleeping for so long. You fought a *naga* to save my life, and here I am..." I want to laugh, but instead, it feels like a sob. "I'm talking to your shadow. I'm pathetic and missing you so badly that I can do nothing else..."

She doesn't hear me. Of course, she doesn't. *She's not really here, no matter how much I want her to be.*

"I'm not a bad person," she whispers, trembling. It's just like it was in the memory. She's acting out a preplanned script, and here I am, pouring my heart out to a marionette puppet of the mind.

I intone the final words like rote. "I am," I say

because, no matter how much Patty Sweeney and the rest of what I can still call my friends tell me, I still believe it. I'm a bad person. What a horrible thought to attempt to burn away. Nobody can be as mean to me as I am to myself.

"This is Hell. But I'm going to do everything in my power to get you out of it, Jo." I spit out the words like an ill-fated prophecy, watching as the memory dissipates into nothingness.

I open my eyes, tired of resting. Tired of hibernating or whatever we immortals do. I open my eyes to an empty bedroom. No glasses of Bloody Mary. No cans of emptied ginger ales poured into tipped-over cups. No soft bed-sheets.

I look to my side, where my arms feel even emptier now that I can see nobody's in them. Everything feels emptier, inside and out.

Jo isn't here. Jo is sleeping, possibly forever. Gone to the place the undead go when they're dying. The unknown place, even to us, the ancient ones.

I hug my arms around my knees. "Jo...I'll wake you up, Jo. I saved the town from the last killer, and I'll do it again. I'll protect everyone. *Everyone.* And then...and then we can drink as many ginger ales as you can handle. I'll do anything to get to you. I'd do anything just to see you smile at me and make everything better. Make me want to make myself better..."

But there's no reply. Of course. *Jo is gone. And it's your fault.*

I want to scream, but instead I just sit there, too tired to do much else. Too tired even to rage, rage at the dying of the light. *Sorry, Dylan Thomas.*

*

Memories suck.

A FEW MOMENTS later, and my mind drifts to another memory, one I visit far less often. I let this one play out. No filters over misty photographs. Just truth.

We're the last two ones at the dinner table. Jo sips at a glass of ice water, the cubes clinking against the glass. She drinks it not because she needs it, being newly undead, but because it offers her a sense of normalcy. We all want that. Normalcy.

I blot at my lip with a napkin, leaving a deep-red stain at its edges from the blood in my cup.

She reaches out her hand suddenly, squeezes her fingers gently over mine. I wouldn't let others touch me like this, but the normal feeling of discomfort doesn't come. Not with Jo. I don't pull away because something blooms inside my chest. Trust. Emotion. I guess a human poet might call it love.

She smiles at me, silver-blue wisps of hair framing dark eyes. Those eyes soften when they see me. It's so different from the way I'm usually looked at. With unbent ferocity, enchanted desire, or disgust.

Soften. Cradle. Caress. Those are how her eyes seem toward me. Like an embrace without holding. Trust without question. Her eyes take me in as she squeezes my hand and whispers, "I know this is all new to you, Lili. We'll take this as slow as you need."

"I don't know," I tell her. "I don't know if I can do this. I've never had anyone trust me before. I've only ever fought for myself, blocking out the whole world. Imagine how big of an ego I must carry to ignore everyone around me for centuries. Hell, millennia."

"Narcissus would be jealous." Jo laughs, then her smile fades into thoughtfulness. "Wait, did you meet Narcissus? Is he real too?"

I grin at that. "Not half so good-looking as he thought."

"Let me try explaining it." She takes her other hand and clasps both my hands in hers. She feels warm, soft. She makes my heart flutter in my chest in the best of ways. Silver-blue hair and black eyes. Golden skin and words like honey. "I didn't start living until I died from a sickness I just couldn't fight. Not many people can say that, can they?" She laughs, a hard laugh, a tinge of smoker in it from when she lived. "I'm glad I died and came back to a world that had you in it."

"I just want to become worthy of you," I tell her.

She laughs so hard she nearly knocks over her water glass, ice cubes and all.

"You don't need to become anything." She speaks low, her lips moving hypnotically as she swears these words like an oath. "You loved me as a washed-up smoker with a shotgun. You loved me when my body was old, when magic made me young. You, Lili? I love you as you are."

Her skin against mine, that feels like a kiss.

She looks into my eyes as she tells me, "You are enough, and I'll love you unconditionally."

And for once, I feel like I am.

Tears in my eyes, I manage a whisper. "I'll love you until the end."

*

Awake

WHEN THE MEMORIES pass in a potent haze of magic and misery, I come to with a searing feeling in my chest. It burns throughout my whole body, but it's not overwhelming. This energy is invigorating. It's electrifying.

I clasp my hands into fists and swing my legs out over the edge of the bed as a new day comes, as the whole world comes into focus.

I'm enough.

I smile, thinking on a former smoker with silver-blue hair and dark eyes who'd held me in her arms when times were tough. And then, I think, *I'm enough.* And I begin the slow, steady trial of believing in it.

Chapter Eight

Stolen goods are good when stolen

I STILL HAVE the *ellyl*'s walnut shell locket in my possession. It burns a hole in my pocket, not literally, of course. It just feels like it's hot still with whatever magic had charmed the *ellyl* to be big enough to kill us.

I run my fingertips against the whorls in the shell, the sharp bite of the cord, its newly empty interior.

I look around the room, Jo's room, and run my fingers against the side table. A light layer of dust comes away with the action. I breathe on it, just a little, and a light cantrip brushes the dust away. I stagger a bit, woozy at the action.

It'd be so much easier if you just took your true form. No magic could be too much for you then.

I snort at the thought. "If I turn thirty feet tall in my true form"—I snicker at the idea of it all—"I'll end up wearing Jo's roof as a hat. And not everyone can rock that look, you know."

I pause, staring at the desk with the evaporated dust. There's a clay pot there, decorated with the Korean tale of

"The Fox Sister," the girl who turns into a fox and devours her parents at night. It was Jo's favorite story, fittingly enough. She always liked the stories with bite to them. The fox girl painted on its edges has red-hued eyes and hair that's turning half to fur. Dead cows litter a field beside her.

Charming. Jo was ever the interior decorator.

Inside the clay pot, a leafy plant holds dominion over the rest of the bedside table. Its leaves fan as innocent as a pothos plant, a "devil's ivy." But the truth is much darker, just like anything that resides in Gamin for long enough.

I open the desk drawer and reach for the vials labeled *Vampir Blut,* Vampire's Blood in German. Since the Sweeneys' coven, the Eye, was out of business while the Sweeneys were sorting out their New York affairs, we'd had to import from a kindly German-American coven in Leavenworth. If mandrakes can't access vampire blood, the other option is that from a freshly hanged man. But, considering that hanged men aren't any easier to access these days, vampire's blood seems a close second as I dash a few droplets onto the plant's leaves.

The whole thing shudders and growls and for a moment, I think the bottom roots of the plant dig themselves upward. From between the leaves, two sleepy, rooted eyes blink at me.

"More," mumbles the mandrake plant.

"Greedy little thing." I stopper the vial. But, because its beige-trunk eyes are so pleading, I dash the vial's edge so that any residue leaks directly into the ghoulish plant's mouth. "Any word from your sister, Tae?"

"You were talking to yourself." Tae, the mandrake plant, chuckles at that, the sound like leaves rustling in the wind. "You were pretending she was here with you." The tree coughs and splutters as I clip a leaf from it, none too gently. "Ouch, what was that for, spiteful demon?"

"Because you're being rude again, bullying the hand that feeds you." I open the walnut shell locket and tap Tae's leaves into it. "Jo was the one who replanted you, you know, saved you from being chopped down in the graveyard. I'd assume you'd keep a better watch over her. She'd watched over you all those years; from the times you were a mighty tree until the times you were no better than an e-garden houseplant."

The plant's features come into view, its roots pulling itself up from the dirt, whorled biceps of bark and stem. It smacks its lips as the *vampir blut* trickles into its mouth, chewing the blood like it's a piece of runny gum, fresh from the sun.

"She never believed my stories back when I was a human." The mandrake sighs. "She didn't believe it until she became a monster too, a *gangshi* no less. Eating souls and breathing their leftover remains onto my mandrake leaves. No fun, no fun at all." Tae opens his mouth and I see a pair of knobby teeth, just like human ones, residing in his tree-trunk mouth. It's a discomfiting sight, even for me.

Before I snap the walnut-shell locket closed, I spy the leaves glowing slightly like they radiate their own spears of moonlight. The locket whispers if I hold it up to my ear, like a seashell whispering the secrets of the ocean's dead.

"But I figured that, since your leaves transport souls,

you might be able to..."

"Talk to Jo? Is that why you took my leaves, because she breathed on them or because they belong to me, her transmogrified brother? Ah, you're getting sentimental." The mandrake raises its eyebrow at me, smirking with a bit of blood at the corner of its lips. "Ah, silly Lili. None of you have souls, you know this, not regular human ones. You'll need to talk to one stronger than me for that. But I have a hint you know that already."

"Baron Samedi, the kin to the *loas*," I sigh, roping the cord of the locket over my neck. The souls whispering on the mandrake's leaves feel warm against my skin, fluttering slightly like butterflies clasped in closed palms. "It was worth a shot, at least. I guess there's no point in avoiding the unpleasantry."

The mandrake shudders at the name, bits of dirt and blood flying off it.

"I grow weary now, demoness. My soul must exit this form and return home." Tae yawns, big and wide, those awful teeth coming back into view. "Time to go back to the Dead Realms. Maybe I can get a kiss from Todd Sweeney or a hug from the lovely Beatrice. I still haven't quite figured out the logistics of kissing as a spirit, you know. Nothing feels quite right."

"You do that, Tae. Rest up."

The mandrake's eyes shutter closed, its mouth returning to a grim line as its face sinks beneath the dirt. The trapped soul returns to being nothing more than a glorified pothos plant for the time being.

A whisper as Tae falls back asleep, his soul to return to the Dead Realms where mortal spirits walk in *mortem*.

Off the leaves, rattling, I hear, "Will you wake her? Will you save Jo?"

"I'll try," I reply, but at this point, there's no one but air to hear me. Air and dust and memories. "I'll try," I say because, sometimes, trying is all you can do. Trying is enough.

I open the drawer and slip the vial of *vampir blut* inside it. Some people might water their lover's sunflower plant while they're away and pet their lonely tabby cat. I feed her mandrake plant with vampire blood and casually talk about transporting souls of the dead. It's the same difference, if you've lived long enough.

I'm distracted from this very Detective Deckard in *Blade Runner* route of thinking when my cell phone starts to hum in my pocket. I pull out the accursed thing, wondering who has the audacity to call me when I spy the icon... *Detective Ikiaq. Of course.*

Sighing, I fumble with a few buttons for a bit to try to silence it. Now, it's humming some banal pop song from a few decades ago and the synth in it is absolutely shearing at my ears. I press another button, and the cursed virtual assistant pops up.

"*Grazie. Come posso aiutarla?*" my cell phone chirps.

"No. No *grazie!*" I press another button and growl with frustration into the receiver. "*Bastardo!*"

"Well now, that's rude even for you." Detective Ikiaq's bemused voice rings through. I can almost see him smirking now.

Great, there goes my chance at looking suave and collected in front of the detective.

But then, he exhales into the receiver. His voice

comes in lower, more serious. "Patty Sweeney is here with me now and our...mutual friend." That must be Bluebell, dammit. "Come to Grid's Griddle for lunch." A long, weary sigh that carries the weight of the world behind it. "We have lots to talk about."

I remain silent, too stunned to respond.

"I'll take that unnerving quiet as a yes. Hurry up, we've already ordered drinks without you. My treat." The detective ends the call, leaving me alone with my oh-so-troublesome thoughts.

Patty warned me she'd do whatever she thought was best in order to help me. I guess she stayed true to her word.

Chapter Nine

Welcome to Grid's Griddle, home of Grid's Griddle, can I take your order?

I TAKE THE back entrance into the Grid's Griddle diner, where I'm greeted with none other than the infamous half giantess who lent the restaurant her name. I catch a pin gleaming over her heart that carries the surnames of the mythical creature who gave her a powerful birthright.

Grid Sibbarayungan-Panganiban.

Sibbarayungan. This giantess's mother. I've heard tales of her. How she was so strong she could move mountains with her bare hands. How she chose mercy instead of rage, to spare a single human's life at risk of her own, at risk of exile by her own kin. It had always confused me, how a powerful entity could take to liking humans so much as to spare them. But I get it now. I, too, have grown soft-hearted for the weak, scrawny mortals.

Grid's Griddle, Gamin's infamous blueberry pie and charred bacon burger diner. Grid the half-giantess carries herself with her shoulders back and eyes wide open, staring at me from where I shuffle my feet awkwardly toward the back entrance of the restaurant. My toes catch over faded white parking paint and cigarette butts.

I wonder if Grid's heard about me like the *loas* did. I wonder if she heard how I skewered a murderer with my talon and grew taller than the trees. I wonder if she'll scream.

Most people do.

I'm a little disappointed when she doesn't react at all.

No, Lili. Remember, you left your theatrical, murdering days behind you. Even if they're fun to think about sometimes. Like remembering the glory days of college, if college included ancient blood rituals and profane worship.

Grid appears to be on break at the moment, leaning against the back door of the diner with her apron untied, chewing some bubblegum. Most of her flesh is human flesh except for her forearms and fists, where gleaming brown skin turns into the rough, sharp edges of a tree giant's flesh, like her skin is formed out of the rough bark of a tree itself, impenetrable and jagged. A pair of gloves sticks out of her apron pockets.

She takes the gloves out when she notices me staring. They're thick, padded things, could be mistaken for oven mitts. Appropriate for a diner, but it leaves me wondering if she has to resort to Fae glamour like Bluebell when she wishes to walk in daylight.

"Take a picture." The lace thread of the glove is caught between her teeth as she laces them tight with a snarl. "It'll last longer."

I close my eyes and will my form to peek to the surface, the names hidden beneath my flesh, the arch of talons beneath my nails. "Don't worry, I'm like you," I reply. "We all have our beauty marks."

"I guess we do." She smiles a little to see an inkling of my true form, edging her way into the diner through the metal back entrance. I dance around a dishwasher with plates licked clean of delicious-looking morsels. "I hope you enjoy your meal."

Steam and gas stoves give way to a long corridor with bathrooms in it, beaded curtains tied over the gender-neutral stalls for a sense of privacy.

A pixie with a tattoo of Tinkerbell on her wrist winks at me as I head in. I curl up inside myself, eyes focused on Grid's well-defined shoulders.

Damn, they really meant "all are welcome" back there, huh? Even Fae. But they look too bewitched by Grid's food to fight. A Fae bewitched by someone else's food. How ironic.

I follow Grid into the main dining area, where she wastes no time tending to the dozens of hungry customers, human, reanimated, and immortal alike. The diner's in full swing for lunch, even as the sun peers in through slivers of cloud outside. The seats are padded in purple vinyl and the whole place has this lavender-hued theme. I spy a vampire drinking a suspiciously red malt on the counter. A hydra toasting with a naga, the hydra curled around the booth while the naga has politely folded in its tail. They split a soft round bread whose contents I dare not mention.

The human customers don't take notice of their magical counterparts. Or, like Bluebell's glamour, maybe they see something else entirely.

Lethe's work. She and her magical river of memory loss that runs through Gamin's land. It hides us from human eyes, keeps them from hunting us for sport. Aside from vengeful murdering, at least the goddess of forgetting did something good for the magically inclined here. Though if the humans knew about me and all I'd done, I'd probably be the first one they tied to a stake.

Detective Ikiaq waves at me across the chaos. He's a taller man with his regular form easily surpassing six feet, though still shorter than the giantess Grid. But something about him always gets my attention. Maybe it's the way he never gives up, even with me.

Even when he should have given up on me long ago.

I go to sit beside him, ducking my head behind my menu. Toothpick and Patty attempt a halfhearted greeting on the other side of the booth.

"We'll have to talk eventually," the detective rumbles kindly.

"And here I was going to just pretend the problem didn't exist until the end of time," I reply, scanning over endless egg options and sides. I look to Patty, where she bats away Toothpick's crumpled napkin. "No Stace today?"

Patty shrugs. "They decided to take the day off and explain to Jason why they're adopting Wilbur as an emotional support pig. Support boar? War boar?" Patty gazes at her nails a moment before shrugging it off. "My brother's taking the news like a champ."

Code for Stace convinced Jason that a world without Wilbur wasn't a world worth considering. Good for them.

Grid runs the diner with a finesse that only experience buys. Her trays are packed high with pancakes so thick and stacked so tall they must have weighed tons with all the cutlery atop it. Whipped butter, cuts of cream, and slathers of jam melt on them.

My arms ache just thinking about it.

She's tall at nearly eight feet, and she has to maneuver her curvy stature around booths and, at times, rambunctious patrons who want a second helping of buttered toast and bacon-wrapped patties.

One white-bearded gentleman says something from the corner of his mouth and sneers in Grid's direction. His buddies laugh and Grid stares him down at the presumably rude joke.

I get up to help, but Detective Ikiaq shakes his head at me and waves me down. "Watch."

The man stops laughing as Grid leans in close and smiles widely for him. Her teeth have braces shaped like skulls. Her eyes, though unmistakably a product of her human half, have *that look* inside them. It's the look I knew all too well. I wear it often.

I'm going to kill you, reads the stare. Grid places her gloved hands on either side of the man. She outweighs him and towers over him like he's a mere child. Her eyes completely empty, devoid of anything but thirst, hunger, and rage.

The bearded man takes out his wallet and adds extra money to Grid's tip, ducking his head low as his buddies quiet to a death knell's silence.

Ah, now that's *customer service.*

I'm the only one who noticed. Toothpick, Ikiaq's part-werewolf detective agency partner in solving crime, is staring at Grid like she has a choir of angels around her.

Angels in Gamin, ha, what a joke.

Oh wait, didn't he mention that he and Grid were school friends or something?

"Gr-Grid?" Toothpick clears his throat and tries waving her over. "We...um, we'd like to order. Please." He looks helplessly at me, crammed next to Detective Ikiaq and the soda container containing Bluebell.

What, is he trying to impress me that he knows the owner or something?

Ah, he's young yet. He'll get over it in a century or two.

"Hey, Gerald!" Grid waves back in our direction.

Toothpick blushes to high heaven, choir of angels and all.

Gerald? Damn, that's a name for a werewolf all right.

No wonder he goes by Toothpick. At least it has the word tooth in it, all sharp and gnarly.

Grid comes over, flashing a big smile at Toothpick/Gerald that makes him blush up to his ears. "My *lola* made a special helping of ube pudding for y'all. I know you like our desserts, Gerald. Oh, wait, you go by Toothpick now, right? How *cute*. Big man out here working on the case. All grown up. Wow, how would our kid selves see us, eh? Me running a diner and you...running." Toothpick sinks into his seat at being called "cute" of all things. Not noticing his obvious embarrassment as he peers over his sticky, laminated menu, Grid just clips on. She turns to face Ikiaq. "Big case, detective?"

Detective Ikiaq shakes Bluebell's plastic soda cup. The fairy rattles around in the container like ice cubes. The detective coughs to cover its angry squeaks. "Something like that. A double burger, raw, for me. Milkshake and loaded fries for Patty. Kid's meal for Toothpick. Sorry, Gerald." Toothpick opens his mouth and shuts it when Ikiaq winks at him. "And, for Lili…"

Grid turns to me, still flashing that smile. I can see each individual skull in her braces. They look like they're screaming in horror. *Nice touch.* "We met. Nice to meet ya properly though, Lili. Let me see." Grid peers at me for a moment before slapping the table for emphasis. "I know. A steak, bloody rare, is that right?"

I blink a few times, look to Patty, and nod. "Is that magic?"

"Nah, just know how to feed people's souls. My human *lola* taught me that, from my dad's side. My dad taught me how to cook." Grid turns around to stick her tongue out at the retreating backs of the bearded man's table. They've left with their tail between their legs, not so much as glancing Grid's way on the way out. "My mom"— she taps on her nametag where it reads *Sibbarayungan*— "she gave me my mettle. Taught me how to fight anybody of any size. Even if I'm smaller than full-blood giants, I can put up one hell of a fight." She points to her gloved hands, sliding them up to show us the sharp bark. Then she smiles wider. "And these too."

I tilt my head to the side, intrigued. "Can you tear through flesh with those teeth?"

She laughs, a hearty laugh, raven hair gleaming thick behind her. "Nah, she just had a pretty smile was all. Why, will you teach me how to hunt when you wolf up?"

Toothpick blushes further. "Uhh..."

I roll my eyes, elbowing him slightly.

"Yes?" he finally squeaks.

"Sounds like a date!" Grid hugs him and I think the poor kid's going to positively *perish* when she finally leans back and takes our menus. She salutes the detective before she goes. "I'll sneak in some ube pudding, on the house. Good luck with the case, detective."

Detective Ikiaq glares at me, giving me that severe side eye. I see antlers peek from his skull. I have to blink a few times to clear the shapeshifter's image back to his regular form. "Oh, I'll need some luck, thank you."

He stares me down and my discomfort only grows as Grid leaves. It's an itch along my arms, a swarm of larvae, my anxiety at this confrontation, digging deep.

"Look, it was only one fight with the Fae," I tell him.

He raises an eyebrow at that. "You fought with the Fae?"

Patty slumps in the booth, bent over with her head in her hands.

Oops.

The detective drum his fingers against the table, leveling his gaze at me like a disappointed parent. My vision swims and I duck my head low.

"They were trying to kill us?" I add.

He raises a thick brow at me. "Is that a question?"

I shake my head *no* and Patty just sighs into her hands; her head still covered by her arms. Toothpick nervously stirs his straw around his water glass, ice cubes clinking against the sides. I tap on Bluebell's cup in consolation.

"This one." I shake the cup and the *ellyl* inside shrieks. "This one tried to kill us."

"It's the size of a wasp," he replies.

"Well...yes. Now. Bluebell had a power enchantment on."

"You named a fairy *Bluebell?*" The detective blinks slowly at my stunned silence and takes a long sip of his syrup-sweetened coffee.

I just can't win today.

Patty finally raises her head. Her hair's molded to her face from where she'd smushed her head into the table for emphasis. She takes in a deep breath and exhales through her nostrils. "Look, detective. I just thought that, since we split up in the last case and things went badly"—I lower my eyes at that, *yeah, like tons of people dead badly*—"I just thought we should be on the same page. We're going to meet with Baron Samedi to find the shade of the Green Prince. We're going to ask Erik Borden to help us since he's one of the last necromancers still working in town."

The detective swallows his coffee with much difficulty, as though it's stuck in his throat. The corner of his eye twitches once as he curves his fingers into his palms, digging into skin.

I think this is one of the few times I've ever seen Detective Ikiaq unnerved. And that scares me.

"You're going to the Crossroads?" His voice is rough, worry unmistakably grating in it.

The Crossroads?

It's then that Grid comes back into the scene. Toothpick, for some ungodly reason, nearly knocks his glass of water over the edge of the table. "Careful, splash zone," Grid teases, handing him a gob of napkins. She lowers down a heavenly array of food. A basket of fries with a medium-rare patty dripping fat onto them and a neon-green pickle for Toothpick. Julienne potatoes smothered in gravy and cheese for Patty. A thick double patty with raw hamburger meat for Detective Ikiaq. And a steak that's bleeding into a mash of tartare and a drizzle of Bloody Mary sauce on top for me.

Toothpick waves at her retreating back, then awkwardly drops his hand when the detective glares at him.

I clear my throat as the detective places a napkin in his lap and, just to be polite, we all follow.

"So, what are these Crossroads?" I ask around a mouthful of deliciously bloody tartare. *Not as good as flesh that's still crawling and screaming, but it's at least a demon's version of tofu substitute.*

The detective takes a bite of the bread, crunching through the toasted butter. He dabs at the blood with a napkin and washes it down with another sip of sugary coffee mixed with hot cocoa residue at the bottom. "The Crossroads are the place between the mortal world and the Dead Realms. Baron Samedi, they're the *loa* of resurrection. They guard that place of in-between. It's where you'll find all sorts of entities that nobody wants to mess with." He sighs, and I stare at the blood seeping into the edge of his napkin. "But why am I surprised you lot want to visit?"

He doesn't think you'll succeed. You're a failure. Just like last time. I close my eyes, trying to will those thoughts away. Except they remain at the back of my mind, haunting me. "We have to try," I tell the detective, breaking through the horrible, eviscerating thoughts for a moment of clarity. *Even if I fail.*

I lower my fork and place it on my napkin, leaving the rest of my food untouched. Patty nods to my mostly full plate, and I just smile at her, explaining nothing. *You can't lose it, Lili, not now.* "I'm sorry." I tense all over, releasing my muscles in a horrible shudder. "I just... I felt weird just now."

Patty moves to squeeze my hand gently with hers. "Was it seeing Jo again?"

No. No, it's something worse. Something I thought I dealt with a while ago. It's come back.

"Lili?" Patty furrows her brows at me. "Are you okay?"

No! "Sure," I lie, and when she removes her hand, I feel it. The gift she's slipped into my open palm. A potion vial of my good old-fashioned demonic antidepressant. Only a talented witch like Patty could make something like this. Only a kind person like her would still be willing to help me after she learned what I am. *What I might become.*

"Is handing me this dose just to play nice again?" I smirk, attempting to play this off as a joke. Even as I know it isn't one, the hurt seeping into my venomous smile. "Or are you going to run off and tell Detective Ikiaq about this problem too?"

"No. I remembered you missed a dose when you went to visit Jo." Patty squeezes my hand again, tapping her fingers over mine with a light hum of worry. "And the detective's on our side, Lili. Goddess, you'd think you'd learn to trust us by now. Working alone is dangerous, Lil. No, not just dangerous. It's *deadly*." Then, bells tolling loudly with a buzzing rushing in my ears, she says, "Jo wouldn't want this."

What do you know about what Jo would want, mortal? I get mad, so mad my stomach wants to retch, and I clench my hands into fists, and I want to... I want to... My stomach immediately turns into knots at the prospect.

I decide to drop my anger. *Just pick your battles, Lil.* "Thank you." I toss a careless smile her way, pocketing the vial as I turn my attention back to the food on the table.

Grid's snuck some ube pudding into crescent-moon-shaped side dishes for us. I sniff at it and take a bite. The pudding melts on my tongue and spreads a creamy sweetness in its wake.

It's all very delicious, but my stomach can't hold a single drop. Like Tantalus punished in the depths of Tartarus, always able to see a grand feast without being able to devour. Always hungry, but never satisfied. Not even humored. All the temptation, none of the sin. *Or was it vice-versa in my case?*

I dig my nails into my palms until my hands ache, willing my nervous stomach to settle. Meanwhile, Detective Ikiaq shakes Bluebell's cup, miffed when the *ellyl* starts screeching.

"*Coc y gath!*" Bluebell squeals, banging its twig arms on the side of the cup, hissing at the cereal flakes burning it with iron.

"Did you just call me a cat's...a cat's...?" Detective Ikiaq shakes his head, mortified.

"I don't play nice with the law." The *ellyl* crosses its

arms and squats down, its silhouette a hard shadow on the plastic Grid's Griddle cup. "I'm Fae. Your rules don't apply to me."

"I'll apply something else if you keep it up," the detective growls back. Bluebell just sticks its tongue out in response, a miniature tongue ring glinting bright against the thin plastic casing. The fairy sparkles against the cup interior, a twinkling lightbulb under a shade.

Push through, Lili. Push through.

For them.

I release my grip on my palms. The wave of queasiness passes me by.

"Lili?" The detective peers into my face, his dark eyes sparkling from up close. "Are you feeling all right?"

I smile wide as I raise my hand to grab Grid's attention. The giantess carries some paper bags and containers over. The bags seep through with her heavenly cooking. I even spy Grid's *lola* from the back, a wide smile with soft, wrinkled skin and twinkling eyes. She's snuck in some extra ube pudding for Toothpick's sake.

"Never better, Ikiaq," I tell him, avoiding his eyes, the sugar-sweet concern. "I've never felt more like a person." I take an extra-large bite of ube pudding for emphasis and swallow it around the anxious feeling burbling in my stomach. "The Crossroads don't stand a chance."

*

I'm at the Grid's Griddle

I'm at the detective's car

I'm at the combination Grid's Griddle and detective's car

THE SKY IN Gamin is always gray. Maybe it's Lethe's river, the eternal mist that shrouds this town and all its inhabitants. Maybe something in the magic keeps the sun from shining through, veiling us from the world like a thin scarf held over all our eyes.

I lift my eyes up to see a splinter of sunlight shine through, an arrow shot before clouds quickly cover us in shadow again.

I stick my hands in my peacoat, the kind of military style with deep pockets and too many buttons. I've had this thing carried through wars, old smoky alleys, and countless knife fights where I had to pay the tailor extra to scrub out mysterious bloodstains from wounds that healed instantly after a quick, gory snack. In one of my pockets, I have a wrapper from candy that quit production in the Victorian era. Not like I need that much shelter from Gamin's gloomy, cold, and misty days, but the jacket helps me feel comfortable in my own skin. It's one extra layer of invisibility, my collar drawn up higher from prying eyes, my dark hair, pulled into a low bun, tucked against my neck.

I catch my reflection in a puddle for a mere moment. Silver eyes. I used to change my eye color more often in my younger days. Had a taste for drama, like all other brash immortals. I've taken to the silver though. Reminds me of Gamin's sky.

I crush my boot against the surface, watching the ripples distort my body. Brown skin, black hair, silver eyes.

All gone.

For just a second, I think I see the hidden me. The one I've carried for far too long.

Lilītu.

The ancient form's smile is a bleeding gash with rows of shark's teeth and eyes deep, empty pockets like a horned owl's gaze. Her names are written all over her skin, blood ink long turned to shadow beneath her flesh. She laughs so loud I almost hear her.

I crush my boot harder until I feel my heel ache.

Stay down.

Stay normal. Or close to it as you get.

Detective Ikiaq bends over from his tall height to stuff his leftovers in the backseat with the *ellyl* strapped into a rat's cage he's got in the back. The bars, fortuitously, are fortified by iron shavings.

Bluebell sticks up a middle claw to flip us off, though since the thing only has four fingers, it's more like second from the left.

Toothpick sips an impulse-buy malt through a too-thin straw, the kind that's guaranteed to get gobs of ice cream stuck halfway through. Patty hops from foot to foot trying to keep warm, a plaid sweater swallowing her up in its knitting.

I think I catch a receipt with a number scrawled on it in pink in Toothpick's hand. He moves it away before I can read it. I thought I saw "G-r-i-d" written on it though.

Lucky dog. I catch myself. *Lucky half-wolf.*

When the detective comes strolling back from his car, we stand apart from each other, in a little uncomfortable circle in the middle of a half-full parking lot. The lunch rush has emptied out, back to quiet work away from Gamin's town center. Away from a world of magical mayhem and murder.

I keep my eyes on the spilled puddle at my feet, avoiding the detective's shrewd gaze.

I was never one for backing down. But still...

In this case, I very bravely address the puddle instead of meeting the detective's impatient gaze.

"We saw Indah."

The detective's laced shoes switch the weight onto his other side. Toothpick's wearing schoolboy loafers and Patty's in platforms with a pair of tights. Intriguing.

"And?" the detective's voice booms.

I turn a little to address Toothpick's loafers. "She told us she was possessed the night of the murder. Someone else, or *something,* it had control over her."

"The bastard prince was far from being innocent too," Patty mutters. "Good riddance."

Ikiaq groans at that. "Bastard or no, the fairies won't stop until they've gotten justice, or a head. Whichever they find first." The detective sighs, the weight of protecting all of Gamin on his shoulders. Must weigh fifty pounds, at least. "You didn't bring Indah in then?"

"Indah's under the *loas'* protection." I pause. *Ah, this part will be a witch to try and confess.* "And she's under my protection too, sir."

Slow words, spoken from a disbelieving feeling of dread. "What are you saying, Lil?"

Ah, screw all. "What I'm saying is...you'll have to go through me to get to her."

I look up again and Detective Ikiaq's face is blank. I

blink and see wide nostrils flaring from a long, furred snout. Antlers breaking through an elongated skull. Just as quickly, the image disappears and I'm staring into regular brown eyes above a jacket bearing a cup of hot cocoa and a caribou patch.

"I see. You've chosen a side then." Detective Ikiaq places his hand on my shoulder, clasping it in a concluding gesture. "Today was a good meal together."

He turns his back on us, shaking his head slowly.

I see, from the edges of my vision, a tall shadow. A shapeshifter with deep eyes, sharp teeth, and a bony caribou's spine broken in three places as it lumbers forth on two legs. Snow perpetually dusting a dark coat and muscular, humanlike torso. The cement gray of the parking lot forms a poor horizon for such a mighty creature.

"We can't meet again, Lili. Not for a long while, I'd expect. I'm sorry," Detective Ikiaq says. Not in admonishment, not in anger. Just a fact that, until this case with the Fae and the *loas* and more are settled. I've chosen to lay down my eternal existence for Indah. Ikiaq's stuck reporting back to the Fae who brought the case of what looks like one-sided murder to him. There are no allies in Gamin.

Not anymore.

"We had to tell him, Lil," Patty says, staring up at me with her amber gaze focused on my left ear so she won't have to stare into my eyes. "We had to."

"I know, Pats. I know."

"Back to the inn then?"

I smirk. "You're letting infamous demons stay at the Sweeney Inn now?"

She shrugs. "We didn't get rated four stars hospitality

for nothing."

Sighing, we turn to walk to her bumblebee-yellow vehicle across the cement expanse. She's parked crookedly between a fire hydrant and an electric scooter. The car's scratched bumper's seen better days, as has this parking spot most likely seen better parking jobs. But I'm not going to tell my free ride that.

Then we hear it.

Heh. Heh. Heh.

Deep exhalations. Guttural with stomach acid and spittle punctuating it. A deep whine from the back of a scared dog's throat.

Heh. Heh. Heh.

The sound of something heavy moving across the cement. A curdled cry, a human cry.

I whip around to see Toothpick clutching his hands to his face, screaming. Hair runs along his arms and ankles, gray and matted.

No, not hair.

Fur.

Then, the awful, strangled whine.

Heh. Heh. Heh.

Toothpick's dropped his malt to the ground. Slipping in the mess, he drops to his stretched-out hands. His face has morphed into a snout. His arms and legs bulge like he's suddenly been deadlifting since he popped out of the womb.

I look to the sky. No, that's the sun still out. No moonlight.

No werewolves. There can't be...

"No moonlight and he's wolfing up. Is this a half-werewolf thing?" Patty asks me, her hands to her sides. She's got the Eye symbol, bleeding like a reopened scar, on her forehead. Her magic surges to her fingertips. A crackle of electricity in the air.

Toothpick's eyes peer out from a strange half-morphed werewolf face. Those eyes…

They're emptier than my soul.

Just like…like…

"I don't want to be right about what I think this is." I shake my head. "But whatever it is, get the hell ready."

I scream as the ink comes forth to my skin, just one line of my old names against my left forearm. Veins pulse with ink on that arm, all my force focused on that one limb. Talons rip out from my nailbeds as I claw at the lunging half-wolf's jaw.

Heh. Heh.

Again, that horrible whine as I strike the morphed Toothpick down. He barely registers it, shaking his head, wolf-like but with human skin stretched over it. He takes his arms, now morphed into claws, and slams them into my shoulders, tearing through flesh.

I can't help myself. I scream.

"Lili!" Patty raises her arms and gathers her strength in red-violet energy overhead. Dark matter drips down from the symbol of the Eye on her forehead as she concentrates her energy on Toothpick.

A shadow hurls itself in front of the wolf before Patty's attack strikes.

I roll away, coughing up blood as, aching, I turn to see who shielded him.

Grid's clutching onto him with a bruise blooming on

her cheek, a singe against her back which, as her clothes have burned from Patty's attack, reveal the hardy element of an expanse of wooden flesh. Her gloves are off, hands formed from tree bark holding him with the strength of the mountains. The strength of the trees.

Heh.

"Toothpick!" she shouts. "Gerald." She whimpers as, unseeing, he swipes at her arm. His claws get trapped in the tree bark. "Can't you recognize me?"

"It's the possession!" I reply, wheezing the answer out, clutching my hurt rib. "He doesn't know you."

Grid holds him tight, wrestling his struggling body against her grip. His whines punctuate in a lonely howl before, finally, he succumbs to his exhaustion and slips downwards.

Grid slumps to the concrete, still clutching him sadly to her.

"Toothpick?" she whispers.

Toothpick breaks free when her grip lessens up and rolls her over, his claws around her abdomen, clutching so tight his fingers, what's left of them, press into her skin.

The damned beast was faking it.

He puts his arms around Grid's throat, pressing down with his whole bodyweight as he squeezes with all his might.

I struggle to crawl toward her. I close my eyes, willing more power to come through. *I'll be damned before I lose someone else. Even if I damn others with me.*

A squeal of tires and the smell of burnt rubber and exhaust as the detective's gray vehicle slams into Toothpick and sends him hurling over Grid's body. He rolls to a stop at a dumpster, his exhausted body melting slowly back into the acne-covered young adult we all know and love.

And something else, something glimmering beneath his lips. Like glitter.

I try to lean in and examine the strange, glittering substance on Toothpick's mouth and chin, but Detective Ikiaq barks an order as loudly as he can and startles me away from doing so.

Detective Ikiaq staggers out of the vehicle. He props silver handcuffs on Toothpick and hauls the young man by his shoulders. Grid follows, holding his legs up.

"The customers were placing bets from inside the diner and when I heard the howl, I knew..." Grid shakes her head as they load him into the back. His chest still moves up and down, luckily, and Wolf Boy looks better than I feel. "He morphed a couple times when we were kids, but he had better control than that. I know he still does. And there's no moonlight..."

Unless...

His eyes. Those empty eyes.

"He's not under his own control." I wince as I shove myself to my feet. My arms feel just about pulled out of their sockets. The wounds on my shoulders are enough to make a doctor in a medical drama wince. And I know Patty's got her patchwork cut out for me for this fight. "I told you, Ikiaq. Something did to him just like Indah. Possessed him like that. Possessing monsters to turn to our full forms, to do murder."

Detective Ikiaq looks slowly into all our faces. He walks up to me, and I'm worried he'll shift into his true form and smack me for being all *I'm right, you're not* when he literally just had to run over his partner with a car. Instead, he presses a box of princess-unicorn-themed bandages into my limp hand and gets close enough to my face to whisper in my ear.

"Stop whoever's doing this at *whatever* cost," he tells me, a grim set in his eyes. He turns away and speaks some words softly to Grid. He waves at Patty, who waves back, the symbol of the Eye disappearing from her forehead as she rushes over to help me get to the car. As I crumple in my seat, I know this for sure: Detective Ikiaq might be on the Fae's side on paper, but he's on our side in his soul. And that's what really counts. *Assuming any of us have souls left in Gamin.*

Chapter Ten

Unicorn bandages are pretty

"AND THAT'S THE last of that."

I glance down and see Patty's smeared some foul-smelling poultice on my shoulder wounds. To add insult to injury, she places a bright neon bandage of a cartoon unicorn in a crown on my forearm.

"There's not even an injury here," I tell her, scratching at the bandage. The saccharine medical tool refuses to peel off. "What kind of doctor are you?"

"A witchy one," she replies with a wink. "And the best you got. Unless you want to share your whole 'I'm a big bad demon, roar' medical history with somebody else in this town."

"Point taken."

Patty grins at me and taps at my hand. "Friends again?"

I nod. Her smile grows even wider. "Cute necklace."

I nod, at a loss for words. *Thanks. I stashed leaves from my girlfriend's mandrake-brother in it, hoping I can speak to the dead. Instead, I just have two walnut shells attached to a cord. Call me romantic. Stupid. Romantic.*

Patty places me in a room next door to Jason Sweeney and Stace. Wilbur sometimes sleeps in the hallways. Luckily, this hall is behind the bar, sectioned off from the rest of the Sweeney Inn. I personally think it's a loss for our marketing team that none of our guests can see Wilbur. Can you imagine how well a battle boar-themed hotel would take off? Pigs in blanket themed sleepovers. Ham it up comedy nights. Fine Swine-Dining. It sells itself.

The room interiors are nicely updated. It screams less hole-in-the-wall and more maybe-if-I-don't-look-too-closely-I-can-take-a-bubble-bath type of stay. Hand-quilted sheets, fresh sprigs of herbs and flower arrangements from Patty's witching garden on a bedside table. New bathrooms with freshwater taps and surfaces done up in green patterned tiles. Wood floors covered in plush rugs.

All paid for thanks to the Sweeney siblings inheriting the Eye Coven from their dead parents and evil successors.

Who knew that selling cursed potions could fund something so blessed?

Patty plops another stoppered vial beside a sprig of lavender. "Take your medicine," she tells me, wagging a finger.

I grin at her, my fingers crossed behind my back. "Scout's honor."

She leaves and I drop the smile immediately. It tastes sour in my mouth, but I have no choice. I can't take this dosage, not with the strange side effects. A twisting in my belly.

Thanks for trying to save my mental health, but I'm hopeless, thanks. No, I'd rather opt for the far less mature option and say nothing. *I don't want to cause trouble.* And then, the secret thought, the one that hurts to even entertain. *I don't...I don't want to be a burden on my friends. I'm scared to ask for help. I'm...I'm scared.*

I dump the vial's contents out in the sink and wash it away with a splash of complimentary mouthwash. I rub cold water over my skin and manage enough vigor to drop my head in the sink and wash my hair out with some shampoo. Brushing my teeth takes too much energy, so I just swish with the leftover soap on my hands and water. I sling a towel around my neck, take off my peacoat and corduroy pants, and throw my belt over the shower rod. Patty left some of Jason's old T-shirts as sleepwear. I choose one that, ironically enough, says "I love New York."

The Midwest boy becomes a city kid, who'd have thought? And now he's trying to take the last train out of Dodge. Witnessing magical murder tends to do that even to the strongest necromancers, who knew?

I drag myself back to the main room but choose to recline on the rug instead of the bed. I drag the comforters down on the floor with me and wrap myself in lavender-scented sheets. I inhale. Exhale.

"As I live and breathe, you're living and breathing. As much as you can anyways." I jump at the sudden sound echoing in this otherwise empty room. A young woman stands in front of me. Silver-blue hair, a butterfly tattooed to half a shaved head. Gold skin and black eyes watching me. A faint blue glow envelops her, and she's fuzzy at the edges.

But I recognize that voice. "Jo...?"

She points to my clavicle, and I turn to the swinging locket there. The faint blue glow enveloping her also surrounds the locket. A thin band of light, like a string, connects from the chain to Jo's ethereal form.

"Shit. The locket actually worked?"

She shakes her head and points, again, at me. I turn around to see the box from the *loas*, the one we're meant to deliver to the necromancer Erik Borden. Blushing, I hide the locket beneath my shirt and crouch over to the box. The lid's been pried off, a wave of something strong and smoky hitting my nostrils. Hidden beneath the random assortment of ingredients—puff pastry that still looks fresh out of the oven, random bottled oils, vials of holy water—I spy it.

It's a cloth bag with a skeletal key wound around it in a tiny charm. I clutch the bag in my palm, and it feels both hot and cold to the touch. Rolled-up parchment and other tiny objects appear to be trapped inside.

I don't dare to open the bag's contents. *Pandora made that mistake, but I won't follow.* Whatever's in there is too menacing. Even for me.

*

A few weeks before

At the healing wing for the magically inclined

SOMETIMES I VISIT Jo Kim where she resides, sleeping forever.

There's a hospital for monsters. A new division of the Eye Coven, a healing ward set up by Patty Sweeney. Because necromancy magic could be used to prevent people from dying at all instead of just bothering the dead, or however Patty put it.

There's a room that bleeds some form of lights resembling the sun. There's a room with stars painted onto the ceiling. This is the room where Jo Kim is kept. Sleeping forever.

At my last visit, I gathered flowers from the riverbank that took her unnatural breath from her. That placed her into this state. The river magic of Lethe, dragging her down into this restless oblivion.

I saw what I did to her. I failed to save her. Even after she succeeded in saving me. She'd call me a fucking idiot for saying that about her. Like I was a prince in the storybooks instead of just some fool who fell in love. She'd probably try to shoot me with a shotgun, then think twice about it, and we'd go out for some nectar instead.

At my last visit, I watched as the shadows deepened beneath her eyes. I don't know how the magic worked, whether it fed her proper. Ever since becoming a gangshi, she needed to devour souls. I don't know what the magical, IV feeding tube equivalent of that was, but it wasn't enough.

So, I saw her. Blue-silver hair like straw around her face. Veins in pale skin. A stomach that caved into bone. All sunk. Sunken in on herself. I put my hand against her shut eyes, felt her eyelids like paper. So still...like a corpse. *Not even a reanimated corpse, just a regular one. Just...almost like... Like she's actually dead.*

Death doesn't happen to beings like us, but to see her like that. To press my face to hers and see her so empty. Unresponsive. A house with all the lights turned off, the curtains drawn.

"I love you," I tell her.

And she doesn't respond. How could she?

I couldn't bring myself to see her like that again.

Chapter Eleven

Rock, paper, scissors, otherwise known as...troll, bridge, goat

TROLL, BRIDGE, GOAT works much the same as rock, paper, scissors.

It's a favorite amongst immortals who decide they're too fancy for simple human games and want to play a fancier, fantasy version of rock, paper, scissors.

Here's the rules of troll, bridge, goat.

The troll beats the goat over the head with a club. And eats it.

The goat trots over the bridge, doing that weird goat noise goats make.

The bridge hangs over the troll's head while the goat goes trap-trap-trap all the way home. Or maybe the goat goes to market or something. Speaking of which, you know that when the little piggy goes to market, they're going to become bacon instead of shopping for groceries? Yeah. I was today years old when I learned that.

I guess this goes to say that Stace played a game of troll, bridge, goat to bargain whether they got to join us on our LARPing urban fantasy murder mystery journey or not. You know, considering yes, they were a good fighter. But just because they possess unearthly charms and strength, doesn't mean they can actually, you know, beat up a minotaur or anything. (Except they could definitely kick Theseus's ass, because screw that guy).

But I played a game of troll, bridge, goat against Stace to decide whether they could come with us or not. You know, to solve the mystery of the possessed monsters thing.

Spoiler alert, Stace is with us now as Patty drives us to go deliver a package to the necromancer Erik Borden. So, you know what that means. Bridge beats troll every time.

*

Did someone order some angst?

WE MEET ERIK Borden at the river. I watch him as we pull Patty's car to the side of a dirt path. The river, Lethe's river. The river that shrouds all of Gamin in mist and keeps humans from discovering our secret.

"Who's Erik?" Stace asks, also watching the brooding figure standing at the side of the river.

Well, most humans anyways.

"The one we need to deliver this package to," I reply, holding up the *loas'* delivery. A small shudder passes through me as its contents slide.

"A friend of ours. Former. A mortal necro, like me," Patty replies. She spins back after she opens the driver's door. "You two. Erm, three. Wait here."

Stace holds a snuffling Wilbur closer while I sink further into the passenger's seat. Most of my wounds have healed. I'd suspect the same mystical force that brought Jo to me might've patched me up, as well. Or maybe I'm just stronger than I thought.

Maybe the demon inside you, Lilītu, *is feeding your power.*

The other demon, the quiet one inside your head, only forces your soul to rot.

I watch as Patty walks over to Erik Borden. His locs have grown down past his shoulders and the fog envelops his figure, umber skin wrapped up in a worn gray bomber jacket. The mark of the Eye is on his forehead, permanently embedded with wire. The mark that shows he's a part of the Eye Coven, same as the Sweeneys...even if he doesn't want to be anymore.

I know that jacket. It was his father's. With a twist of nausea in my stomach, the next thoughts rushes, unbidden. *I wonder how he fished it out of the bottom of that river...*

Patty exchanges a few words. Erik stares past her at the car, his gaze narrowing. He clenches his fists, then unclenches them. He speaks to Patty, his lips moving quick. Short.

Patty gets back to the car and speaks through a crack in the driver's window. "He wants you, Lili."

Yeah, he wants me. He wants me at the bottom of the river...where our last murder investigation left his dad.

I replaced my trademark peacoat and corduroy pants. I didn't have enough energy to wash them, and they still smelled like Grid's diner, like oil and sticky sweet. I place my hands into my pockets, embrace the chilly air of Gamin. The fog runs off the river, braiding through leaves off heavy trees. I remember when I last was at this river. When my inner demon unleashed. The world looked so small then. *As small as I feel now. What is this, guilt?*

I walk slowly to Erik, standing at the river's edge, one foot in front of the other, sinking into the mud. Erik Borden, to his credit, doesn't take his eyes off me. The other eye, the one run through with wires, has magic coursing through the modified tech, neon pulsating with magic. Wires feed the magic and the arcane feeds the technology, making Erik a literal tech-wizard.

Erik extends one gloved hand to me. I remember now, the moment I first saw that gray bomber jacket. I remember Erik's father, how he looked when we first met the infamous monster hunter, Dakari Borden. Iron knives strapped beneath a gray bomber jacket. A cap pulled low over his head. He had hired us to help save his son.

Saved the son, killed the father. Chasing after murderers, playing hero. Will you do the same to them?

I take his hand. Neon magic, the selfsame wires pulsating on his gloves. They're hot to the touch. Hot and cold. Burning. Freezing. All at once. The power. *The* loas *were right. He's powerful. He really is Marie Laveau's kin. Erik Borden will get us to the Crossroads if he has to kill us himself.*

"Erik."

"Lili."

We exchange names. The power shifts. The river keeps flowing. Cold in the water, piercing through the spray that hits our legs. The mud beneath us, soft and ply-ing.

"You should punch me," I say, the words thorny in my throat. "I'd deserve it. Worse."

He laughs a little at that. "Why should I torture you when you do it so perfectly already?" He kicks his foot in the dirt, shaking his head. The burning and freezing feeling in my hand lets go. Instead, there's a soft pulse as the magic relents. The fog disperses in a semicircle around us, the power of the river respecting power in us. "My dad said you lot would be visiting. He says you can't do shit right by yourself. You need us to fix your problems. You always do."

"You talked to...?"

He points to the wired-neon eye on his forehead. "I'm a necromancer, Lili. We talk to dead people, it's what we do."

"Why help us? Aren't you upset?"

He turns his full attention to me, the power in his eyes, the shifting in the quiet as the river flows. I swear I could hear a leaf falling right now, feel it brushing past me, sharp edges hurting. "I get sad. I get mad. I feel so many emotions at once on some days that I wonder if the true hell is the one on earth. I was upset with you for the longest time. I was blaming everyone for my father's death, including myself."

There's a beating inside me, a rhythm that goes. Of worry. Of nerves. Of feeling so much that, at the same time, I feel absolutely nothing at all. It doesn't feel real. Did anything ever feel real?

"Emotions are tricky little things, aren't they? Truth

is, we were friends once, Lili. I don't know if we can be friends so easily again, not with all the emotions in the way. The hurting. But I'll help you because you aren't my enemy either, Lili."

The next words, he sends the message directly inside my head. The eye on his forehead gleams so bright, it's as if the words are spelled out in front of my eyes, burned into my retina with magic and strengthened with whatever wired, magic conduit he's implanted into his skin and gloves. The strengthener, pulsating thoughts in bright neon into the air. He speaks thoughts into my aching mind.

You'll know if you're my enemy, Lili. You just will.

*

A necromancer, a demon, a human, a witch, and a ghost walk into a coven...

Wait, where's the punchline?

"HONEY, I'M HOME!" Erik calls into the empty laboratories of what once was, as I fondly liked to call it, Evil Eye Inc.

Evil Eye Incorporated. Has a nice ring to it, doesn't it?

Patty and Jason Sweeney's parents, Todd and Beatrice, had started this coven in an attempt to unite the local necromancing community under a single cause: profit.

It was a corporate office from which Gamin's resident necromancy coven sold all manner of potions, ghoul contracts, and reanimation licenses. However, a few botched attempts at summoning a demon, razing a poltergeist, and bringing zombies back to life later had put a considerable damper on business deals. The labs had fallen silent.

Last time we'd entered this space, it had been guns blazing to save Erik Borden from some of the zombie workers' grasps. Now, the place was eerily sanitized. The zombie workers were mostly gone except for one with a crooked nametag, "Frank," a play on Frankenstein, on its stomach. This Frank holds open a door for us as we enter.

The interior of the Eye Coven building is white tile and plain, geometrical wallpaper under fluorescents. The front desk is empty, the same front desk Erik used to work at before being promoted to running the place. Entirely online since it was destroyed, of course. A line of high-tech computers, running lines of simultaneous code, are plugged into databases teeming with a fair bit of magic.

Techno-wizard, indeed. I'd hate to meet IT.

The main lobby elevator hisses to a stop and a figure steps out from it as the doors open with a metallic grunt. The newcomer wears a beeping contraption around his neck. He has a haircut like Nirvana in the '90s, the shaggy part down the middle of dark-brown hair. A duster jacket over distressed jeans completes the whole pirate-rocker look alongside circular metal rims and an ever-present smirk I know all too well.

Well, knew all too well. Before we made inadvertent frenemies.

"Byron?" Patty fights the look of shock, her eyes widening to see him. "How are you...how?"

He takes a bow, looking wholly...corporeal. "Byron López, at your service." He knocks on his own shoulder. His fingers don't just float through. "Like my new flesh suit? It works. Most the time. Can't tell me apart from the real thing, eh? Almost mortal. Which means I can't use my flashy poltergeist powers and go exorcist on your asses, but I look alive and hot when the device is on, so potato, po-tah-to."

He presses a button on the techno-choker and now it's Stace's turn to panic. Byron rises a foot into the air, hovering with a translucent glow to his skin. "Where...?" Stace shudders as the temperature in the room grows noticeably cooler. "Where'd he go?"

They can't see him anymore. Made himself incorporeal just as easily as he made himself tangible. Impressive.

Wilbur whimpers nervously, flattening his wings against his back as he presses to Stace's side. Byron presses a button and he's back to appearing, well, *alive.* The pig squeals.

Stace's eyes focus on him with a new distrust evident, nervousness sparking in the tension around their lips. I imagine it must be quite terrifying, seeing the figure in front of their human eyes vanish then reappear in an instant. Like pigs flying.

Oh wait.

"What are you?" Stace stares at Byron for another moment. Shaking their head, trying to clear their vision, maybe.

"*Who* am I, you mean?" Byron chuckles. "I'm Byron López, poltergeist."

"He's the first friend I made in Gamin," I reply.

"Was. I *was* your friend." He walks toward me, feet firmly planted on the ground. Damn, I don't think I'll ever get used to seeing him walk around. Like seeing your boss wear a golf tee and khakis. Just not a natural setting whatsoever.

"You're…" And I try my hardest not to be an ass, I really do. But old habits die hard. "So, what, you're alive now?"

Byron points at the choker again. "At least until the battery runs out."

"Battery-powered corporeality device! And it runs on clean energy. Magic funneled through gryphon-urine-fed mycelium networks," Erik Borden calls out, beaming with pride at his handiwork. "Take that, Apple."

"See? You didn't even need me. You had Erik. And he has science," I tell Byron.

Judging by the sheer hatred seething on Byron's face, this was *not* the thing to say. "You made a promise to bring me back to life, Lili! And you never followed through. If it wasn't for my genius necromancer boyfriend, I might still be floating around twenty-four/seven like a Macy's balloon." He glances at Erik, who comes in for a quick peck on the cheek. "But you're used to unresolved issues, aren't you, Lil?"

"First off, resurrection is a difficult task. Secondly…" I shrug. "What can I say? Immortality's a long time, and I'm no completist."

Patty, wearing thick, padded gloves, lifts the crate given to us by the *loas*. "Speak for yourself. This witch, for one, wants this little side quest over with as soon as possible. When I learned I was a witch, I was hoping more for the chill vibes of the *Sabrina* comics, not the dark and edgy reboot. But we all can't get what we want, eh?"

Our resident Sabrina-reboot witch, Patty, goes to what was once the front desk of these offices, the same place that Erik used to work before he got a promotion. Now, Erik Borden is the techno-wizard running the laboratories and the online coven spaces.

And the coven is decorated like Silicon Valley meets Westeros. Fun.

I step on one of Erik's mycelium magic network cables. A ring of toadstools is plugged into roots digging into the ground. I think I see a human fingernail clawing out the end of one and tapping into a crystal vial that glows and sparks as a Tesla coil, rims of blue around ribbons of metal.

Patty clears an empty area for the parcel, the yellow folders pushed to a rollaway chair while silhouetted in some dust, her gloves trembling as she holds it.

Yeah, I'd be scared of the loas' *power too.*

Dropping the *loas'* parcel on the table feels terribly anticlimactic. There's no lone spotlight with filtered light through dust motes shining on it. No swell of dramatic, fantastical music for our heroes' journey.

Just a bunch of tired immortals and necromancers and dead and living humans staring at a box on a dusty table.

Oh, be still, my un-beating heart.

Erik walks toward the box, his hurried footsteps echoing in the tiny space. His badge gleams on his jacket, the label reading "ERIK BORDEN, HEAD TECHNO-

WIZARD." He wears his new role well, a chipped monocle with a silver card in its side overlaying his right eye. A faint, green-blue gleam of light appears over his eye, a monitor reading digitized numbers and a steady stream of code.

"It's calling to me, I feel it inside." He taps the side of his head and the screen in front of his eye gleams violet, magic streaming from his hands. "According to the data, the magic energy readings are off the charts."

He reaches into the box and his entire hand gets subsumed inside it, pulling him in.

"Argh!" he screams, the sound curdling in the back of his throat, fermenting there.

We all jump back in a panic, adrenaline coursing. Blood pounding in our ears.

"Got you," he says, smirking at us.

Byron smacks him good-naturedly on the shoulder, pulling him in for a quick kiss on the neck. The techno-wizard blushes profusely.

Grinning widely, Erik pulls a small bag out from the box's contents. It's wrapped with two drawstring cords pulled tight. The bag is black, luxurious silk, soft and hushing. It seems to have transmogrified from plain cloth to silk in Erik Borden's fist; his face illuminated by the moonlit glow emanating from the bag.

"Whoa... A gris-gris bag. My mom made some when she was younger," he whispers, bringing it closer to his face. The bag rolls on his palm, almost like it's alive. It's playing with him. "She told me to never mess with them. Sorry, Mom."

Byron, the now-tangible phantom, slings his arms

around Erik's neck. Peering close. "What is it, love?"

Erik tugs his fingernails at the drawstrings, trying to loosen the bag's lip. The bag refuses to open, sealed tight by ancient magic. "I can't see inside..." The digitized monocle over his eye sparks. His eyes glow brightly with an inner light, the symbol of the coven burning on his forehead with digitized wires running to the monocle. "I *can* see it."

He takes in a breath, leaning back into Byron's touch. He sways on his feet, his heavy boots barely keeping him steady. "Water from the River Styx, of the goddess of forgetting, the waters where my father met his end. Dirt from the grave of my mother who sacrificed herself for me in New Orleans. The bag itself was made by my many-greats grandmother, spirit in blood, Marie Laveau. And..." He gasps, nearly choking on the words, his lips dry and skin flaking like they physically pain him to have the Sight like this. "In a secret compartment of the box, there's gifts for him, the Baron Samedi. The *loa* of the Crossroads. Cigars, thick as thieves. Coffee, black as night. And a pair of dark shades that can manifest the Ancient Sight."

He suddenly pushes himself from the table, the bag still tight in his palm, as though taped to his skin. Even Byron jumps back, the ghost terrified of power beyond his comprehension. Erik's eyes are still aflame as he throws his head back, the power strong within him.

"The Crossroads," he rasps, every muscle tense in his jaw. Bulging in his neck. And then, his lip twists into a smile. He laughs in a voice not his own. Neither feminine nor masculine, but so sweet that it'd convince you to walk off a cliff if it wanted to.

The being laughs, turning those eyes, not Erik's eyes but someone else's, to me.

"Well, well, well, *bèl. Koman ou ye jodia*?"

The figure holds out its hand, and from Erik's grasp stretches a beam of red light, burning hot as a star. It sears itself down into a pattern of a spade, a shovel, spitting sparks and fumes until it cools, all at once, into a shining metal not of this world. The being, wearing Erik's skin like a flesh suit of possession, holds this shovel out to me. I step forward, gritting my teeth, preparing to be burned.

The metal, blessedly, is cool to the touch. The being pulls me in close, its/Erik's hand over mine on the shovel's hilt. "Dig and don't stop. Dig where a living mortal's nose bleeds and that's where the Crossroads will find you. You don't find me. I find you, that's how it goes."

The being/Erik winks at me, and for some reason, I find myself appreciating the aesthetic beauty of this being's eyes. It's like looking into something so dangerous it's beautiful. Like staring at forbidden fruit.

Just like that, Erik, *just Erik,* throws himself forward, pushing me and the shovel away. He stumbles for an office table, the gris-gris bag still tied around his wrist. Byron rushes over to him, his spectacles half-sliding off his long nose, his hair falling in front of his eyes. He pulls his arms around Erik's chest, fingers locked together in desperation.

"Love, love?" Byron asks, holding Erik close, so close that Byron hides his face in Erik's neck.

The techno-wizard coughs once. Twice. He rolls his shoulders back, wincing as though a great spasm overtakes him. He pushes himself up, eyes soft, normal now.

"Dammit," he splutters. "I need a drink."

Chapter Twelve

Chilling in the Coven Corporation

Shots, shots, shots, shots, shots!

...of magical espresso.

Yes, that's really a thing.

PATTY BREWS THE finest potions known to magic-kind. She makes a mean buttercream coffee doused with a hint of invigorating elixir. I'm not sure if it's magic exactly or the caffeine or both, but Erik comes back from the (figurative) dead in no time, the brew reviving him from the shock of a *loa* possession. He takes a few sips and his vibrancy returns, the techno-wizard's monocle sparking again and shifting back to its regular, stream-of-code functioning. He taps one hand against his leg and bounces from foot to foot. The gris-gris bag is looped to his belt for safe keeping, but he's slightly more hesitant to touch it this time.

Byron drifts over and massages Erik's shoulders. "Are

you back then, love?"

Erik shudders, clenching his jaw to keep himself together. "Yeah. Yeah, I'm all right. Thank you, darling." He reaches back to kiss Byron's cheek, but his mouth drifts through Byron's semi-translucent skin. "The charger, darling. It'll need a boost soon for you to keep your physical form."

Byron sighs, his fingers going through Erik's skin as the magical tech revitalization device fades. "Ah, to have a literally *dying* battery, all fit for a ghost. It'd be funny if it wasn't so cruel."

Byron flickers for a moment, the collar's light turning red like a phone low on battery.

Stace blinks twice, turning noticeably paler and staring at the spot where Byron used to be. They sigh, biting the inside of their cheek as Wilbur shakes and presses his sides into them for support. "I'll never get used to Byron disappearing like that."

Byron laughs, floating past Stace. Stace jumps, shivering at the sudden gust of invisible cold. "Me neither, newbie," Byron quips and Stace jumps sky-high.

Erik hands Stace a bit of the magical buttercream drink. "Try this. It should comfort you from the whole magic-exists-and-monsters-are-real shock thing. Or, at the very least, it'll taste delicious."

Stace takes a sip and licks the foam off their lips with a smile. "I'm never waiting in the Mooncash drive-through again. Thanks, cyber necromancer dude."

"You're welcome..." Erik stares at Stace blankly for a few moments, trying desperately to place them. "I'm sorry. Who are you again?"

"Stace, my brother's partner. They're mortal. Though everyone thinks they aren't. Boxer. Badass. Botanist," Patty explains, slamming her empty glass of foamy, sweet-smelling coffee on one of the lab tables populating the Eye Corporation desks. A zombified Frank servant/worker bustles the empty cups off to a break room sink. This Frank, number 5001 from the nametag, even wears a charming collar and tie over their white T-shirt. Another Frank wears a hoodie and sandals.

Ahh, casual Thursday.

"Yup. I'm a badass botanist boxer. The three Bs," Stace amends. "Four if you include bi—"

Wilbur squeals, cutting Stace off from the rest of that charming sentence.

The walls surrounding us hold streams of computers plugged into dormant mandrake roots, fairy circles, and strings of charms growing out from underneath the desks in miniature, glowing terrariums. The lab station smells like a mix of wet earth, overheated computers, some form of formaldehyde from the undead zombie workers, and aerosol fresheners.

"Charming. Like your average tech startup mashed up with something out of some sick fairy tale." I run my finger over one of the countertops, frowning at the rust color coming up from it. A Frank with a staple attached to its arm seems to be the culprit of the bloodstains.

I wipe my hand clean on an office chair. Fairly surreptitiously, or so I believe...

"I saw that. Your keeping-secrets game is getting weaker since we last met, Lil," Byron chides, rolling his eyes. He plugs his techno-collar into a portable battery.

The red light gleams a faint yellow and he flashes into a stronger corporeal existence again.

Wilbur squeals until Stace feeds him some carrots from a discarded lab tray. The battle hog burps a cloud of lavender-colored smoke that, for some ungodly reason, sparkles.

"Oh yeah, maybe I wanted you to see it. I like an audience." I try to recover and lean nonchalantly against Baron Samedi's shovel. But the cold feeling emanating from the metal deters me. I awkwardly lean against a table instead. "Look, are you going to hate me for the rest of however long we have to spend together? I didn't mean to keep secrets from you."

"But you did. And they led to so many, many bad things, Lil." Byron checks his nails, buffing them against his shirt. He looks up with the most severe side eye I've ever seen. Like, honestly, I feel more chills coming from him than I do the demonic shovel. "You've seen the lab. Fully functioning computers powered by bio-tech magic. Franks all reprogrammed to be, well, *not* evil. That amount of work can only be done by someone trying desperately to forget, Lil. Erik was hurting so bad from his father's death, from you lying to us..." Byron sighs, wringing his hands together, his dark hair getting caught up in his glasses. "I was hurting too."

"I didn't kill Erik's father, Byron. Alethea did. She was a *serial killer*, Byron, and she would've gotten everyone. Patty. Jason. Erik. Detective Ikiaq..." I close my eyes, remembering Dakari Borden, how he looked at his son, the spitting image of his mother. How Dakari's ghost came back, and his eyes...those tormented eyes that wanted to do so much more but were trapped in the eternal realm of a mortal's end. "I would've given up my eternal life to stop her from hurting you. I very nearly did if I hadn't *changed*. Unfortunately, Dax had the same idea in his head and beat me to it."

"It seems lots of people die around you." Byron glances down, his collar light beeping green at his neck. He screws up his eyebrows, energy spent on picking up a pen, marveling at his newfound corporeality. "Or stay dead."

"I know, and I'm sorry. I'm sorry I hurt you." I pick a flower growing from a petri dish. Two flowers spring up in its place, petals shaped like fangs, like a two-headed hydra. I hand him the flower and he places it behind his ear. Byron pauses, glancing down. "I was a bad friend for not keeping my side of the bargain, for trying to handle it all by myself and not asking for help. But let me make it up to you all. Help me keep this from happening to somebody else. Alethea, she might be locked up but...she has a copycat."

"It's happening again?"

I dig my nails into my fists. "That's why we want to go to the Crossroads and see Baron Samedi. A Fae prince was killed by a *Kuntilanak* in a strip club. Her name's Indah. But we suspect she was, I don't know, somehow mind-controlled? Same with him. We need to find the Green Prince in the lands of the between-dead. We need to get his side of the story to find out who the real killer is. Who's trying to get us to kill each other."

Byron bites his lower lip, pushing his spectacles back up his nose. "Fine. But I'm not doing this for you." He reaches for the shovel and grips it with intense concentration flashing in his eyes. He lifts it off the ground, huffing slightly. The collar glows steady green. "I'm doing this for Indah, mostly."

"Same." I smile at that, helping the poltergeist, my unwitting friend once again, to hoist the shovel higher. "Then let's get digging."

*

Nose goes at the River Lethe

"SO, I...I just have to...bleed?" Stace motions to the ground outside as we walk along the riverbank, the crunch of cold frost sinking into the ground. The awkward melt of mud and slush sitting above soft green shoots trying to reach for the sun. Stace walks with Wilbur at their side, holding onto the battle boar's broad shoulders, their fingers digging in above their folded wings. The river itself smells like magic and rot and...

And old blood. Blood magic. Blood calling. But don't think about that, Lili. Don't think on it.

"And this nosebleed..." Stace falters again, wrinkling their nose. "Will it help you?"

"It's what Baron Samedi said when he had his little visit. Dig where a living mortal's nose bleeds and, boom, Crossroads." Erik shrugs, holding the shovel with a fingerless glove on his hand. The glove has wires running past the cloth up to his elbow. They sink into a band tied beneath his skin where the magic thrums, the violet cyber-magic glowing within his blood. The monocle over his gaze reflects the glow of the Eye on his forehead, the Coven's symbol.

Stace sniffs and everyone leans in closer.

Oh, to be an ancient demonic entity reduced to this. Nosebleed watching. What job fulfillment.

Stace awkwardly pinches the bridge of their nose. "No, that wasn't a nosebleed. I just... I have to sneeze..."

Stace leaves the group to sneeze in peace. During this period, I notice Patty holding a perfume-scented card in her hand. It bears the name of the Kraken Club, and beneath it, a blurry sketch of a certain charming *Kuntilanak* we all know.

"She has a calling card? I wasn't aware people still did that." I smirk as Patty blushes a bright red, brighter than seeing the sun through your eyelids.

"I..." Patty stuffs the card into her pocket. "Well, Indah does."

"And you like what Indah does?"

"I..." Patty grins back at me, shoving me slightly. "Yes. I hope she likes what I do too. And at the end of it all, Lili, I hope she's..."

I'm about to rib her more when Wilbur suddenly takes off at a breakneck pace. He flaps his wings a few times and his hooves catch the gleam of the sun, snow melting on his giant back. A stream of butterflies, a faint blue flash against the mud and snow, catches a particularly fierce gust of wind and rushes quickly along the river. The battle boar follows them, Wilbur squealing up to high heaven.

So much for a stealth mission.

"Wilbur!" Stace takes off at a run, awkward sneeze

forgotten as their pet chases after something we can't see.

And we, in turn, take off after one very frazzled botanist.

"Stace!" I shout my throat raw as we run after them. *Dammit, why do they have to be so in shape?* "Stace..." I gather my strength, legs pounding into the earth. Knees jolting from fighting the riverside earth.

My eyes home in on Stace's muscular shoulders, flexing back and forth as their strong legs propel them forward, rushing after Wilbur. Wilbur's really leaning into his haunches, his wings occasionally lifting his front legs off the ground. Patty jogs at my side, Erik and Byron taking up the rear. The poltergeist takes the longest time, flashing between ethereality and corporeality at intervals as his battery flickers, the magic tech readjusting to the movement.

Wilbur stops all at once, digging his hooves into the muddy riverbank, wings sloshed with rushing water. The jet of cold spray seems to calm the battle boar. He snuffles lazily into Stace's grasp as they inhale deeply to catch their breath.

"Never do that again, huh?" Stace leans into Wilbur, pressing their nose against his snout. "Don't scare me like that, buddy. We're in this together, right?"

Wilbur whimpers softly as Stace pulls away, sniffing hard and pinching at their nose.

I glance down, watching, mesmerized, as a few drops of blood stain Stace's skin. They seep, slowly into the earth. I walk forward, carried by something within me, smelling the tang of the blood. Suddenly, I can hear Stace's strong heartbeat. Their heart. A fighter's heart. A warrior's heart.

How long has it been since I've feasted on proper mortal flesh? Animal flesh. Raw flesh. Not even hunted. How long has it been since the hunt, oh Mother of Anathema? Too many years, since the last empire went to dust... Too many years since they've screamed your names to the heavens. Too many...

"Okay, champ." Patty grips my shoulder, hard. Her fingernails dig into my skin, and I shake my head, a sudden feeling of clouded sleep come upon me. "Earth to Lili! You good, fam?"

I lick my lips, staring guiltily away, turning to face the riverbank. Lethe's waters hit me; the river magic a potent drug against my skin. The magic quiets my thoughts for now, leaving me with that unnatural blanket of calm. Leaving me just Lili, minus the whole Mother of Anathema part. Untransformed. Unmoving. *And 100 percent unnatural.*

"I'm glad we've found the place to start digging is all."

But when I look into Patty's eyes, her soft amber gaze pulls into a gentle smile, the kind that knows more than she lets on. "All right, Lil. Hang in there, okay?"

I nod, leaning into her touch as the solid grip to keep me back from Stace melts into a half-hug instead. "I will. Thank you."

"This thing..." Patty licks her lips, pausing. "It isn't you."

I nod.

But what if it is? What if there really is no escape?

Erik leans forward, breathing equally hard as the rest of us. Like me, he quiets in the presence of the river, the magic soaking into his blood. Baron Samedi's shovel glows here with a faint luminescence, a ringing like a song sounding in our ears.

"Yep, this is it." He kicks his boot into the spade, the metal part sinking into the earth like a knife through flesh. He leans into the dirt, tearing the earth out with a tension in his shoulders, putting his legs into the movement. He swipes a hand across his brow, stale sweat mingling with the damp from running and the perpetual chill in Gamin's air. "Welcome to the Crossroads."

"Welcome to an early Christmas present too," Byron mutters, winking appreciatively at Erik. "You look even prettier doing exercise, you know that?"

Erik grins back at him, his face softening from his usual seriousness when dealing with me to something, well, something softer. Something in love. Something wholesomely smitten. "Are you going to help me see how far I have to dig, ghost lover, or just stare at my biceps all day?"

"Fine." Byron sticks his tongue out at Erik before being pulled in for a quick kiss. "But you owe me double the bicep flexing after this."

"Deal," Erik laughs, an easy smile on his face. When he notices me staring, he drops the smile immediately, eyes settling into a cold stare.

I don't even know why he's mad at me. Scratch that, his father's at the bottom of the river behind us. I know perfectly well why. You know what, I take everything back. He deserves to be mad at me. You have a lot to fix, Lili. More than just a bippidi-boppidi-boo would do.

Byron rolls his eyes but comes over to help Erik mark

a path with his shovel. He presses a button on his corpo-reality collar, his bronze complexion taking on the violet-blue glow of the dead. Newly ghostly, he sinks down into the ground, his semi-transparent head disappearing amongst a rush of leaves and slugs. He pops back up a moment later, just his eyes visible. He waves at us, half out of the ground and half into it. Stace blinks a couple of times, staring confusedly at nothing in particular.

"It doesn't go on forever," Byron says. "I can see... something. Or rather, *not* see something. It's like the earth, the worms, everything. It all just vanishes about six feet under."

Six feet under. Fitting for the guardian of the dead.

Byron rises above the ground, flipping the switch back on. His body warms to the air around us as he hugs Erik quick, leaving Stace and Wilbur staring in awe again at him flashing back into regular purview. Erik leans into Byron's embrace for a moment before sinking the spade back into the earth, kicking it down with a newfound gusto with his boot.

I walk forward despite Patty's nervous grip on my fingers, pulling away as I hold my hand out to Erik. "Ahem," I say, pointing to the shovel.

Erik levels his gaze at me. "Yes, Lili?"

"Use your words," Byron adds in a singsong voice.

I sigh, nodding to the ground again. "Come on. You need to save your strength. Let me help you." When he doesn't relinquish his grip on the shovel, the words come rushing out of my mouth in a nervous plea. "You're the only one with Marie Laveau's magic in you, Erik. You're too important to get tired out on a simple digging job."

Erik pushes the shovel into my hand, the metal eerily cool to the touch, like clammy flesh. "Don't break it," he warns as he leans back into Byron's touch. I look to Byron, who nods at me in that *you did well* kind of way. Patty sighs with relief, slumping in the corner of my eye. Stace is busy trying to staunch their mystical nosebleed while Wilbur snuffles around in the dirt, probably finding truffles or something.

Baron Samedi's shovel meets the earth. The earth gets excavated. And for six wonderful, dense, constricting feet, I dig. Past the layer like dust above. Past the cakey, muddy mulch in the middle. Past the roots and the places where secrets lie. Past the spaces where bodies are buried, where the trees meet the fungus meet the water and sand.

Past the places where my regular form, with its strong yet untransformed body aches...

The Crossroads and the slaughtered Green Prince waits.

And waits...and waits...

For us to tumble in.

"Koman ou ye jodia, bèl?"

Chapter Thirteen

Six feet under

"KOMAN OU YE jodia, bèl?"

"How are you doing, beautiful?"

Byron, the semi-ghost who now, thankfully, only semi-hates me, was right in saying there's just a big, old *nothing* down six feet below the ground. Six feet below, even the rushing of Lethe's magical waters disappears. No crunch of frost. No bite of an insect against wood. Not even squirrels, who just don't know how to quit.

It feels like nothing. Smells like nothing. Tastes like nothing on your tongue, not even air.

Six feet under the space where Stace's nose bled like Old Faithful, the Crossroads began. And I stare into the sparkling, glittering eyes of none other than the *loa* of Resurrection, the infamous Baron Samedi. Their figure is drenched in this nothingness. And I cannot see their beauty so much as sense it. Encapsulating, like dirt sinking into my throat. The void becomes my canopy with decay as my bed.

They stare at me and hold out their hand. I try to take

their fingers in mine, but their palm slips away, a leaf running downriver.

"Nuh uh, beautiful." They smile at me, tipping their head low to reveal a top hat and a long, flowing skirt. Their eyes hold mine a moment longer. I try to avoid their gaze. There's something there I don't like seeing.

My spine prickles, as I remember what it feels like. Like a curtain rushing down to crash against a mahogany stage before the rush of applause. Like a clock ticking down to the inevitable alarm. Like the last day of summer before the first leaf falls.

Their eyes look like The End.

"My shades, *bèl,* where are they?" They tap their fingers against the side of their forehead, all angles that meet up into something too beautiful to be named.

Something else, another figure, appears at my back. I can feel it from how my skin tingles there, the space of nothingness taken up by solid mass. The shadows sinking down into a beacon of artificial glow.

Erik Borden bears a lamp synced into his monocle. A lamp whose light bleeds into his gloves and jacket. The reflective surface gleams against the nothingness, part tech and part magic. The pair of spectacles he wears slides down his nose and bumps up against the monocle. The two circular dark lenses are stark against a rim of thin, trimmed gold.

Baron Samedi's spectacles. He's wearing the loa's *spectacles.*

Byron flashes into half-corporeality behind Erik. The semi-ghost is split directly down the middle, half his body comprised of seemingly living flesh, the other half of a pale blue-violet glow. He melts half-into Erik, who leans into his whispering touch.

Then arrive the reinforcements. Stace sitting atop Wilbur's hunched shoulders, leaning into their pet for support. Patty with her cardigan drawn about her like a cape with buttons from Little Red Riding Hood in the stories, the hood pushed back against her red-fire hair.

Baron Samedi smiles, redirecting their gaze to Erik, their eyes flashing as they notice the gris-gris bag looped against his thigh. "Ah, so *you* have my shades, do you? Young, genius blood of Marie Laveau." And then, a brief smile. "I'd recognize that body anywhere. I couldn't help but notice the fine muscles I was in, if only for a time."

Byron snarls, but Erik holds out his hand to brush Byron's ghostly one.

"We're not here for that now, milord. A trade." Erik bows his head respectfully, just enough to get his point across. "A trade for a conversation with the Green Prince, son of the Green Man, King of Summerland."

"Oh." Baron Samedi leans back on their polished leather shoes. "The one who got killed in a club bathroom? Now why'd you want to talk to a jackass like that?"

"It's me!" I raise my hand, much to Patty's chagrin. She keeps trying to wave me desperately back, but I'm too stupid to know better right now, and the adrenaline coursing through me doesn't help my case. "I'm the jackass who wants to talk to the jackass, please."

Baron Samedi levels their glittering gaze back on me. I swallow, but I can't seem to get rid of the sudden lump that's developed in my throat, bravado be extra damned. Baron Samedi laughs, a sound like teaspoons against porcelain. "The Mother of Anathema, first demon queen, calling herself a jackass? Has Revelations happened for your lot, yet, or am I hearing things?"

"I'm, um, I'm good now. Clean of the whole 'burn villages, salt the earth' thing. Went to Assholes Anonymous and got to leave with my 'I'm a Reformed Killer Immortal' chip." I sigh, chewing on my lip when I catch myself rambling too much. I can't help it. The feeling of the pressing *nothingness,* the constant ringing in my ears in this place in between something and beyond. The glittering, cruelly beautiful eyes of Baron Samedi. It makes my skin crawl. It makes the transformation feel oh-so-much nearer as my regular body senses we're in perpetual danger. "I'm the good guy now, Baron Samedi. I'm trying to solve a serial killer case for the humans...again. I think I'm a glutton for punishment."

"The best ones are." Baron Samedi tilts their head to the side, pausing a moment before they bend their head the other way to take a closer look at me, their neck so twisted that their ear aligns with my chin. "Huh, you got so bored of eternal life that now you're playing savior for the ones you hunted, are you, Lilītu?" Baron Samedi holds out their hand again, waiting for Erik's lead. "One tour of the Crossroads and one Green Prince coming right up. Price of admission, my seeing eyeglasses, taken by my cousin Damballa if I remember rightly and returned by you." They bow with their palm held open in a flourish, waiting as they turn to Erik. "If you please, blood of Laveau."

Hesitant, Erik turns to Byron, who nods his assent. He scans quickly for others' reactions. Finally, he turns to me, and his gaze hardens.

Come on, Erik. Do this for Indah if not for me...

After a long moment, Erik tears the spectacles away and folds them into Baron Samedi's hand.

The *loa* grins and slides on the spectacles. The space suddenly feels less in-between and more tangible. The ringing in my ears sears into a crackle, a fire being lit over gasoline. A light comes up, piercing through the uncomfortable dark. We speed through the in-between, sinking through the eerie sensation, dark matter sliding over our skin.

All at once, a *pop,* like we've been reborn. We stand on an expanse of sand beneath a gray sky, a gray sun. The air tastes like the color gray even, like pudding cups of an indeterminate expiration date or fruit when it's a bit too ripe. Like things that should be better than they are. Promises not kept. Moments lost. Memories forgotten.

I'm so busy watching the gray sands beneath the gray skies, tasting the pudding gray thick on my tongue. I'm so busy trying to remember if I'd been here, trying to remember dreams that are barely in my memory. Dreams like memories. Memories like dreams. All quicksilver, salmon swimming upstream.

"I like the Crossroads because it's in between, like me." Baron Samedi is beside me then, all at once. My friends, or non-enemies for the time being, are a few feet behind us. Patty stares, bewildered, at her hands. Stace hugs Wilbur tight for comfort. Byron looks bored. Erik reaches, instinctively, for the gris-gris bag at his hip. The power of Laveau.

"What do you mean?" I ask, shaking my head, staring

at my worn boots instead of the uncertainty of the horizon.

Baron Samedi points to their skirt, their blazer, their top hat. They run their hands along the curves of their body, the flatness in others. The mountains, the valleys. "The Crossroads are both. Not living. Not dead. Me? I am both. Male. Female. In between." They tell me with a wink. "See, *cheri*? The Crossroads are just like me." They pause, staring at me another moment with that too-tilted stare. "You are too. In here." They tap their head.

I swallow, the pudding sensation now thickening my throat like phlegm. "I don't know what you mean."

"What you mean, what you mean. You're at an impasse, *cheri,* a permanent fork in the road. You're a broken record, beautiful, because you don't want my answers. But you need them." They point to Patty, who waves uncertainly at me. I force a smile and wave back. "You been hiding your secret from your friends. You need their help, but big, bad Mother of Anathema doesn't want to admit you need their help."

I squeeze my hand into a fist, feel nails bite into palms. So easily, they could turn into talons. I could rip the world to shreds. But how can someone rip something that's neither here nor there? "It's not like that. I'm just...I don't want to be a burden."

Baron Samedi looks at me for a long moment, sparkling eyes staring deep into mine. Intimate. Accusatory. Both scathing and comforting all at once. Like being strapped down to a gurney while being spoon-fed the sweetest porridge. A trap, but one with a feathered pillow and too many sweets.

"You're scared of getting better," Baron Samedi says. "You're scared the medicine will stop working or, worse, start working, and you'll lose yourself."

"What, I...?" I shake my head, cursing myself mentally for really acting like a broken record. For proving the ageless *loa* right. "I'm fine."

I blink again. My friends are all staring at me, watching. Waiting. Silent.

The sand blows past them. I wave my hand, and no one reacts. They're statues, staring.

Neither living nor dead.

"Fun, huh? Like Simon Says, except all they can do is play statue."

"What do you want, Baron Samedi?"

Baron Samedi crosses their arms and sticks their hip out with a meandering sigh. "My dear. I want you to get back in the game. I will give your witch a spark of inspiration, have her brew medicines that will work for your immortal, demon blood. But you have to take the medicine and get better, *konprann*?"

"I didn't think the *loas* cared so much for what happened to us folk. Much less a demon trying to find their heart." I laugh. "It's like a Satanic Hallmark commercial or something."

Baron Samedi does another flourish. They push their spectacles over their eyes and their pupils glow in golden hues, glittering like the sun against the endless expanse of gray. "We don't care much about your walking on water and your birthday parties, no, that's true. Just you, Lilītu. We care because *you* are *special.*"

"Why do you want me to get better all of a sudden?"

Baron Samedi pinches my cheek. "Why does the gentle moon want the vicious sun to rise? Because, secretly, it wants to see the world burn."

They snap their fingers and the statues of my friends come back to life. Or rather, not death or whatever state of impermanent permanence the Baron had them frozen in while we chatted. Wilbur whimpers and huffs until Stace sneaks him a bit of an apple chew they had in their pocket. The battle boar snuffles this down gratefully and licks Stace's palm in return.

"I've had the most wonderful idea for a new potion for you, Lili. It's remarkable. And we can even make it cherry flavored." Patty's practically bouncing on her heels. The sudden energy seems wrong, somehow. Especially considering she was a statue under Baron Samedi's spell a moment ago.

Baron Samedi winks at me. *How convenient.*

Patty grins, ignoring my nervous glance at Baron Samedi. Her eyes are not quite here nor there. Enraptured by the gray expanse, the Baron's spell. "Wait...where are we?"

"The Crossroads. The *real* Crossroads." I shake my head, hugging her tight as she falters in her step and nearly falls to the ground entirely. "Time works differently here." I sneak a glance at the Baron, who holds up a finger to shush me. A slow smile accompanies that gleeful wink. "Or maybe time doesn't work at all. Not when you need it to."

Baron Samedi claps their hands, and a path sinks into the sand, revealing gray cobblestone beneath the shifting dunes. A road appears, solid and firm beneath our feet.

Walls of sand at either side of us. "All on the yellow brick road to Oz. Or in our case, awes, as in the awesome case of one dead fairy man. We got to get you to the Green Prince." They wink back at Erik Borden, flashing their spectacles. "Much appreciated for the trade, young Laveau."

"Not a new Laveau, just old me. Erik Borden," Erik replies.

Baron Samedi looks Erik over, their eyes seeing something the rest of us could not. Something only someone in between could see. Something beneath the layers of skin we fashion so carefully to hide truth. "Suit yourself. *Erik*. Legacies aren't easy, are they? Living up to dead people's expectations, tut, tut."

Erik's expression sours, brows drawn low and lips pulled tight. Byron hovers over him, massaging Erik's shoulders with his ghostly fingers. Erik shudders, leaning into Byron's ethereal touch, the whispers of kisses only half-there.

Baron Samedi cracks their knuckles, each sound somehow more visceral than the last. They swing a cane out in front of them as their skirts sweep out dramatically behind on the cobblestone roads. Their suit jacket smart and sharp, padded corners triangular on their shoulders. Like wings. "Most everyone comes to me when they don't know where to go. Immortals, especially, have a hard time accepting that their eternal life wasn't as eternal as they thought."

Baron Samedi points to the side and we see shades of figures against the clouds of gray, mere silhouettes. Some big as dragons, some as tiny as seahorses. They grasp for us, squealing when Baron Samedi glances their way. Their eyes beneath their spectacles flash that brilliant gold, searing away the desperate gray figures. Searing away the damned. "Those who never lived don't know how to die. So, they come to the places in between to try to figure it out. *Kaka,* I'm still trying to figure it out myself. Plenty of room though. It's like how motels always somehow have vacancies on empty stretches of highways. Never shut down even when the gas stations and the grocery stores all pack up and go. The Crossroads are the gift that just keeps on giving when your car engines give out, ha!"

"So...the Green Prince never died?" Stace shakes their head at that. "Forgive me, I'm new at this whole magic thing. But that doesn't seem helpful for a murder mystery."

"Oh, he's dead all right. He just doesn't know it or want to know it." Baron Samedi glances slyly at me. "I know a few immortals who are just like that."

The gray sand builds itself up into a grand castle with spires reaching upward into that gray horizon. Staircases shift in and out of existence. A swirl of wind brings a chandelier swooping down toward us. I raise my hand to touch a spire and it breaks as though into shattered glass, and just as quickly, dissipates into glittering dust. It flows harmlessly off my skin, even if it looks lethal.

Like everything in this place. Lethally beautiful.

"I'll leave you now. Thus...remember," Baron Samedi says even as they fade into that strange in-between, until just their eyes glow in the mist. "Remember that saying the Jesus fan club has? Ashes to ashes, dust to dust...until you simply *must.*"

And with that, they leave us even more confused than where we began.

Alone at the in-between home of the Green Prince.

The castle builds itself into more of a church, spires reaching heaven. But instead of crosses, there's the face of a man covered in vines. He stares solemnly out as the sand shifts itself into glass bells playing a merry tune. Wilbur stares up into the sky and makes a noise, almost musical, in response. Stace pets his wings with delight at the boar's strange singing.

Patty gets closer to the rune and runs her fingers against it. The face widens into a sort of lopsided grin, the sleeping man yawns. "It's the Green Man's symbol, king of the fairies. This must be his castle. Or a replication of it." She frowns, her amber eyes aflame now. She looks ready to go full *Kill Bill* at any second. "I want his bastard son to feel pain at what he did to Indah."

"We aren't here for revenge." Thing is, I want revenge, same as Patty. I want to taste the Green Prince's throat between my teeth for violating Indah. But I promised the Baron I'd try to live a more fulfilling immortal life. So, here we are. Calm Lili. Let's call it my anti-rebellious phase. "We're here for answers."

I look back at Erik and Byron, who are too busy trying to measure the properties of the Crossroads' gray sands and/or sneak more kisses to pay attention. And Stace is feeding Wilbur more apples.

"Answers, not revenge," I reiterate, my voice cracking this time.

"Speak for yourself." Patty huffs. "I'm here for Indah." She knocks on the door of the gray-sanded castle.

The surface, by some twist of strange magic, makes a sound much like the echo of old wood. "Hey, Green Prince! Asshole, open up. We need to talk to you."

The door creaks, opening on streaks of silver and an empty hallway leading into nothingness. Nothing save for that selfsame cold, gray light.

"Patty…" I whisper.

But I whisper too late. Patty rushes into those cold, gray halls. I slip in just in time before the door slams shut behind us.

I take a step down this endless hallway. My weight shifts. My leg runs into something cold, damp, and squealing.

"You!"

Wilbur squeals again and Stace coughs a couple of times. Stace staggers to their feet as I help them up. They lean a little on me before they regain their bearings.

"It was just supposed to be me," Patty mutters, flexing her fist a couple of times. She stares angrily ahead of us, her eyes burning a hole into the cubed, gray sand walls surrounding us. The palatial space feels very claustrophobic with all the sand dripping down, leaking like water.

"Yeah, well, I didn't want to be here either." Stace sniffles, some dried blood crusted in their nose. They wipe their hands against their knees, the gray dust caking their palms. "Wilbur shoved me in here while the rest of you were bickering and…" Stace runs their hand against the gray sand, sees it flow and reform into something like stone around their fingers. They break away with a shudder. "You know, I wasn't really the religious type. I went for the pavê and brigadeiros my nana would make after the service, you know? But, after this..." Stace makes a sign. "Just in case."

Wilbur snuffs his agreement, pausing dutifully for a crumpled apple treat from Stace's pockets. His giant wings buffet some of the sands.

The entire hallway trembles beneath our feet. My hand sinks into a cool spire, the gray sand nipping at my fingers as I try to regain my footing.

"Who dares?" echoes the voice from above. *"Who dares disturb the Green Prince? This is my castle here, and I see all."*

I cover Patty's mouth with my other hand before she can say anything. I grimace as she licks my palm and attempts to bite me in defiance.

"I dare. My friends call me Lili."

"What do your enemies call you?" the echo asks.

"Nothing." I smirk, leaning back on my heels as the trembling subsides. "They're all dead."

The echo pauses a moment before erupting into pealing laughter mingled with the sound of those unnatural bells. Wilbur squeals again as I wipe Patty's spit from my hand and dry it onto my pants to avoid smearing my favorite peacoat.

Because we all want to look like the admiral sea captain lost in the war. Or at least...I do.

The Green Prince seems to be appeased by my humor and my peacoat, because something shifts. A gray sand wall shimmers and vanishes, collapsing like water, crashing into nothingness. The "endless" hallway ends in a semicircular throne room. Ghostly figures created from the sands dance in front of a lone figure, seated on a throne fashioned of a century plant, fabled to only ever bloom once in a hundred years, a tall stalk with a rosette of gray-green leaves, striped with embedded silver. The center of the great hall bears a floor cradled in a nest of vines. The Green Man's face peers up at us, scowling, his eyes buffeted by tiny leaves as his eyelashes. The throne's leafy backing curls around him like a cloak.

"Like it?" The Green Prince waves his hand airily at the mural of the Green Man carved into the floor. Every one of the prince's fingers bears a thick, silver ring. Diamonds sparkle like moonlight. "My father follows me everywhere, even in this strange, boring world. He'll come looking for me soon. I know it."

What did Baron Samedi say?

"Oh, he's dead all right. He just doesn't know it or want to know it. I know a few immortals just like that..."

The Green Prince lounges on a throne. He wears a gray silk suit and cape. At odds with the rest of his attire, he sports the latest mortal line of sneakers on his feet, laced up in silver and a marbled thread. From his head sprouts a laurel wreath of leaves set atop soft ferns for hair. His eyes are of emerald coloration, with eyelashes like the stems of young dandelion shoots. His eyebrows are moss, his green stomach bare where his suit ends in a laced crop. A raw opal glints like moonlight from his bellybutton.

Around his throat, gentle threads linger, connecting his head to the rest of his body. A marionette poorly patched together.

Good for you, Indah. Good for you.

He bounds forward, too fast for a living soul. Too unnatural, like time slipping through your fingers, gray sands through an hourglass.

Patty holds up her hands, the mark of the coven, the Eye, glowing bright hot on her forehead. She presses forward...

Only for her magic to fizzle out. Water over a candle flame, and nothing sputtering into existence. Patty shakes her hands once...twice...

The Green Prince smirks from his willow lips. "You don't think I tried? No magic unless the Baron says so in this awful realm. Baron of what, I asked them. They just laughed at me. *Laughed* at me, as though I'm not the most powerful prince of Summerland. Then they said something else, but I couldn't understand it."

He pauses, staring down at his fingernails, coarse with more of that same gray sand. His emerald eyes flicker a bit at that, the light in them dimming. Gears turning in his head, clicking steadily against an expanse of clouds of grief and denial. "But Father will come for me. I know it. Just drank too much fairy liquor. Whisked away after a bad night at the club, that's all. That's all..." He turns to his throne, the gray-sanded figures, dancing for nobody at all. "He always comes for me. I know it."

"Uh-huh..." I lean back a bit, hiding my words behind my hand as I tug Patty closer. "So...we both agree he's lost it, huh?"

Patty nods slightly, really leading more with her eyes than anything else. "I'd almost feel bad for killing him. It'd be a mercy."

"Almost," I reply, and we both smirk at that. Patty's

lips tug upward ever so slightly. I just frown less. "Green Prince?" He shakes his head at both of us, walking so close that I can smell the faint scent, like the sweet rot of a plant when its roots go bad, petals wilting. He leans in close, so I'm forced to stare at those emerald eyes. "While we're waiting for your father, how do you feel about another dance? Unless your dance card's full of, you know"—I point to the gray-sand figures—"shadow demons."

He raises an eyebrow at that, the leaves of his hair fluttering. "Why would you wish to dance with me?"

I lean to the ground then and pull my hand up. The sand fails to follow my movement. What did Baron Samedi say?

"Remember... Ashes to ashes, dust to dust...until you simply must."

What is must?

"What did you say?" I ask the Green Prince, still folding my hands into the creases of the ever-shifting floor.

He pauses. Even as befuddled as he is right now, anyone would question why a random siren would be making sandcastles in the floor. "Why?"

"Because I'm hot for you, handsome." Patty stifles a laugh of disbelief at my words. The Green Prince smiles at her, in a way I don't like. Self-satisfied. I tilt my chin up at him. "So, repeat what you said."

Well, *I know I'm ace. He doesn't. Besides, Indah hinted that the asshole likes a power trip. Me too, douchebag.*

"Why would you dance with me?" he asks. He poses a little bit this time, I notice. Like he's on the cover of some poor human kid's fairy stories. He stretches one leg out in front of the other, flexing so the green chlorophyll veins of his skin are more defined.

Ashes to ashes, dust to dust...

Until...

Why *would* I dance?

"Because I must," I reply.

And, just like that, the gray sands of the makeshift throne room around us shift. They gather and fold into the creases of the room, bearing a strange, vibrating energy within them. Just like that, the gray dust and ashes form into a ring of fine, silver mushrooms. When they sway, they dance like they're living. Hopping around like frogs. Never in the same place twice.

Patty scrambles backward with her eyes, panicked, locked on me.

"Lili..."

But she doesn't have to finish that sentence. I follow her gaze, her fingernail hovering over the circle of silver fungi surrounding us. Like Baron Samedi had hinted, the ashes had formed from my obligation to the Green Prince. By saying I must dance with him, the ashes made it impossible for me to resist my obligation.

The gray sands around here thrive on obligation. The home was the Green Prince's manifestation of his obligation to the trappings of royalty. To being his daddy's favorite over in Summerland. The fairy circle, well, now that's my debt to him.

"A fairy circle..." I shake the remaining dust off my hands, frowning when it gets in the cracks. "If I remember my lore correctly, that means I'm in your hands now. So, how's about it?" I hold my hand out, waiting. I tug my smile even wider, until my teeth are shaking from the effort. *Damn, it's been a while since I laid it on this thick. Or maybe it's just his stench.* "Spare a dance?"

He takes this in stride, the plant-based ass. "I'd suppose Father will take a bit of time to travel here all the way from Summerland." The Green Prince takes my hand, a shadow hovering over his face even as his lips still smile in that sneering, sadistic way. "It would be my pleasure."

The way he says "my" indicates he only ever thinks of his own pleasure. Typical of a douchebag. But is he the one who set Indah up as his murderer? I mean, I can think of multiple reasons offhand why someone would want him dead.

But did he?

"Madam." He pulls me in by the waist until I'm toe-to-toe with his damn, laced-up sneakers. My heavy boots, oh, how I have to resist the urge to stomp on his ankle bones. But I keep it together. For Indah's sake. "May I have this dance, seductress?"

You may, but you won't like it.

I push his hand backward, twisting my other fingers around his. I pull him with me into the dance, the center of the fairy ring our performance theater. "All right then." He might be taller than me, but by pulling him into this dance position, I force him to my height, neck craning down to mine. "But I lead."

The fairy circle hums and vibrates a simple tune. A waltz memory, held to the lone strings of a violin, singing out in this echoing chamber.

I pull the Green Prince along behind me, not caring if he smells like broken flower petals strewed along the earth. Not caring if his lashes are close enough to mine to let me see where the spots of his emerald eyes turn eerily dark. Not caring if I feel every inch of his cold, deceased, green-tinged skin. Every step I take in this dance to the sound of this sad violin.

Every step isn't mine. They're Indah's.

So, sue me, even immortals have hearts. When we aren't eating them, I guess.

"Tell me who you are."

"Prince Sam Hain," he replies, "son of the Green Man. And you..." He trails one hand along my cheek, nearly causing me to miss a step as he breaks our dance form. "You are Lili."

I crunch his fingers back against my hand. He winces as I close my hands around his like a vice. "Nuh-uh, Sam. I lead, remember?"

He laughs then. The sound, thankfully, is drowned out by the violin, playing based solely on the will of the air itself. "That eager, huh?"

I push down so hard that, satisfyingly, I feel one of his finger muscles strain. Bone already feels so close to twigs. I wonder if snapping a plant fairy's hand would cause it to break like a twig too. I wonder if they sound the same. *You can't die twice in the in-between, can you?*

He bites the inside of his cheek, so hard I see the indentation from the outside. "Shit." He gasps. *"Mallacht na baintrí ort!* Widow curse you." His eyes flash as he spits this last part out at me. "Easy, Lili."

"This whole dance is easy." I let him fall into a dip, enthusiastic to be the one staring him down this time. "You're just a bad dancer."

He tries to break away, but I have him in my grip now. My ribs heaving hard, and all my strength focused to my arms, I can feel the change coming. The urge of blood pumping under my skin. It's not magic for me to change, not like with Patty's spells, able to be blocked by Baron Samedi's wards. The transformation is simply power. A code written into my bloodline since the dawn of time, since the first One said there should be light and someone called Lilith, who the One immediately regretted making.

I press my thumb down a bit more against his finger, and he howls.

"What do you want?" Sam Hain asks, glaring up at me with a growl in his voice. I can see the ring around his neck clearer now, from where his head was liberated from his body back in the living world.

"I need your memories," I reply, pulling him back to his feet. The violin hums faster now, the tune almost merry. We whirl faster and faster around the fairy circle. We pass the throne that Patty leans against, staring on. Uncertain. I spin on my heel, the world a spinning top beneath me, going faster and faster. "I need your memories of what happened before you ended up here."

"I can't..." He winces, his tongue flopping around his mouth, unable to lift. "I don't want to remember."

Oh right. Fairies cannot lie. So, it's just as Baron Samedi says. Sam Hain really doesn't want to remember.

"Indah didn't want to deal with you either, but here we both are, huh?"

A snarl at his lips then. A flash of dastardly recognition in his eyes. "Indah?"

Ah shit. I did it. I ran my mouth again.

"Yeah, Indah. A dancer at the Kraken Club." He tries to step on my foot, but I push back on my toes, leading him further into the dance. Our bodies swaying, I see his muscles tense. "You won't want to hear this, Prince Sam Hain. But you didn't just stumble home from the club drunk."

"No, no! It cannot be." He strikes out at me with his elbows bent in. Trying to twist my arms to unleash him. Trying to hurt me. Throttle me. Run. Maybe all the above.

"You died. That's how you got here. You. Are. Dead. Or, trapped in the in-between. Whatever it is, it's as close as an immortal gets."

Sam Hain stops dancing then. I finally let him go. He falls to his knees, head bent in supplication, appealing to powers that no longer work for him. The veins at his neck are tensed, his head thrown back, hair like ferns curling over bony shoulders. Skin stretched over them, skin like the sun shining through a pile of leaves, decaying on the earth. Roots, white and dangling, grow in spurts from beneath his feet. They curl around his wrists and ankles, positioning him like a puppet on a string.

"No, it can't be..." he mutters, even as the roots tie around his neck. They drag more of the gray sand from the in-between, acting much as plant roots do in the living world, drawing water into their core, trying to take nutrients in to survive. But here, there is nothing but infinite gray sand and imagination and the horrible things that too much time and too much memory does to endless souls. The roots start to pull at him, leading him around like a puppet on strings. He turns his head up at me then, all at once. His chin jerks to reveal those emerald eyes, barren in shadow, with fern lashes dusting over those pollen-speckled cheeks.

"Whatever I was. I *ended* at the Kraken Club, didn't I?" he asks, holding one thin, green-tinged hand out at me. "Something ended me. It should be impossible for a fairy, especially a fairy prince, to die. Impossible things ending impossible things. How funny."

"Hilarious, so..." I try to walk closer to him, but one of the roots... They branch out into something that spits out thorns as a thousand tiny quills along its end. It whips out at me, cutting my cheek.

"Lili!" Patty raises her hand again, willing her magic to break free. But, alas, Baron Samedi's wards hold still. "Frogger in a duck hole." She spits out the most adorable curses for being the scariest of witches sometimes.

"Fuck you!" I shout, tamping my palm against the wound. "I might be bajillion years old, but I still feel things, you know. Even paper cuts!"

"But I'm talking to you, Lili, right? So, I'm not ended. I'm not. Not yet. If I keep talking, then I'm alive. What did that mortal say? I think therefore I am. Yes, if I keep talking, then I'm not dead. I'm not ended yet." Sam Hain's eyes stare off somewhere, the pretty emeralds marred by the silver sands' shadows. He raises a hand, the nails ending in bits of tree bark, and when he opens his mouth, even his tongue and teeth look fashioned of some sort of seeds, the inside of his mouth like sliced-open fruit. "The night I ended, before that dancer girl ended me..."

"Indah, her name was Indah, asswipe."

He looks at me blankly for a moment. "Yes, that one.

Indah. There was something sparkling in the air. Glittering. Something that smelled like poisons and powders, something I recognized from the apothecary who bore all those tattoos and that strange hairstyle…"

Apothecary? Ah, his drug dealer. Gods, fairy language. I'm old, but at least I don't sound like him.

"Whoa, whoa. Wait. Describe this apothecary more." This comes from Patty.

Helpful Patty, paying attention when I'm too busy thinking about fairy verbiage.

"The apothecary." Sam Hain's lip curls in distaste. "Eyes green like mine, except not. More shining like a cat's, a mischievous color. The back of her skull shaved like a warrior's helmet. And ink all over her hands and neck. Lots of patterns with swords and rivers…"

"Lethe." I spit at the name, then apologetically wipe the fairy circle floor clean with my boot because even the in-between sands don't deserve getting dirtied with *her* name. "You had the displeasure of meeting Alethea Styx, didn't you?"

Patty and I exchange a glance.

"Impossible," she tells me. "We confined her in the basement of the coven."

"He's dead," I say, responding by sticking my thumb out at Sam Hain's rooted, marionette self. "Who else does impossible things like she does? A serial killer who kills dead people again. Come on."

"She's confined indefinitely," Patty repeats, shaking her red hair back from her pale face.

"Then she got out." I insist, wiping the blood away

from my cheek, getting it all over my nice peacoat by accident. *Shit. I hope Erik invented some magical stain remover.*

"She couldn't have..."

"She moved like the river in the morning." Sam Hain lurches forward, his arms and ankles bound with the strange, twined roots, undulating and delving into the silver earth. He is a creature on strings, a puppet detached and tied up in his own little world. "And she walked like a swordsperson, a fencer. She walked like she knew how to kill, even as she peddled her wares."

I throw my hands into the air. "Who do we know who loves swords?"

"I mean, I like swords, so..." I glare at her until she cracks. A moment later, Patty sighs, shrugging a bit. "Okay, okay, she sounds a lot like Alethea." Patty pushes her hair out of her face, her eyes glowing bright now, sparking with adrenaline, as she turns on the Green Prince. "Sam Hain, tell me. Tell me what Alethea sold to you that night."

The Green Prince smiles, and from between each gap in his teeth oozes mud from the silver dust, mixed in with a pinkish, viscous fluid. "Just a little bit of pixie dust. Made of actual pixies' teeth and bone. People in my kingdom only get it if you're rich, and you become it if you piss off my father." The Green Prince turns that eerie, leering gaze to me, staring deep into my eyes. "One hit and it'll change your immortal life, forever."

Sam Hain holds his hands into a ball, cupping around the gray sands. They shift into an illusion, shimmering and bright. Translucent flakes like diamond shavings glitter in his palm. They whirl like a torrent of feathers and lace, and when they move quickly, I think I hear tiny pixies singing...or screaming.

"Yeah. The pixie dust changed your life so much, it ended it." I grind my boot against the ground, smothering a root that gets far too close to my ankle for comfort, the rounded vessel crunching beneath my heel. The root winds back like a serpent with a mind of its own, squealing into the dark. "Come on, Patty. We've gotten what we wanted from here."

The Green Prince rises then. Sam Hain spreads his arms out wide, the roots following, suspending him like a ragdoll in the air. "Take me with you. I know an old one when I see them, another with immortal blood in their veins. You're powerful enough to get me out of here, aren't you?"

"I probably could." I turn back to face him. A single tendril, the root so close I can see the hairs on it, curls curiously to my cheek. The vine lingers, a smooth caress across my skin. I snap at it, biting down so hard on grayness and dust that my teeth clack against each other. "But I won't. And I hope you see Indah's face every day you're down here, you pitiful little shithead."

"The dancer?" Sam Hain laughs, the walls trembling with the force of it, the peals of unnatural laughter shaking these unnatural walls. "The dancer liked me well enough. I always give the dancers extra pixie dust before they perform. Only the best for the Kraken Club girls."

"Patty..."

"You and all others like you, you fuckers on your

power trips with your too-high opinion of yourself. You tell yourselves the same story every night. That your quarries liked you. That they secretly wanted you. But every sentence, no matter how often you rewrite them, is nothing but a fucking lie." Patty's fists tremble at her sides, her eyes sparking like coal at the bottom of a pit, yearning to be unleashed into a vacuum of gasoline and tinder. The power trapped inside by Baron Samedi's wards, every drop of it courses through her veins, writhing, desperate to be released. Though she cannot use magic here, she doesn't need magic to face Sam Hain, for this is power of a different kind. She stomps forward, crushing a mushroom on the fairy circle to dust beneath her feet. "Indah never wanted you. She never liked you. She hated your guts. And, at the end of the day, I'm glad she took your head off, you fucking pig!"

"I can never die..." Sam Hain splutters.

"But you did," Patty says. "And I wish you'd go back just so I can kill you twice."

Sam Hain releases this desperate, caterwauling howl. I try to pull Patty back, but it's too late. Sam Hain raises his arms to the ceiling and the fairy circle collapses all at once. The force of the broken ring sends us skittering upon the floor until I thud into the gray wall behind me. I'm fortunate enough to serve as the cushion that breaks Patty's slide. She crashes into me, barely missing one of Sam Hain's roots that's trying desperately to lash out at us, whipping forth angrily.

Sam Hain rises like a tentacled creature, the throne room collapsing as he whips about madly to reach us. I tug Patty to her feet as we go back to the main halls. But the hall is shifting and tumbling around us, spinning slowly like a cement mixer. The gray dust attempts to place some semblance of normalcy back on the place, at least to let the structure accept some sort of physics, but it's no use. Magic and all else is broken in these halls.

But to turn and see the triumphant grin on Patty's face, it almost makes an eternity of being trapped in the in-between seem worth it. Almost, but not today.

We sprint through the collapsing, trembling halls of the Green Prince's reimagined castle. The shadowy Fae figures dance and spit around us, twirling around in the never-ending dance of Summerland, the endless court affairs. Donkey-headed creatures dancing with winged beings. Goat-legged characters leaping about with figures with hair so long that it wraps around them like a cloak. We leap over crashed banisters and trample upon tapestries with the gray-embroidered face of the Green Man, the prince's father, wearing a crown of holly and thorns.

"The door!" Patty cries out as I tug her along behind me. "We made it."

Just then, a single root bursts from the ground below us and curls around Patty's calf. It tries to drag her into the shifting sands, thin and leaking like water. I reach down to pull her back up, scrabbling at the roots.

"I cannot die." Sam Hain is behind us like the chase was nothing. He raises one arm, and from that arm extends a root, an appendage currently dragging Patty down, so she sputters beneath the sand. This is his world we live in, his little slice of unending reality in the in-between. "Father will come for me, I know it. And when he does, he'll torture you for a hundred thousand years until you wish you were dead." Sam Hain grins nice and widely then, his emerald eyes looking murky as sludge at the bottom of a pond. His eyes hung heavy with shadows. "I am forever."

I spit at him, watching, satisfied, as a glob lands at his cheek. "But this isn't."

And with a mighty heave, I reach down and sink my teeth into his arm, like overripe fruit and pulp, gnashing down so hard that I think I can almost taste something like fermented papaya. *Oh, the things I'll do for my friends.*

He howls again, a pitiful thing. He struggles to lift his arm again, but the damage is done. I kick him in the ribs as I pick Patty up from the ground, pulling her free from the sands. We hurl ourselves at the gray-sanded doors, the edges slick with falling sand.

And, just like that, the nightmare is over. We blink wearily, staring up at an endless gray expanse with brighter, silver lighting filtered against the same, gray sky.

The gray halls, the gray throne room and the muddied root appendages are all gone. No more staring into the sickly green eyes of Sam Hain.

The Green Prince, for now, cannot reach us. Not here. Not at this moment.

We've escaped...back into the endless in-between.

So, halfway escaped.

Erik, Byron, Stace, and Wilbur walk toward us, covering the distance over the sloping gray dunes at a much more normal pace than the strange temporal unreality within the Green Prince's twisted domain. Stace pulls us both into a hug, smelling like apples.

They give excellent hugs. I wish I was half so cool as to give hugs as good as Stace's.

"What happened? One minute, you were at the doors of some castle. The next...just gone. Where did you go? And what happened to your face, Lili, you're bleeding!" Stace hovers worriedly around us, glaring an accusation with those galaxy-nebula-exploding contacts of theirs.

Stace looks so cool, even when they're scolding us. Maybe I should start wearing contacts. Yeah, I could change my eye colors with a cantrip or something, but still...contacts.

If Jason ever hurts them, I'll throw him into the Pits of Tartarus...assuming I'm not still banned from there.

"Good news, I'd expect?" Erik asks. He's fiddling with a square metal contraption in his pocket, wires connected to tiny chips and pieces of what appears to be bleached bone.

"That's my man, always expecting good news." Byron sticks his tongue out at me. "But knowing Lili, it's probably bad."

"Oh, ye of little faith." I stick my tongue out right back at Byron. "You were more pleasant when you were fully dead instead of half-alive, Mr. Semi-Ghost." I unwrap a piece of cloth I had in my pocket. An old handkerchief I'd kept around after some Victorian poetess fell in love with me and wrote a book about me or something. It happened more often than one might think. "Three cheers and three beers for me because I found a piece of evidence." I unwrap this handkerchief, and inside, somehow still bespelled and not morphing back into the gray sand of its birth, is a tiny pile of pixie dust. "Voila. Pixie dust. Pinched off one headless prince."

Stace shrugs, pinching at the napkin. "I mean, it's been a while since I partook. Probably since my last time at Burning Man, but if it's for a mystery..."

"No, it's not for *that*." I barely pull the napkin away from Stace in time. "We have a lead on the dealer who sold to the Green Prince the night he died. Made his head all fuzzy."

"Fuzzy. And no longer on his neck," Patty adds, smirking a little at that. "Thank the gods."

"Yes, that too." I hold the napkin aloft, feeling it settle snugly into the palm of my hand, a dangerous little bauble. "They were selling to all the dancers at the Kraken Club that night, including Indah. And we've heard Indah's testimony from that night. She lost control of herself." I scrounge my fingers into the cloth, feeling the tiny crystals tumbling there. "She was drugged that night. Perhaps mind-controlled into killing Sam Hain. And I might've been seeing things after the fight. But I've seen it a few other times, as well. A glittering substance on Toothpick's lips after he wolfed up at the diner."

Erik Borden takes the handkerchief from me and shakes a few crystals into the air. They chime like bells...or high-pitched pixie screams. He blinks a few times, his monocle readjusting to the few flakes that have gotten on his palm. He wipes them back on the handkerchief with a mild look of discomfort, lip twisted inward slightly.

"Fascinating. Pixie dust made from literal pixies. I've tried to implement a liquid form of this into bio-magic-therapy for the Franks." Erik shakes his head. "But this substance, it's too unwieldly. Makes Franks calmer, yes, but also...makes some lose their brains altogether.”

“They have brains? They’re zombies.” Byron raises an eyebrow at that. He flickers out of existence for a moment. His skin goes translucent, and I think I spy a bit of muscle and bone as we see *through* him for a moment. Like one of those skeleton fish in an aquarium. X-ray fish, I think they’re called. It’s quite uncomfortable to witness it on Byron.

“Zombies can’t have brains.” Byron tilts on his tiptoes to throw his arms around Erik’s neck. Erik leans back into his arms, grinning.

“Yes of course they have brains, dear.” Erik places the palm of his hand on Byron’s cheek, his fingers going through Byron’s skin for a blink of an instant. “They eat them, after all.”

Byron chuckles a little at the joke and nuzzles into Erik’s side as he hands the napkin of pixie dust back to me.

Stace just looks perturbed, but for another matter entirely.

“Ground-up pixies, like Tinkerbell?” Stace shakes their head as Wilbur snuffles sadly into their palm. “They’d best not get near Wilbur if they’re crushing up winged magical creatures for their drugs or whatever.”

“They won’t get to him. I’ll die first. I mean, I’ve done it once and come back from the dead. I can do it again.” Patty glares at me for that joke, and I studiously avoid her gaze, my cheeks flushed with the discomfort. “Just kidding, I’ll be careful.” I stuff the napkin back in my pocket. On the corner are two initials: *V* and something else that’s been worn by time. I wonder who fell in love with me then.

Back when I didn't understand how I loved differently. Back when I didn't understand how to love myself. I was just a siren then, taking hearts and eating them. Killing for sport. Who am I now? Who is anyone?

I curl my free hand into a fist, nails biting into my palms. The pixie dust hums in my pocket, literal crushed hopes and dreams. "If we want to keep everyone safe, we have to get back to the living world. We have to track down whoever's selling this product and trying to manipulate Gamin's magical population into an early grave."

Did somebody call for a ride?

A flash beneath us and a plume of violet smoke, like the blooms of an orchid spreading out beneath water. The particles form a shadow, a beauteous silhouette. Speaking in that melodic way, with their figure neither here nor there. Blink, and they'd be right by your side in an instant.

Blink again, and you might stop existing.

They wield a cane this time, resting their weight against it. Their silk skirts billow out behind them, a sharp-shouldered blazer like wings on their shoulders. Baron Samedi stares out with those sparkling eyes. When they walk, they smell of coffee, cigars, and rum.

"Oh, *bebe*, I hear people want to go back to the world of the living. That's where I come in." They shift their weight to the other side, one hand curled on the cane while the other places their spectacles back over their dazzling eyes with a flourish. "Need a lift back to the extra boring world, darlings?"

Baron Samedi holds out their hand, fingernails shimmering between colors like the night sky in paint and a purple so deep it looks liquid still. Like wine you could fall into. They smile, dip their head. Their stylish ribboned top hat slides a bit forward.

"*Mon amour.* It's time to return to the surface."

Rings glint on every finger. They wiggle their fingers, and the nail polish glistens brighter. Gray sand falls from their fingertips, dancing through the air.

I take their hand and they pull me to them. Something strong. Sheer power. It radiates off them, filling the spaces in between. "Remember, *amour.* Remember why we're helping you and your covenant kin." Their voice carries clear as day even as they don't move their lips. They smile at me, black spectacles sliding down their nose and running into their hoop ring.

"I'll take it that it's not my people skills," I shoot back.

But they just keep on smiling as they speak without speaking.

"Take your new medicine. Drink your water. Eat your heart-healthy food and get some exercise by running after that killer. Because my darling..." And they laugh, still holding their smile still, but the sound carries into my ears. Into myself. "If we help you get better, well, let's just say we help ourselves, *konprann*?"

I scoff a little at that, digging my toe into the sand. "What if I don't care about myself?"

They raise a painted, thick eyebrow at that. "But you care about her, the soul-eater, don't you?"

"Is Jo...? She told me she was staying in the Crossroads."

"Oh, she was, but she isn't. Not anymore." They shake their head. "Not here, darling. Your love's escaped the usual fate. But, darling, she's not exactly *her*, anymore.

You understand?"

"I don't. What are you saying?"

They look to me and those eyes... Their hands take both of mine. The power radiates further now, to encompass all of us. I think I hear my friends, faintly calling my name. Calling for us both. But those eyes are all I can see. The in-between caught in them. A gateway from the living to the dead to the places where neither lie.

"I'm saying it's time to wake up for you, Lili, to find your little dreamer."

Their eyes burn brightly, piercing all, but just as their power nearly becomes unbearable...

"Baron Samedi, wait!"

They pause, and the world drifts into focus around us as I wave them forth with one finger.

"If I may, great Baron Samedi, I have one more request..."

"The request?"

I lean in close to whisper in their ear, watching as their smile grows wider. "That young man, Erik Borden...he lost his father. *I* lost his father during our last case. I want you to bring him back, if only for a day."

"Are you admitting your wrongs, demon mother?"

I pull my lips back tight, almost baring my teeth. *Calm, Lili.* "If I did, I wouldn't repeat myself now, would I?"

"Well, with a request as interesting as that," they cackle, eyes bright, "I can pull more strings than a puppeteer."

*

THE OTHER SIDE of the river is cloaked in a thick fog, a magic fog that covers all.

Erik goes into the unknown, determination writ heavy on his face. There's a voice calling out his name from the other side of the river.

"Erik. Erik…"

The voice sounds familiar. We watch Erik go to it. All is silent, save for the voice.

On the other side of the river, Baron Samedi winks at me. I see those sparkling eyes behind the mirrored glasses and the towering top hat. He holds one finger to his lips, demanding secrecy.

A moment later, or perhaps an eternity, Erik Borden emerges from the foggy plane. He places his hand on my shoulder.

"I saw my father," he tells me, his voice thick as blood. "Did you do that?"

I remain silent.

Erik smiles at me before he goes, melting into Byron's embrace. Tears streak from the metal wires merged in his eyes. I look across the river. Baron Samedi is gone.

Chapter Fourteen

Just a spoonful of sugar makes the medicine still taste like piss

"DAMN."

...urgh.

This medicine won't go down easy.

I slam the empty crystal vial on the hotel front desk. I nearly knock down a bell, except I must not have pissed off the goddess of luck because I catch it on my thigh before it dings.

I swallow the medicine from that silly vial. The taste of syrupy red and whatever unearthly compound Baron Samedi slipped in, it sluices down my throat and stays for a moment before dropping into the pit of my stomach. My head, I don't know if it's my desperation for this to work this time, but it feels...different somehow. I hold on to my skepticism before I admit to it being better just yet. *But I'll try...for Jo. For Indah. For my friends.* I shake the last few drops of medicine from the vial before stoppering it.

"Better?" Patty asks.

I studiously avoid the question, glaring daggers at the

little medical vial. "Why do humans like making their medicine taste fake? This doesn't taste like cherries. It tastes like air freshener."

"We like to be enchanted by the fakery." Patty laughs. "Even necromancers get enchanted sometimes."

"Yeah, with those goo-goo eyes of yours." One edge of my mouth creeps up into a teasing smile. "Enchanted by long, dark hair. Soulful eyes. Glitter across her cheekbones..."

"Enough about my crush on Indah. Let's talk about you." Patty crosses her arms and leans back over our lunch. Blended heart and a sprinkle of unicorn horn shavings sourced from the bits of horn they sharpened themselves. Patty made sure to be ethical for a coven dealer. Even if unicorns are vicious, biting bastards that don't deserve the hype, Patty wanted them living. Not dead, undead, or anything in between. I digress. Again. "Lili, you haven't been taking your medicine until we got back from the Crossroads. Why?"

Shit. "How'd you know?"

"My Spidey senses. And I found the vials you'd been hoarding in your room." Patty kicks her feet up to rest on the side of the desk I'm leaning on. Her new lace-up boots have very dramatic, deadly looking sharp heels on them. I wonder if she borrowed from Stace. Oh shit, she's glaring at me. "So, I'll ask you again. Why didn't you tell me you'd stopped?"'

"I..." I sniff, slumping over. Patty scoots over on the bench behind the counter, staring over a nearly empty lobby except for one tired-looking cross-country driver who had fondly told us earlier they'd stopped by Grid's waffle house and met a whole host of edgy characters who looked like they'd walked out of *Twilight*. Oh, if only they knew. They seemed happy enough, probably appeased by Lethe's River. They currently sit on a couch in the lobby, facing away from us, their eyes following the golden triangles etched into the wallpaper. At this exact moment, they are sniffing their hair for chlorine from our pool.

We should really have the water demons clean the pool better next time. I beat them in poker, so they owe me a favor. Granted, I was cheating. But they're also immortal. They have no excuse not to learn how to count cards.

"Lili. Focus." Patty gestures, once more, for me to sit on the bench.

Shit. Why is it so hard to pay attention when admitting your guilt? I sit on the available space beside Patty, having to awkwardly move over when I crush part of the uneaten tomato and cheese that Patty was saving up in brown paper packaging. "I was scared to tell you that I wanted to switch meds again. I was scared that...maybe I wasn't *made* to get better. Maybe creatures like me don't get a second chance. Or a thousandth, in my case. I didn't want to drag you into that. I didn't want to drag you down with me."

Patty holds out her hand and takes mine into hers. I lean into her touch a bit, feeling her warmth. So mortal. So kind. So...so Patty. "You are dragging me into nothing, Lili. I'm here for you, got it?" Patty hugs me close, and I exhale, releasing all my tension. Feeling stress flow out of me as I hug her back.

"I think even an immortal's life is too short *not* to tell

your friends you love them. I… I love you, Pats," I tell her. I laugh a bit. "I guess I don't say that enough. Sometimes, I think I have forever with everyone. But if living in Gamin has taught me anything, forever means jack shit." I shake slightly until I focus on the feeling of the bench beneath me. I try, so hard, to center myself.

I look at the lobby in front of us with the soft red carpet. The brown bar hidden in the back of the Sweeney Inn. The smell of cedar and wood shavings from the building and rebuilding. The smell of the dried plants Patty set in the corners. Parsley, sage, rosemary, and thyme from Scarborough Fair (the Simon & Garfunkel song *and* the fair that King Henry III started in the late Middle Ages. I was around for the inception of both, mind you). The scents and dried flora were made to keep the guests peaceful and the toilets smelling less toilet-y. I feel the bench beneath me, the legs digging into my calves. The air from an overhead fan brushing my cheeks like a whisper.

And focusing on it all, I feel centered. Less shaky. Almost…

Normal as an immortal being can get.

Patty smiles at me, freckles and dimples cutting into her pale skin. Red hair curling around her face. I see my reflection in her glasses. The age-old peacoat. The dark hair. The curious, scared eyes, more terrified to admit to caring about someone than I'd been to face off against an overzealous knight back in the age of Charlemagne.

"I love you too, Lili…you dumbass."

Close enough.

I watch the cross-country guest sniff their hair, loudly again.

I wink at Patty. "Another chlorine-scented customer. Time to..."

"Clean the pool?" Patty suggests.

"Threaten a water demon," I reply with a shrug.

Patty rolls her eyes, unwraps her cheese sandwich, and takes a large, razor bite. "Typical Lili."

"But you love me?" I try.

She tosses a gum wrapper at me and, before the customer can notice it, she snaps her fingers, and the paper shrivels and rots away in a second. *Typical necromancer,* I think, before marching off to threaten another water demon at the pool.

*

Yes. We now have a pool at the Sweeney Inn

Rate us five stars!

THE POOL AREA of the Sweeney Inn is a poor imitation of the Ayasofya Hurrem Sultan Hamam, the largest bathhouse built by Hurrem Sultan, the wife of Suleiman the Magnificent back in 1556 in Istanbul. And that, in turn, was a bathhouse built over the Baths of Zeuxippus that were built over the Temple of Zeus the Greeks and then Romans had for a while. And they, in turn, had taken the land from Thracian tribes...

I'm sorry, dear reader. Am I boring you with this timeline? I'm immortal, remember. I have all the time in the world.

I never visited the Baths of Zeuxippus as I'd been a hothead back in 526 and had compared a young man named Justinian to an unfavorable anatomical part of a donkey. One year later, Justinian became an emperor, and it was *I* who became the unfavorable anatomical part of a donkey.

I did have a chance to check out the baths in Istanbul a thousand years later. They were gorgeous. Magnificent tiles. Intricate geometric designs hewn into the walls. Sunlight filtered through cutout ceilings that made you think the stars had fallen from the heavens.

I'd gushed all about the bathhouse one night after an embarrassing amount of pixie liquor I'd taken from Jason Sweeney on a bet.

Patty had heard some of my speech and she told me: *I'll do in one day what took empires centuries!*

I asked her how and she said: *With magic!*

But, dear reader, she was no episode of *Bewitched*.

The Sweeney Inn pool had reached for the stars in trying to imitate those Turkish baths but ended up dropping faster than an asteroid on the dinosaurs.

The resulting space is currently occupied by a bored-looking naga sleeping in the center fountain, her serpentine tail wrapped about the lowest tier. The fountain comes up to about as high as one's waist and features faceless stone figures spitting water outward. The tile on the floor is placed crookedly. The construction Franks, being zombies and all, gnawed down the tile with their teeth when the tiles didn't fit right in order to mash them into place. There is a changing area woven by helpful elves with wooden folding screens set to the far side of the room. Burgundy and velveteen cushions lie around the actual bathing area, a deep octagonal bath surrounded by a smooth stone surface.

The pool is maintained by a water demon, a vodyanoy, an old man with a frog's face, kelp for his beard, and tiny swim trunks (usually a vodyanoy travels naked, but Patty struck a deal before hiring him for our pool). He flips me off cheerfully as I toss him a pack of sweet, sticky pink taffy, his favorite. "Same time next week for blackjack, Pabel?" I ask him, watching him dip a measuring stick into the pool and frown as he looks at the chlorine meter.

"Fuck you and your card-counting, Lili," Pabel the frog-faced, pool-cleaning vodyanoy replies sweetly, accepting the taffy besides. The gills on his neck tremble when he's feeling particularly passionate.

"Learn card-counting, Pabel. You have eternity!" I chuckle, watching him take out the trash bins and change the cucumber water on the way out. "It might take you eternity and a year though, with that attitude." I pat my pockets, which are filled with a few more crisp dollar bills than I had before. *Ah, trusty, gambling Pabel. Always good for a few laughs and cash.*

I inhale, smelling a bit less chlorine than last time. It's not as severe, which tells me Pabel cleans pools better than he plays cards. The floors are also newly mopped, and the deck chairs are sparkling and a deep, polished black.

The large pool looks, unnervingly, like it goes on until infinity, a portal leading to another dimension. I go to the edge of the pool to stare at my reflection and find it smiling back at me though I had no intention of smiling in the first place.

I lean back from the edge, suppressing a shudder as I agitate the water with my right hand. The reflection goes away for an instant, but the smile does not.

Stace and Jason walk in from the steam room where we keep a tiny dragon under the coals to belch steam occasionally. He's a sweet enough fellow, a friendlier sort for dragons. Sometimes, he steals a tiny earring or swipes a coin here or there to build his miniature dragon hoard beneath the coals. He's quite cute actually, named Smaug like his larger namesake from *The Hobbit*. Fearsome, yet insanely cute when tucked in the palm of your hand.

Stace looks pleasantly relaxed from the steam room, dressed in a black plaid muscle tank and shorts. I think tiny Smaug must have stolen one of their hoops, because the cuff around their left ear is noticeably missing.

Jason is so wrapped up in staring adoringly at Stace that he fails to notice me. He cups his hand around their cheek, leaning in for a kiss. His swimsuit trunks, adorably, match Stace's in black and gray plaid. He wears a towel around his neck that slides down to reveal scars on his chest. Near his right shoulder, he's tattooed a symbol of an eye, the symbol of his and Patty's coven.

The symbol of a coven leader.

From Midwest boy to coven leader. To NYC runaway now. We've changed each other, after all. We had to when Lethe threatened to destroy us.

He looks to me and the softness in his eyes, it all fades. There's only wariness and weariness, to be apprehensive and incredibly tired all at once. He looks at me and he holds on to Stace's hands tighter, squeezing their fingers into his, wanting to never let go. "Lili," he intones, and even the naga in the fountain has the good sense to leave the space for the steam room. Even being belched on by a tiny dragon named Smaug is better than being caught up in found family drama. "What a pleasant surprise."

I raise an eyebrow. "Is it?"

He shrugs, and Stace squeezes his hand gently back. He gives, fiddling with the towel around his neck. "I heard y'all went to the Crossroads with the *loas*. You survived, clearly. Congratulations." He stops fiddling for a moment and levels his gaze at me, glassy eyes seeing more than they let on. He sighs, taking in a deep breath. A rush of cool air powers against the steam from Smaug's steam room. The naga must've opened a window to slither out, as I catch a few scales of her glorious tail slipping past my sight. Glinting blue and green in the outside sun.

Jason begins anew. "I'm sorry, Lili. I'm just stressed with us leaving Gamin and you still traipsing around the place, trying to solve a mystery. But you did good. You protected Patty. And, as much as I claim to be irritated by her, she's my sister, you know?" He folds his hand into a fist, then awkwardly holds it out for a high five instead. "So...thank you."

I high five him. The echo of a halfhearted slap sounds through the pool room. It is, indeed, from the grimace on Stace's face, quite awkward.

"Don't mention it." I rub my hand against my cheek, feel the steam cool against my skin. Try to root myself here. The words come rushing out at once. It's better that way, feels less painful to keep it in. "The lead we got from our time in the Crossroads... He told us Alethea was there the night of the murders." I see how Jason tenses at my words, how his whole jaw goes so rigid, I'm afraid he'll bite his tongue. But still, I continue. "She's selling some drug that brings monsters back to their original, most murderous selves. To their truest, harshest form."

"Back up." Jason holds on to Stace tighter. They lean opposite his weight, literally supporting him in his disbelief. "I… Alethea Styx is behind this? I…" He closes his eyes and takes a deep, shuddering breath.

Stace brings him to the deep pool in the center with the raised, smooth stone benches. He sits on the edge of the infinite waters. His reflection doesn't smile while mine flickers to a hesitant smirk.

Narcissus's reflection damned him. Does it bring out the worst in me? Or does it just highlight the bad part? The part that hurts others no matter how I try to stop it…

"You're okay, babe," Stace tells Jason, running their palms against his back and shoulders. They turn to me next. "Lili, are you okay?"

"Yes."

No. You're not bad, Lili. You're trying to be better. Or maybe that's worse.

"I'm sorry…" Jason squeezes his eyes, his forehead all wrinkled up in pain. He presses his thumb to the bridge of his nose. "It's just… It's only been three months, you know. Since the murders. And I get this tightness in my chest to think it'll happen all over again. We're stuck in this endless loop in Gamin, doomed to repeat the same thing over and over until our uses are all spent up. I just want to get Patty out of here. I want to be there for her, but I can't do it again, Lili."

He reaches out for my hand then, waiting for me to take it. I slip my cool palm into his. I feel the blood beating there. Warm, mortal blood. I feel the determination in each line on his skin, the weathering of time that will only increase as he ages. Slower than most mortals due to his magic, true, but still.

For him, time passes.

I wonder what that's like. To not be caught up in forever.

"Please, Lili. I can't fight this fight. My body...the nightmares alone...you know? And I thought to myself that the nightmares couldn't chase me if I ran away to New York." He turns those eyes to me, the shadows darkening within those pale eyes. "But Patty, she believes in this town, in Gamin. She loves this inn. She wants to fight for it. But if I can't fight with her..."

I place my other hand atop of his, sealing it from the cool air, the steam, the reflections. I stare into his eyes, will the shadows to seep from his gaze into mine.

After all, I've had a whole millennia's worth of nightmares. What's one more to take on?

I see the shadows lifted, replaced by a brighter, softer thing. A tender sparkle in his eye.

"I'll fight."

But it's not my voice that declares it first. It's Stace, hugging their arms tight around Jason. He looks up at them with wonder, at Stace's determined stance. At the way they lean in, preparing for a fight.

I smile at them, and they return my gaze, all-in.

Stace holds their hand out and takes Jason's free one in theirs. We all join hands in that strange little pattern, crisscrossing and smiling slightly at the pomp and ceremony of it all. It's silly, but it's a little victory amongst all this fear.

I look to the pool and my reflection's stopped smiling. In fact, it's staring directly at the steam room. The door's ajar. A tiny figure flies forth, squealing.

It's baby Smaug, crying and bleating terribly for such a scaly, beastly thing. The size of a small puppy, it folds its wings up and nestles in Jason's arms.

"What is it?" he asks, the Eye mark already glowing on his forehead as he stares forth into the rolls of vapor.

I walk toward the steam room and my toes tap against the glass door. I push it open. The door stops with a bump against a large, fleshy thing.

A corpse.

I make out features on the body; a few piercings glint in the light against ears that come to a point. Platinum hair over see-through skin. An undercut with long hair half tied up and half strewn across his open eyes. He wears a bathrobe, but it's clear his body was moved after his untimely demise. He's still fully clothed in pleather and suede beneath the terry cloth.

"Pelle..." I bend down and close his eyes. I can't have him staring at me. He's probably calling me a bitch even from the afterlife. Or the Crossroads. Wherever he went for whoever was forgiving enough to take him.

In the steam room, there's a whole mess of envelopes in the damp. Luckily, their wax seals kept their contents from seeping. I take one of them that's half opened already and peer at it, see the lines and numbers characteristic of a written check.

The front of the envelope bears a cross and a logo for a St. Benedict's Church. The address is too blurry to make out. On the back, in firm, red print are the words: *Vade retro satana.*

I run my fingers beneath his nostrils, past the bite of the piercings. When my fingertip comes back, I see the telltale sparkle of a little faith, trust, and pixie dust.

Pixie dust, the party favor that just keeps on giving in Gamin.

"Oh no...no..." Jason moans, turning away from the scene. "Not again. Not again."

Stace holds Jason tight in their arms as he, in turn, holds a trembling Smaug against his chest. I try to block as much of Pelle as possible from their sight.

"A souvenir." I hold up the envelopes I've gathered from the floor and Pelle's pockets, all bearing the same name as the first, all addressed to this church. "Let's see if Gamin's up-and-coming drug boss can tell us a little bit more about it. She used calling cards in her murders too. She can probably tell us something about this one."

I leave the room to go tell Patty and Pabel about cleaning up the mess and being as discreet as possible. But mainly, I just see her. *Alethea.* I hear her all over again, remembering what happened in Gamin three months ago.

The last murders. The blood on my hands. On hers.

Her face in my mind, over and over. Flashes of our last encounter, when she promised me the world, then tried to end my infinite life once and for all. Held me beneath the river right after pledging her undying loyalty to me.

Alethea. Lethe.

Lethe...oh, Lethe...
I'm coming for you.

Chapter Fifteen

We're in Jason's bedroom now

Just a city boy

Born and raised in (not) Detroit

He took the midnight train going gods know where.

"IT WAS JUST a little body. I mean, Pelle was an asshole to his employees, anyways." I scoff. "Well, seriously, the world should be grateful to have one less asshole in it."

From the way Stace is crossing their arms and Jason is biting his tongue, something tells me that was not the right thing to say.

Jason glares at me over the edge of his suitcase. He is currently trying to smush some folded button-downs together, wrinkling all their nice, patterned surfaces. The plane ticket to New York City is set right beside it. Jason's scowl is not nice, but his room is. It's newly fixed up and everything, the symbol of the Eye burned into his ceilings, hanging out next to a Lara Croft poster.

I think the walls of his room escaped renovation, still having little scrawl marks from where the Sweeneys marked Jason's and Patty's heights. Patty wrote "ha-ha, I'm taller" next to one crayon line while Jason wrote "ha-ha, not anymore" next to the other one in childish script. The rest of the room is outfitted with newer furniture that still smells like polished, minimalistic, Swedish furniture stores. An older, shorter desk is crammed full of photographs. Some of the handsome Todd Sweeney hugging his arms around a smiling Beatrice, Patty and Jason sunburnt in front of their parents. Tae Kim, still in human form before he fell in love with Todd Sweeney and got turned into a mandrake because of it. Tae, the third of the throuple that was Patty and Jason's childhood, poses shyly behind Beatrice, trying to drag him into the photograph.

First Tae gets punished for getting involved with the Sweeneys, then Jo.

No, not the Sweeneys. Jo was my fault. I'm so sorry, my love. My Jo.

"Hello?" Jason waves his hand in front of my face. "It was *not* just a little body, Lili. I don't even know how the hell a whole body just plopped into the steam room without us noticing. I...I mean, did it teleport there like out of *Star Trek* or something? Are we going to have to fight a vampiric Spock now or something?" Jason shakes his head. Ever the nerd, even when angry. "Here we go. Fighting all over again. Not even back from the city for three months, and already, we have to fight some villain!"

"You need to be there for yourself first, babe." Stace runs their fingers along Jason's neck, massaging the tension away. "Mental health and dealing with trauma aren't to be taken lightly, not by humans or Dracula or whoever. You find yourself in New York, and you come back to us as *you*, understand?"

Stace claps their hands together and tosses Jason a pair of boxers that he wedges with all the others on the opposite side of his giant, black roller case. Some of the edges are taped up, and I think I can hear the suitcase's material groaning for mercy.

"You're right, Stace. You are." He stuffs a foldable piece of exercise equipment in next to the vials of Patty's traveling-size potions, a fishhook charm against evil, and some toothpaste. "You three can handle this while I'm in NYC. Thanks to Erik's wonderful tech wizardry, we still have some credibility in the necromancy market. They're hoping to borrow elements of our tech. This could be big for Erik's role in the coven, for all of us."

I raise an eyebrow at that, dodging a pack of toothpicks Stace tosses our way. "There's a whole board of corporate necromancers in NYC?"

Jason sighs. He packs a tie complete with tie clip and a re-tailored and tailored again suit with some gold thread sewing up a tear. "Unfortunately, yes. Like *Social Network* backstabbing, just with the occasional murder and revenge reanimation necromancy sort of thing."

"Oh, so *American Psycho*," Stace pipes up.

Jason nods with a tight smile. "Regrettably." He stops smiling for a moment, his fingers scrunched up around the tie clip. "When Stace told me they knew about magic, about *everything* in Gamin, I…" He takes in a deep breath, the exhale a slow hiss, a sting across the silence. "I got so scared. Stace, you, and Patty, you're all strong as hell, but I feel like I should do something more. Help you more. I want to, but when I think about three months ago...that trip to the Dead Realms...and I lost my...my..."

He fumbles with a notch on his prosthetic, the casing drops away, energy radiating forth. For a moment, the casing turns transparent, leaving only the phantom limb, literally. He'd lost his arm in the Dead Realms, fighting back reanimated zombies when we were sprinting through Gamin trying to find the murderer in the last case. A phantom limb is what's left behind; the feeling of loss new amputees experience. Potentially able to feel fingers move, to feel an itch on their elbow when there's nothing there.

Except, Jason's powers had filled the gap with a magical prosthesis, his power able to rival an immortal's on a good day. But the darkness in his eyes, the shadows there after it happened, after he returned from the Dead Realms...

He lost his parents, his arm, and nearly his life to the magical underbelly of Gamin. What else did he leave behind in the Dead Realms?

Stace runs their fingers along the prosthetic before planting a kiss there. They run their fingers along his arm, ending at his neck. They pull Jason into them, murmuring into his hair as he shudders. "My love," Stace begins, whispering soft as a lullaby, "you have done enough. I may be new to all this, but I have some idea of what I'm getting into." They turn to me, smiling widely, their piercings shiny and their tattoos freshly oiled, showing patterns of vines leaping across their skin, almost like they were growing there, always moving. A pattern of a forest living in their veins. "Besides, love, I have Lili to show me the ropes."

I smile sheepishly at Jason. Try as he might to stifle it, I still catch it, the flicker of mistrust. The glimmer in his eyes as he glances at me for the briefest moment before his eyes slide guiltily away.

"Of course," he murmurs, low and short, the words tumbling out in a dismissive rush. "I have nothing to worry about." But the way he digs his fingernails into his palms tells another story.

I pause, stare at the floor for a bit, before holding out my hand to him. He gets up from where he'd been tackling his suitcase, trying to get the zipper to stop catching in his blanket. "I give you full permission to straight-up murder me if I fail to protect your sister and your lover."

Stace's jaw drops nearly to the floor. "Lili!" they squeak. I'm a little proud to have thrown them off their game for a bit.

Jason, on the other hand... My promise manages to startle a laugh out of him. "Worst thing is, she means it, Stace." He shakes his head, a smile still wrinkling his face. "Fine." He takes my hand firmly in his grip. "I'll take you up on that bet."

One would think I'd learn to stop making bets after making one with a poltergeist who turned me into Paranormal Sherlock. Ah well, I'll put that on my to-do list for next century.

"But, Lili." Jason stares deeply into my eyes, and I see the weariness in his. The white hairs trailing from his scalp where there used to be only strawberry blond. The shadows in his papery skin. "Lili, I want you to end this. *To end it.*"

I squeeze his hand, unsure what I'm promising.

Unsure if even Jason knows what he's asking of me and doubting if even I'm powerful enough to stop it.

Chapter Sixteen

(To the tune of an annoyingly catchy jingle, circa the '60s) Evil Eye Coven Incorporated!

THE EYE COVEN corporate building has an elevator that makes you feel like you're entering the bowels of hell.

It's a wonderful gray corporate box with a touchpad you press on that will take you directly to your floor with a sharp *ding* and some lovely, electronica techno music. However, most of the necromancers going in and out don't even need to use the touchpad. Their eye symbols just glow on their foreheads or shoulders or necks above their crisply ironed ties and pressed collars as they *think* of a floor. And the elevator whizzes them safely to their destination, magic included, and the occasional reanimated poodle, kitten, or Frank in tow.

All the magicians are properly licensed for having reanimated pets, of course, though resident tech-wizard Erik Borden is much more lenient than his power-hungry predecessor, Sabrina, in this regard.

The interior of the elevator, I notice, seems to expand according to how many people are willing to step inside and share the space. The smooth, mirrored surfaces promptly whoosh open and arrive, large enough to fit Stace, Patty, Wilbur, Erik, Byron, and me all inside with a little bit of leg room just to keep things spacey. The doors close so seamlessly that they fold into a mirror, any indentations or memory of where a door was disappearing into that fluid, waterlike mirror surface.

Still, somehow, Byron finds his way to stand next to me.

I glance over, seeing how I can count the hundred sub-level buttons through his see-through skin. The tech-collar on Byron's neck, noticeably, is missing.

"No more flashing in and out of mortal view?" I ask him.

"I wanted to try something new. Like a new shirt, but you know, looking like you're made of flesh and blood or...not. Besides, Erik fashioned some contacts for Stace, like heat-sensing, ghost-hunter things. Now, they can at least see me as a really cold, human-shaped spot in their vision. I've always wanted to be an air-conditioner. A dream come true."

I laugh a little at that. Stace, startled, glances back and places their hand protectively on Wilbur's back. The boar snuffles their black-and-silver painted nails.

"Can Stace not hear you in that form?" I notice another piercing on Stace's ear, really just a hugging, silver ring pinching next to their ear lobe.

"The ghost-hearing earring uses a sort of magical hotspot system." Byron shrugs, glancing around the elevator. "Bad signal. Must use Jiminy Cricket cellular."

Again, I have to stifle a snicker as everyone else in the

elevator looks quite solemn. As they rightfully should be considering we're visiting a serial killer and drug dealer in a high-security, magical corporate prison.

But still…

I dig my fingers into my arm, wondering how to phrase this. I plunge in. "I miss you, Byron. And I'm sorry I couldn't do it. Couldn't find a way to bring you back to life." I stare at my feet. "I…I have to admit it. I fucked up."

"Yeah, you did." My heart plummets at that. Byron sighs, rubbing his nails against his ghostly, long, pirate-like jacket. Patches on black wool lining, fingerless gloves ensemble and all. "But I heard what you did for Erik, asking that *loa* to bring Erik's dead dad back from the Crossroads for a day. That was cool. It was even…kind of you, to do that." Byron rubs his lips together, trying to glance anywhere but at me. "You aren't a total *pendeja*, I guess."

"Thanks." I pause a moment before glancing between him and Erik, who's watching the elevator levels counter with a grim, shadowed expression in his eyes. "So, does Erik also think I'm not a *pendeja?*"

"Let's go for one milestone at a time," Byron shoots back. "I'll just say *better*, for now."

Fair enough.

The levels counter is a shimmering outline of red light against the mirrored surface, floating a way away from the spot that once held the doors. The numbers drop lower and lower at subterranean levels, some floors marked with numbers, other with strange symbols that go by too quick to contemplate. Sometimes, we hear screams through the doors, drowned out by the steady pulse of elevator music sounding above us.

Erik moves his gloved, wired hands behind his back, resting his intertwined fingers at the small of his spine. His nails are black, shining with a coat that occasionally glows when the lights flicker in the elevator. The symbol of his Eye, rewritten with code and wired at the base of his hairline with neon-colored gadgets embedded into his skin, illuminates the space over his forehead. His monocle reads as a string of ever-changing stats. He waves his hand once and the elevator jerks to the side, the pressure leaving us unbalanced. *Are we going at a diagonal now?*

"When we arrive at the captivity chamber," Erik murmurs, fixing the dangling key earring from his left side, "you can't bring liquids into there."

"So, we don't have to pee?" Patty suggests wryly.

"All good on my end," Byron chimes in. "No need for bathrooms when you're dead." Byron laughs at his own joke, but for his level of bravado, it works.

Stace eases slightly at the jest, though I notice their fingers are dug tight into Wilbur's back bristles. Stace's ear cuff crackles a bit in response. *Guess the magical hotspot works better when we're closer to Hell levels.*

"For the newbies"—here, Erik's gaze slides over to Stace, who snaps to attention—"Alethea Styx, aka the goddess Lethe, was brought into our facility by none other than Lili a few months ago." I perk up at that, shoulders back and leaning on one hip, really peacocking for the benefit of our small posse. "Aside from Lili's *unusual* methods, Alethea is mostly under control." I deflate at Erik's wry tone.

Okay, so I grew to the size of a small forest, impaled Alethea with my own talon, and lost a couple people in the process. You try being an immortal demon creature with slight memory loss and see if you can do better.

"What did Alethea do again?" Stace asks. "Like, why is she so bad she needs to be kept a bajillion levels beneath some tech startup witch coven?"

Erik presses a few markings on his arm. There's a faint buzz, like the ringtone on a cell phone, with each mark he presses. *Buttons, he's embedded gemstone buttons into the side of his arm. Techno-wizard, indeed.* An image pulls upward, a 3D reenactment model of the horrific events of the past.

The faces, floating past me like spirits from thin air. Haunting my memories. My waking nightmares. *All those children. Anna Snow. Anatol, the grandfatherly vampire mortician. Some unlucky siren. And Dakari Borden, Erik's father, murdered point-blank trying to save his son.*

After the array of bodies come the non-fatalities. The injuries. Some, civilians who were hurt long before I breezed into town. An array of sleuth stabbings and/or kidnappings.

And then, her. A young woman with blue-silver hair like starlight cropped short. Sparkling eyes that go on forever. Arms crossed and a cocky smile on her face.

My heart.

Jo Kim.

"But...why?" Stace asks. "Human children. The magic creatures of Gamin. So many deaths. So much suffering. Why?"

Everyone in the elevator falls uncomfortably silent.

I raise my head a little, my voice aching. "Alethea was

courting me. She believed I was still my old self. Lilītu, the one who did the whole sacrifice-to-me-and-worship-me-as-your-god thing." I laugh at that, the sound echoing for an unfortunate amount of time in the confined, metallic quarters. "Maybe Lethe's...Alethea's greatest strength was also her greatest weakness. The goddess of forgetting made me forget I was a vengeful god. I...I found my family here in Gamin. I stopped wanting that, the power. The bloodshed."

Stace scoffs at that, even startling Wilbur into a stunned sitting position. "So, the power of friendship made you the good guy all of a sudden?"

"Stace..." Patty hisses, dismayed.

"Yeah"—I smile back at Stace—"that's pretty much it. Wild, huh?"

The elevator stops whirring, the gears outside grinding to a halt. The mirrored doors deepen and open, peeling back into a long strip of shadowed hallway. Bare bulbs illuminate our path, naked light spilling above us.

A figure waits in front of a twice-sealed, bolted door far ahead of us. A large creature, he wears the same badge and office-lite uniform as the Franks above us and leans on a cane.

As my eyes adjust to this new lighting, I see a sword is embedded into the place where his arm was. The sharpened blade hangs down to the floor, scraping along the tiled halls to keep his giant figure upright. Each lurching step he takes, the blade keeps skittering along the halls, drawing sparks along with it.

Skiiiiiii. Skiiiiiii. Skiiiiiii.

The lone figure's head almost scrapes the twelve-foot

ceiling and takes up half the unusually spacious halls. When he yawns, he reveals a long red tongue and fangs with stones embedded in them, a lip piercing on his lower jaw. Symbols are carved into his lower lip, a sealing spell of some kind. His head is shaved down to a crew cut, though the rest of him is covered in curling, thick hair with a blue button-down buttoned crookedly halfway with sailor's shorts and brown sandals. His eyes have no pupils, yet I still feel his gaze tracking us in the space even if I can't tell where it's directed.

"Boss!" The figure waves amiably enough, lumbering toward us. He holds out his hand, large palm and fingers splayed, to Erik. "About time you visited us in the sub levels. Is it inspection time already? I swear I don't bring the mermaid magazines anymore after the kraken girl complained."

"Her name is Katja," Erik sighs in reply.

"Katja the kraken! Lovely," the hairy fellow bellows. "Hey, boss, I've been having troubles with my cell phone. Can't log in. Figure since you're one with the tech..." He points a square-cut claw to Erik's monocle and wires.

"What's your password?" Erik asks.

"G-R-E-N-D-E-L," the figure replies.

Erik stares incredulously into the creature's stubbly face. "You made your password your first name?"

"Yeah!" The hairy, giant, sword-armed Grendel laughs, and the lightbulbs swing and flicker above us. "Can't forget it that way. Oh, *scittan!* Pardon me. Me and my big mouth, blocking your way again." He steps out of our path as we all filter out of the elevator. "Oh, that's a nice sized piglet, isn't it? Who's a good piggy?"

Wilbur snuffles cautiously in reply to Grendel patting him with a large palm.

The fluid metal doors close behind us, and the wall is left only with that unnatural, mirrored surface. I think my reflection winks at me, eyes flickering hot red. Iron in a fire.

I turn away, blushing furiously.

"Yeah, yeah, he's a nice battle boar." I pull Wilbur back a bit. The coddled boar snuffles to hide behind Stace's back, far from Grendel's aggressive back pats. "Where's Alethea?"

Grendel scratches his belly from where his button-down doesn't know whether to push up to his neck or down to his clawed feet. "Humm," Grendel hums a bit of a pub tune I remember vaguely from my more self-de-structive youth. *Barkeeps taste great in summer. Something about marinating in beer and boredom.* "Humm, drum, tum. Well, she's back there like she always is."

Here, he jerks a large finger back in the direction of the double-sealed doors. The symbol of the Eye is burned into its center, from which radiates fiery streaks of red to all edges of the seal. The pupil of the Eye is bright as smeared, fresh blood.

"Pleasant," Stace squeaks, absentmindedly fiddling with their brass knuckles in their pocket. I note there's a strong whiff of Jason's magic on them.

Charmed to better fight against us magical beasties. Fishhook earring charms, brass knuckles forged from some Fae metal mix. Jason should start selling his acces-sories on the internet. He'd make a killing, metaphori-cally speaking.

From the way Stace slips the brass knuckles on, as though the weapon is a part of their body, something tells me that Jason's magic is just icing on Stace's power-punching cake.

"And Alethea stays there?" I glance away from the sealed doors, unimpressed. "Never leaving once? Not even for bathroom breaks? Selling illicit drugs, maybe."

Grendel shakes his head. "Nuh-uh. Can't remember. And bathroom, eh. Not really."

Not...really...?

"That doesn't seem up to code." Erik frowns, a line creasing his forehead. "Perhaps I really should've performed more inspections on the sub levels if the tech enhancements above didn't take all my time."

"I'll show him a surprise inspection..." I growl. Grendel's eyes widen in bemusement in response.

I step forward, flexing my fingers and already planning how to wring this giant fool's neck. But Patty holds her hand out to stop me.

She smiles widely at Grendel, opening her palm. I'm astonished to see some rolled-up candies lying there. "Come on, hard work or hardly working?" But when Grendel picks one up, the wrappers dissolve into tiny shot glasses.

No, not shot glasses.

Vials. Potion vials.

"Come on," Patty continues, holding out the disguised potions. "It's happy hour somewhere."

Erik raises a single eyebrow, but the frown still marring the edges of his lips mean he'll probably let this pass.

"Don't mind if I do. Ahh, I'll bet Katja would love

some of these. Cracking good times with krakens, eh?" He guzzles the liquor-potions down in an instant. The gleam of recognition in his eyes dulls as the tension in his jaw slackens. His tongue lolls against his fangs, hanging at the bottom of his slightly parted mouth.

He sways once, twice, before Erik mutters something beneath his breath. The power in these chambers, the power radiating from the doorway. It pushes outward a bit, righting the swaying Grendel.

"Ahh, my head feels funny," Grendel mutters.

"It should with twenty ccs of Sphinx fur coursing through you. The lion who guards secrets will unroll your tongue." Patty slowly navigates Grendel against the wall, where he slumps into a half-squatting position. "Now, tell us, Grendel..." She leans in so close that her spectacles nearly brush against his thick eyebrows. "Has Alethea ever left her chamber?"

Grendel yawns, showing his red tongue and fangs again. "Trivia...night at the shiny bar. With all the glitter and the pretty..." He yawns again. "Pretty pixies."

"What bar?" I ask, already suspecting the answer.

"Cracking...good time..." Grendel yawns again. "At the Kraken Club." His head lolls over to his shoulder as he shuts his eyes. "Katja...we're going to win trivia night. The answer is B. Unicorns!" And with that, the big, scary guardian of Alethea's door, and apparently her trivia night score, falls fast asleep. Whenever he snores, the hair running down his arms seems to shift with his breathing, ripples like waves.

"Jeopardy." I barely restrain myself from kicking Grendel's serum-drunk body five times in succession.

"This giant released a damn serial killer just to win a fucking glowstick at trivia night!"

Byron floats by, staring curiously down at Grendel. "Eh. I took Erik's bingo card once when he had the winning hand. We all do things we aren't proud of for game night."

"Yeah, he...wait, you did that? Hey!" Erik whirls around on Byron, who just blows a kiss at the frazzled tech-wizard.

All of a sudden, we hear a familiar sound of laughter from behind the sealed doors. The laughter goes on and on, near hysterical with little breath to pause between inhales. It sounds low, pitched and gasping like a ship tossed to sea. Waves battering the edges, trying to drag everyone down with them.

"Alethea?" I call, already speeding down the hallway. "Alethea! Get out here where I can see you." I break out into a sprint, running full tilt at the sealed door.

Gods forgive me if this is how I die. But I'm angry... Their faces flash in my mind's eye again. Anatol. Dakari Borden. Anna Snow. Jo. Jo Kim. All dead or hurting because of what Alethea did. Continues to do with this pixie dust. But no more...

"Lili!"

I try to ignore the voice, to keep going and throw myself at Alethea's chamber. To knock her down so that she never gets up again. Never hurts anyone I love again.

"*Lili!*" Patty's voice. Desperate. Screaming at me to stop.

So, I stop. I push down on my heels just as I'm about to bash the door with my entire upper body.

"There's *better* ways to open doors, Lil." Patty's voice echoes down the halls as she lifts a set of bone keys, fashioned from real bone, from Grendel's slumped body. She bounds into view as she jogs at a much more normal pace down the hall. Stace, Wilbur, and Erik walk calmly to join her. Byron floats.

"Oh right, keys. Yeah, that's how normal people do things. That was, uh, my second option after Hulk-smashing the door open, am I right?"

Patty just rolls her eyes at me.

We wait for a moment for Byron and Erik to follow us. But Erik just shakes his head. "Go on." He waves us on, and his ghostly boyfriend hovers close to his side. "I have business to discuss with our head of security when he wakes."

Stace glances nervously between us and Wilbur. "Um..." they begin, "where's the bathroom?"

Erik blinks a little at that. "Down the hall. Behind the vending machines," he replies.

"Okay, cool. Cool." Stace waves and tries to walk casually in the direction of the bathroom. However, a few steps in, they've increased their pace to a full-on sprint. Wilbur dutifully follows. A moment later, a lock clicks shut, and the vending machine drops its saturated-fat treasure. Wilbur squeals happily.

"I guess that leaves us and Alethea." Patty brushes closer to me, taking in a deep breath. I can feel her heartbeat from so close; how strange. I forget, sometimes, how she's a mortal. How her blood beats, her skin cells shed, her heart slows steadily over time. I forget.

To me, time so quickly ceases its meaning. But to

her...it never stops.

I step aside as Patty jiggles the bone key directly into the doorway's lock. The lock is in the Eye's pupil, where a notch gives way with a click. Blood lines pulsate from the center of the door, reaching in a trickle to all segments of the locks and bars sealing the doorway. Faint clicking sounds, like skittering beetles, sound off as the door hums with a burning energy.

The door creaks open into what feels like another world. An all-white room with no visible light source, yet it's perfectly lit. A single figure sits in the center with her arms and legs tied to a central column, rising from the room as a bird in flight.

She crouches low to the ground, eyes sparkling in the dimness. Half a shaved head, emerald eyes, tattoos criss-crossing with scars over her skin. An empty scabbard where a monster-hunting sword usually lay on her back. Muscles tensed; a panther ready to unleash.

"Hello..." Alethea Styx whispers. A muzzle is strapped over her chin, complete with tiny bars so I can see her sharpened teeth glint like daggers. She can speak but not try to tear our throats out with her teeth. At least, I hope she can't.

"Hello," she spits, licking something that looks suspiciously like blood from her lips, "old friend."

Chapter Seventeen

*The uncomfortably long, awkward silence of the
lambs*

"AH, IT'S HANDSOME Hannibal Lecter." Patty sends over a peace sign and then a middle finger, stepping calmly over a step to enter the vault's space. "I thought you were cute too. Guess all the good ones in Gamin are vicious killers, right?"

I stare uncomfortably at my feet. I remember the different being I was, all those centuries ago, when people bowed down in worship. Or I'd do horrible things to them if they didn't. I'd torment them at night, screaming at odd hours so nobody slept. Nail travelers to trees. Threaten to slice their children's fingers.

"Maybe I should be in here with Alethea then," I offer, but it's less an offer and more a suggestion as I fear recalling the monster I used to be.

"Not you," Patty says. "You did your vicious killing when you were all 'rah, rah, I'm the mother of all demons.' Which, I mean you still are now. But now you're...uh..."

"Boring?" Alethea suggests.

I growl at that. *Patty can make astute statements about my grayish morality, but I draw the line at Alethea.* "I gained a conscience. They were on sale." I skirt the edges of the room, eyeing the stake at its center, drilled down to the chains hanging from Alethea's ankles and wrists. "Two for one deal, interested?"

"Keep your conscience. It suits you." Alethea trails her eyes over my body for an uncomfortably long time, until I feel cold dripping down my spine. She chuckles. "I heard you've been talking to preachers. Seems you really had a change of heart for the heartless, huh?"

"Preachers? What preacher are you talking about?" Then, I remember the envelope on Pelle's dead body. I remember the man in the hotel lobby, the cryptic words. The murmuring eyes. "You mean the priest we had at the inn... He was in training or something. Father Adam...Adam Gay?"

"Adam Way, not Gay." Patty stifles a laugh. "Though everyone in this town is pretty gay, so I'd agree with that one. And hot." Again, she glares at Alethea. "Except for you. You're a disappointment."

"Ah yes." Alethea sniffs, her lip curling so I see a flash of teeth beneath those bars. "Father Way of St. Benedict's Church. The rising star there. How could I forget? They tried to bring him in to do an exorcism on me."

St. Benedict's. The words scrawled on that envelope. Smeared by the steam room, by tiny Smaug's breath. But still there. Still legible. Vade retro satana. The words written on the paper plastered to Pelle's corpse.

Something passes through me then. It's like a disconnect. Like everything's shifted all at once and my body's stopped shifting with it. I look to my fingers, my nails. And nothing feels real. Like it ever has been. I'm a ship without anchor. Adrift on waves of sand, no water in sight. I'm drowning, drowning, and when I open my mouth, all the air leaves my being, rushing to the shadow waters.

"I know you've been talking to preachers," Alethea repeats.

Patty crosses her arms, freckles showing as her bubblegum-pink long-sleeve slides up her forearms. "The only way you'd know info like that is if you escaped."

Alethea rolls her eyes, bucking her shoulders a bit so her chains clink on the ground. Scraping so loud I can feel the noise vibrate in my teeth. "Yeah, so that idiot Grendel took me out to trivia night at the Kraken Club. Big whoop." She extends her fingers in a mocking plea, her nails painted with a fresh coat of black polish. *Seems she has access to contraband nail polish alongside the drugs.* "If my biggest sin was knowing the answer to what causes the holes in Swiss cheese, then consider me guilty."

"Stop playing around!" I slam my fist into the wall, feel the pain vibrate all the way up my bones, feel the power coursing through my fingertips. The raw strength, begging to be released. "We know you're selling pixie dust at the Kraken Club."

"Yeah." Patty kneels just outside Alethea's ring of movement, her restraints pulling her back like a dog on a leash. Alethea strains to strangle Patty in anger, but Patty just smirks as Alethea's polished nails fall short of scratching her. "You've been selling under Grendel's nose."

Alethea looks first to Patty, then she settles those

flashing emerald eyes on me. It feels too intense, to the point I have to look away. But when I gather the willpower to look into her gaze again, I see only a glimmer there. A faint scrunch at the edges of her lips. A dark glitter in her eye. "Oh, this is rich." She chuckles, and again, the sound echoes harshly in this tiny chamber. It bounces off white walls and lands on our skin, puddling and collecting in our ears as Alethea just laughs and laughs louder. The laugh of a killer.

The laugh of a forgotten god.

"You think I'd sell pixie dust for my own pleasure? Damn, you're even stupider than before. And I managed to kill like twelve people in a row without you realizing. But this? This takes the cake." Alethea falls to a squat, staring up at us from this crouching position, poised to launch at us if we come any closer.

"Then..." I clear my throat. "Then who are you selling it for?"

Alethea sniffs then rubs her hand against her nose. Her fingers come away glimmering with a gold-flecked blood. "I swore not to say, but...the trivia question. I never gave you an answer. Why are there holes in Swiss cheese?"

"Oh, enough with the games, fu—" I start, all ready to risk it all and walk right into Alethea's range just so I can scream in her face properly.

"No. We'll humor her." Patty holds me back, hothead-edness and all. "Why are there holes in Swiss cheese?"

Alethea spreads her hands to her side, grinning wide as the Cheshire cat, her tattoos gleaming on her arms and the exposed skin on her clavicle. The mark of the monster hunting order she quite literally shot in the back when they didn't suit her style. A sketch of a sword following her spine. A literal backstabber. "The bacteria will eat away at the cheese to survive. It'll look like the cheese cannibalizes itself."

But Alethea's eyes aren't locked on to us anymore. No, that emerald gaze seeks beyond us, boring through her pale-painted prison to see the shadow looming at the door, crawling on three limbs, the fourth a blade, screeching along the door.

Grendel carries himself to the door, heaving with his one hand in a fist, pounding bloody into the flooring. He releases a breath, and it sounds like the grating of a metal pipe against bars, mashing of teeth, and clawing of hair.

Alethea's voice carries stronger now. "Bacteria will stop at nothing to survive. Even gnawing off its own arm, drilling holes into it." She smirks, her sharp teeth shadowed by the bars on her muzzle. Her emerald eyes fired through with rage. Cut through on promises and too much pixie dust. "If it isn't careful, it'll have nothing left. But, then again, it's very stupid. Reminds me of someone I know."

Grendel is breathing hard, the giant's skin exposed along his spine from where his hair parts, raised as though electricity runs along it. He opens his mouth so wide that I see his protruding tongue, the gemstones cut into his teeth. "I'm not stupid!" The runes, again, carved into his bottom lip with a clumsy pen and brush.

"No, you're right." Alethea grins, her gaze still locked on Grendel. "You're damned."

"Erik! Byron!" I try to keep my voice level but find I'm shouting as I try to track Alethea and Grendel's movements.

Patty shakes her head at me, and when I spy what Patty does, I realize why.

Past Grendel's contorted frame, I see that Erik Borden and Byron are both staring off at a wall with glassy-eyed expressions. Patty's potions, the vials lay in a puddle of glass shards at their feet. The potions are uncorked, leaking a blue-green gas toward Erik's and Byron's face. Byron's collar's been rigged to solely have him in his corporeal form, the button jammed forcibly so his body absorbs the enchantment in the vials. The magic seeps into their skin, tinging them with that strange, glowing smoke. Their pinkies are curled lazily together, holding tight despite the stiff, unseeing state of their bodies.

Patty's face grows ever paler when Grendel looks between her and her potions. His lips slowly peel back from his lips in a smile; his breath pushes Patty's hair back from her face.

"Your liquor smelled bad. I threw the rest of them at your friends." Grendel groans, flashing his teeth again in that eerie smile, his lips all stretched over gums. "I guess they didn't like them much either."

"Grendel, we can discuss this..." Patty tries to hold her arms out, but Grendel thrashes on the ground and we're all taken off balance save for Alethea. Alethea's been crouched in fighting position this whole time.

I roll myself against the wall, half-bruised but still balanced enough to avoid Grendel's blade arm.

"No!" Again, Grendel throws himself against the ground, causing the whole earth to tremble. I wonder if the coven building feels this as an earthquake above us.

"No more lies from you, witch!"

"Grendel, all we have are lies." Alethea gets steadily to her feet. "It's over. Detective Dee and Dum over here have figured out about the pixie dust. I won't sell for you anymore. Prison isn't looking so bad compared to what anger issues over there will do to you."

Here she glares at me, her hand subconsciously going over her heart…

Where I'd stabbed my claw through it and left her impaled for days.

"You won't talk to anyone else, fake god. We made a deal," Grendel starts, and he roars so loudly I have to pull myself up using all my strength. "I'll rip your tongue out so you won't talk at all!"

Grendel throws his whole torso forward, his bladed arm pointed at the delicately tattooed throat of none other than the grinning Alethea Styx.

Alethea holds her hands in the air, the manacles glinting.

Grendel's blade swoops down against her manacles, loosening one of the links in the chain. A wide smile spreads across Alethea's face.

She's trying to escape.

Patty rushes Alethea all at once, screaming a spell into the air. The words dissolve into light and heat. Patty's mark of the Eye burns into her forehead, a bloody red scar of magic carved into flesh, carving power out of it. Alethea grunts from the impact as Patty, her arms flowing with veins of power, pins Alethea to the earth.

Alethea struggles to lift herself from the ground, thrashing her torso, but Patty holds firm. Her magic coils like serpents around her fingers, binding Alethea in ropes.

If she's bound, Alethea can't reach her true form, her most powerful form. She's no threat to us.

But Grendel, on the other hand…

"Lili!"

Patty's voice registers just in time for me to duck as Grendel's blade embeds itself into the wall above me. The whole room shudders and vibrations knock through my teeth at the impact. I feel it, the fight calling to me. The old power coming through my blood.

In those few seconds she had to call my name, Patty had to stop her spellcasting. Alethea's rolling her body upward, struggling to sink her nails or teeth into Patty's soft flesh. But the witch only doubles down on her spell. She screams at the top of her lungs, her power weaving restraints of magic to fortify Alethea's physical chains.

She's got this.

And I look back at Grendel, hear the blade ring as it slides out of the walls, hear the scraping of metal. See him tower above me, the sheer massive size of him…

But do I got this?

I can't dodge him this time. Grendel's free hand whips across my cheek, the backhand leaving my face burning and freezing all at once. I taste my own flesh as my teeth tear into my tongue. I shake my head to clear it, but it just makes the rattling in my skull worse.

I spit out the blood thick in my mouth before rolling back to my fighting stance. I crouch low, let myself have one of my names crawl up on my skin. I hear the singing of those who once worshipped me; taste the salted earth of a battlefield on my tongue. Hear the cries of fear.

I am one to be feared, not *fearful.*

I launch myself at the midsection of the giant, dodging his blade and his fist to latch onto his sensitive underbelly. I slide underneath his hunched-over form just to hook my arms around his throat. To dig my bootheels into his flesh, curling my whole lower body up to try to make any contact I can. I kick and sink my talons into his neck. My arms can't reach all the way around, so this serves as a poor handhold. Like I'm trying to battle a living mountain, one that moves and breathes and curses and, apparently, loves a good round of trivia night.

Grendel yelps and jerks and all I can do is hold on for dear life, like a pitiful mortal riding a mechanical bull. He throws his weight into the wall, knocking one of my hands from his neck. I kick off then, tearing my other hand free.

My nails are good as knives. He hisses and uses his fist to staunch the bleeding from the new marks in his flesh. Now he has only one side of him free to attack.

His blade.

"Hey, Grendel!"

We both turn at that.

Patty has Alethea in her magically fortified arms in a sort of bear hug, and in the next moment, she's shoved the bloodthirsty goddess at the giant like she's nothing more than a meat shield.

Alethea falls as gracefully as she can to the ground. Grendel raises his blade...

I take a running leap at the hilt of the blade where it's connected to his shoulder with thick leather straps. I have no time for unclasping it, so I do the next best thing that comes to mind. In that...it was less of a thought and more of a concept.

I sink my newly double-rowed teeth into the device. I might have more teeth now in this form, but I break a couple with the force. I tear and gnash at the leather straps, ignoring the pain soaking through my gums as I tear the blade arm directly from Grendel's shoulders.

The giant, unbalanced, gropes wildly for his fallen sword-arm. But this uncovers his neck wound and the resulting mess leaves even more sweat pouring into his eyes. The giant swoons once, twice, before falling to the floor with a dull thud. His sword follows with a metallic clatter.

I clamber off him and spit out a tooth or so, returning to my regular form. They'll grow back eventually, but for a while...Patty might have to give me her potions through a straw.

"What about me?" Alethea whines. Amusingly enough, she's currently crushed beneath the belly of the sniveling giant. She kicks, but the chains combined with Grendel's burden just drag her back down. "I helped you, you fucks! What about me?"

Patty and I exchange a quick look. A look wherein flashes every single person Alethea killed. A look that won't soon forget the horrors we saw three months ago. The killer who inspires the copycat killer now, the one who tries to wreak havoc in her imprisoned wake.

Young. Old. Children, promises of what was to come.

She thought they were disposable just because they were human. I used to think that way, once. But now... I've grown quite fond of humans. It took a millennium or so to learn I was the disposable one, an immortal going on forever. But them? They were precious, finite beings full of promise. I had to protect them. To make up for those who were lost.

When Alethea asks, "what about me?" all Patty and I can remember is *what of them?*

"We'll get back to you," Patty murmurs, glaring at Alethea with a fire that burns stronger as the mark of her Eye fades. That power is solely Patty's; no coven could match it. "I think these are yours, Lili." Patty segues, handing me a couple of teeth.

"Thanks," I reply, pocketing them as we make for the door.

Patty mutters the spell and closes the vault behind us, cutting off the anguish and betrayal of Alethea Styx's cursed screams.

"I'll murder you all!" Alethea screams. "And I'll make you watch, Lili!"

We glance back at the door as, one by one, the locks re-engage. Sealing that horror in there with Grendel.

Footsteps ring down the hall, a break from the screams.

"Hey. Sorry, had a bathroom emergency." Stace walks casually toward us, nibbling on a candy bar from the vending machine and surreptitiously feeding Wilbur bits of the nougat. "What did I miss?"

Stace turns to the door. To my horror, I see Alethea's burning eyes from the open slit in the keyhole.

"When I get out..." Alethea rasps. "I'll devour you all."

Wilbur whimpers and hides beneath his hooves.

Stace calmly goes over there and jams the lock shut with such power that, yet again, I'm left marveling at their strength. *I bet Superman grew up wanting to be Stace someday and not the other way around.*

Alethea cries out, a squeal of pain this time as the lock's probably been jammed in their eye. *They'll heal. They aren't a murderous, forgotten god for nothing, right?*

"Missed one," Stace mutters, a new determined set to their jaw as they glance warily back at the one barrier between us and the infamous Alethea Styx.

Chapter Eighteen

Holes

Why does Swiss cheese have holes in it?

That's a trick question—we ate all the cheese and Alethea's still locked up in the vault with Grendel.

PATTY KNEELS BY Erik's slumped-over body to check for a pulse as Stace elevates the necromancer's head. Patty breathes a sigh of relief as I, holding my breath doubly even if I don't *have* to breathe to keep living, toss all the potions down the elevator shaft for good measure.

"Come on." Patty gently nudges Erik awake. "I'm so sorry that gigantic trivia-loving asswipe used my potions on you..." Patty pauses to beam with pride for a moment. "But I've got to say, the potions did work excellently. You two haven't stirred for like, an hour."

"Patty..." I warn, a growl deep in my throat as I check on Byron, frozen in his own, chilling ectoplasm. I fiddle with the tech collar until, blessedly, the damn switch un-jams and sets Byron to his ghostly self again.

"*Mierda*! Potions somehow hurt worse with this tech collar on all the time." The ghost yells to lowest heaven and highest hell, rising to the short ceiling with his eyes aflame. "That's it. I'm through with this half-life thing. It's too much of a liability. For now, I am a ghost, and I'm proud of it."

He takes Erik's tech collar, dyed a dark, oozing violet from all the potions and sparkling with magical electricity, between his fingers and smashes it thoroughly in a poltergeist rage. Streaks of orange lightning hiss from his transparent fingertips, setting the collar into a singed, buzzing mess of crackle and pop.

The collar falls onto the ground. A melted, desperate thing. A plume of smoke erupts from the potions leaking on it, a plume in the shape of a skull.

Stace blinks once. Twice.

"By-Byron? I can't see you anymore. I can't see you without the tech magic." Their eyes are filled with swirls of anxiety as they curiously run their fingertips to where Byron was with the collar. They grasp his bootheels by accident.

Byron drifts down, holds his hand out in midair. "If you try..." he murmurs, and I hear his voice coming through from the tinny speakers in Stace's ears. "You can sense where I am, Stace." Stace holds onto their earpiece to hear Byron better. And then, with sadness thick in his voice, he adds, "It's where life is not. A shadow of vitality."

Stace holds their fingers outstretched and moves their hand close enough their nails touch Byron's wrist. "Ah." Stace gasps, withdrawing their hand before firming themself. They stare straight ahead with their brows down as they reach for Byron's cheek. "You're not a shadow, Byron." They smile, their palm gently resting on Byron's shoulder now, their skin erupting into gooseflesh in the cold. "You shine too brightly for that. You're a star."

"I agree." A rasping cough as Erik turns to the side. Life returns to his eyes as the potion wears away with Patty's incantation. The tech-wizard shifts to his side to spit up the last of the potion. "You are a star, my darling. You don't need some tech-collar to prove it. I love you perfectly well, living or no." Erik turns left, right, and finally stares with a tight-lipped expression at the locked vault door. "So, Grendel betrayed us, didn't he?"

Patty shrugs. "Turns out he's a sore loser at trivia night."

I move to help Erik to his feet. He considers my outstretched hand for a bit before finally taking it.

"Over there." Erik gestures to Grendel's desk. I help him make his way over there.

Erik bends over the desk. His tech monocle activates, and a magnifying lens overlays the virtual one over his forehead. A beam of magic like a laser scans the desk quickly. For a moment, there's a blaze of blue light. A brash beeping sound. And then silence.

"In there." Erik points with the utmost surety. At the end of his freshly polished nails lies a desk drawer covered with a gargoyle knocker.

I reach down and accidentally rip off the handle, patiently screw it back in, and finally open the drawer to the strong smell of alcohol and, beneath the mystery flask, a stack of cosplay and swimsuit magazines.

I pinch the magazines to the side with my fingers,

wiping my hand after scanning the titles quick. "*Mer-person Monthly. Kitsune Kitties. Sexy Satyrs*? Goodness. Grendel really covered his bases, huh?"

"A disturbing amount of Beowulf cosplays. Old grudges, eh?" Byron snickers.

Stace pauses. "That wasn't in *Beowulf* when I read it..." they mutter, cheeks hot with embarrassment.

Erik's monocle beeps sadly. "It's all my fault we let Grendel in to take Alethea to gods knows where. I should've paid better attention to who we were hiring." He lets out a sigh that carries the weight of the world—and the grief over his father—in it. It sounds from his chest. No, deeper than that.

It carries the weight of an overburdened soul.

I lick my lips, pause a bit, before continuing. "I think you're a great leader, Erik. A great leader dealing with a very shitty situation." I tell him this and the intensity in my voice only confirms my truthful admiration.

Erik keeps his face cool, but his eyes, I see them upturn. He's smiling.

"Beneath this stack..." Another *click* from Erik's monocle as the laser scans. "That's what you need. It'll aid your investigation."

Beneath the stack of dirty magazines is a wide, rectangular book bound in thin animal hide yet laminated in fun, orange plastic. Inside the ledger, in surprisingly neat, cursive script, is a tally of prices and items bought and sold.

Unicorn Horn. Dragon Scale. Newt Eye and Rat Tail.

And most importantly...

Pixie Dust.

At the end of the accompanying checkbook are stubs made out from Grendel Cain. Surprise, surprise.

"Grendel's been selling drugs with Alethea. No shit." I huff, and when I turn the page, my eyes widen so much that I think I'll have my face permanently etched this way. They could replace the gargoyle drawer handles with my head if I keep up this expression.

"What is it?" Patty and Stace crowd closer.

I hold my index finger beneath the latest entry for Pixie Dust. An envelope is taped between the pages. *RE-CIPIENT: St. Benedict's Church.* The church that was on the same envelope we found on Pelle's body.

And yes, witchy Watson, the plot thickens as we add another connection to this circle of death. The address on this envelope though, unlike the ones on Pelle's body, is in perfectly clear print. *None of Pelle's odor or blood in the steam room to smear it.*

"Seventy-seven Paradise Park. Gamin, Minnesota." I snort. "One more seven and they probably get a free angelic choir in the mix."

"Are you sure you'd want to go, Lili?" Patty raises an eyebrow.

"Why? Concerned for my lack of a soul?" I try to play it off with a smile but, for all intents and purposes, I'm nervous.

Because it's then I remember why *Vade Retro Satana* sounds so dreadfully familiar.

I once knew a nun named Catalina de Erauso. If you actually enjoy technology and that damned devil box of a cellular device, then you might want to search her up. She was quite fun in life, not like all the other nuns. She wore men's clothing, seduced women, and killed men.

A fun Sunday night for us both.

She was so clever that she got the Pope to pardon her misdeeds.

My point is that Sister Catalina did, in fact, know her prayers. And while smuggled into the monastery and feasting on the hearts of the men she killed and acting as her personal janitorial cleanup crew (sometimes, I got lazy in hunting), I picked up a bit of Latin.

Vade Retro Satana.

Go back, Satan.

The Catholic formula for exorcism.

*

In which we leave a place (the Eye Coven) better than we found it

(If slightly smashed up because let's face it. It's not a Lili story without some random fight scenes)

GRENDEL IS FIRED for making his coworkers uncomfortable and exploiting the dangerous murderer he was supposed to be guarding. Being fired from a necromantic Coven, even a corporate Coven, is an interesting process. Because HR is run by zombies who will eat your eyeballs if you don't cooperate and being fired means you will literally be set on fire if you fail to comply. Trust me when I say that the bored junior-level necromancers, while sick of spiking coffee with revenge potions, will *not* hesitate to set you on fire. Grendel doesn't stand a chance against bored necromancer teenagers.

He is banished from the workplace and the Eye Coven. The young woman he made uncomfortable, the kraken, Katja, is given a welcome surprise. Tech-wizard boss Erik's prepared a special gift for her.

"Katja." Erik sets Grendel's papers aflame with a snap of his fingers. We stand in front of Grendel's desk, emptied of its contents. His metal nameplate GRENDEL CAIN stares dully on. Erik etches a new name into the metal with a laser coursing from his monocle.

KATJA HAFGUGA.

He holds this nameplate out to her. "You are now the Head of Security at the Eye Coven. Congratulations."

Katja stands at eight feet tall, slithering on octopus' legs as a sort of gliding motion. She wears a gown made from shimmering scales and takes the name tag in one pincered claw. She stares with large, damp black eyes and speaks without moving her beaklike mouth using some sort of soothing telepathy that tickles the brain like ocean waves.

"Thank you for removing Grendel." Katja's eyes darken at that. And then, another moment. "Did you catch the killers yet, detectives?"

"Oh, I'm not a..." But I pause at Patty's glance. *I guess I am as good as a detective for these paranormal peeps.* "Not yet. But we found many clues thanks to Erik and Byron allowing us in here for our investigation. Thank you for trusting us." I hesitantly reach out a hand to Katja. "Guard her well, Katja."

"We have a saying in the ocean deep," Katja tells me, taking my hand in hers. I feel a slight suction against my palm, the strength of limbs that dragged entire ships and skeletons of sailors out to sea. "*Å få blod på tann.* Get blood on one's tooth. It means a hunger, a sense of drive. Once you sink your teeth in something, don't let go, detective." I cannot tell whether Katja smiles from her beak-like mouth, but something tells me she does from the glimmer in her dark eyes. "I won't ever let go of Alethea Styx. You don't need to worry about that."

As she lets me go, sensation returns to my palm. The momentary paralysis passes. "I know you will, Katja." I try to hide that I need to massage my hand to bring feeling back to it.

"A word, detective?" Erik waves to me, as friendly a gesture as it goes between us. "Thank you, Lili. If it wasn't for your investigation, who knows what harm Grendel and Alethea would've caused if they weren't found out." Erik leans in closer. "And for letting me see my father again. I don't know how you pulled it off with the *loas*, but I'm grateful."

Byron presses his cold phantom fingertips lightly to my forearm. "You might've made some mistakes, but you never forgot about us, Sherlock." He presses his fingertips harder, and when he removes his hand, the shadow of blue fingerprints slowly fades on my arm. "You're a good friend, Lili. Even if you're still a bit of a *pendeja.* Now go solve this case and drop the bad guys deep into Hell."

*

77 Paradise Park, Gamin MN

(One more seven and you get cherubs on clouds sitting on top of rainbows)

THE CHURCH OF St. Benedict sits on a gray hill with purple flowers planted in a dull field of languor behind it. The church itself is built of wood and stone, rising in a belltower that has no bell. I watch the time change from Patty's bumblebee-yellow vehicle, the green numbers with their sickly hue. The church belltower emits a metallic chime. It's probably preprogrammed, and it sounds a bit like a street organ. You know, the kind where a tiny monkey or dog in a top hat carries around a bucket for tips. A kind of metallic, hand-cranked music.

Patty parks beneath a dramatically weeping willow, branches all asunder like a set of skirts seeking respite at a ballroom party. Erik and Byron are busy renovating and reexamining their hiring practices at the Eye Coven, leaving the usual reformed Scooby gang to solve this mystery. Me and Patty and Stacey and Wilbur pile out of the backseat.

Yes, they beat me in a game of troll, bridge, goat. Don't mention it again.

Stace wrinkles their nose. "What's that smell? Is something burning?"

I shrug. "Maybe some vampires got too close."

"Vampires?" Stace widens their eyes, aghast.

Patty gives me some heavy side-eye, her freckles more pronounced against a fierce flush. "Come on, Pats. It's Gamin. It's not entirely unlikely that…"

"We have company," Patty hisses, a little too pleased when I go silent.

Walking from the front of the building is none other than Father Adam Way. His hands are smeared with red. I inhale deeply, but it's not the salt tang of blood accompanying him. No, it's...it's more chemical. Acidic, even. *Paint.* Behind him lies a rectangular wooden sign bearing the name of the building. It's damp with fresh paint. *St. Benedict Church.* And beneath it, the sign reads the church's battle cry. *Vade retro satana.*

Father Way looks even more charming than he did back when we met at the Sweeney Inn. It feels like centuries ago that we saw him, sitting in the hotel lobby, making bored bachelorettes swoon. He has dark eyes and a neatly trimmed shadow of a beard against his face. He's not particularly tall, yet he walks in his square-cut black cassock with purpose. And there's an intensity to the set of his jaw. The way his eyes hold on to yours and refuse to let go. Not until you wish you could pray. Only the most foolish of demons would confront an exorcist on his own turf.

Who knows if being the mother of all demons can save me now?

"Ah, Miss Patty Sweeney. You run the inn here, don't you? And you've brought your friends." He shakes Patty's hand first. And when he smiles, all that intensity is swept away by charm and bright teeth. The fearsome exterior turns to sunlight and the organ grinder music starts resembling actual church bells. I blink and the purple flowers blossom into lavender and the world seems brighter. Hopeful, even.

"We've come on business," Patty responds, keeping her cool even as, damn his charm, she returns his easy smile.

"Oh." He frowns at that, brows drawn low. "I thought the church settled my account once I moved here. If I owe you anything, I'd be happy to pay from my personal fund…" His eyes then settle on me. "Ah, Lili. You, I remember. A fellow wanderer without a home, but you have a new family. *Marhaba!*"

"I'm afraid it's more serious than that." Patty sighs. "We've been sent out as part of a private investigation."

"Oh dear." His eyes widen, a little set of unease in them. "How can I help?"

I pull out the envelope from Grendel's ledger and hand it to him in silence. His easy smile disappears, leaving the grim, shadowed priest in his wake.

"What is this?" He shakes out the envelope and a few hardened pieces of rock, honey-brown and crystallized like sugar, fall into his palm. They smell both spicy and sweet, and they sting my nostrils to witness. *Frankincense.* My sacrifices were bathed in it back in my days of empire and glory. It's hard to forget the smell of such luxury.

He turns the envelope over.

And his smile returns, but it isn't easygoing.

No, far from it. His smile is clouded by the curse of knowledge. A thief whose hand has been marked in red. He drops the frankincense back into the envelope, shakes it a moment, and drops the contents again into his open palm.

This time, the contents shine in the sun and sing a different tune.

Pixie dust.

"What is this?" he asks, his lip curling in mock disgust.

I step forward, staring him down. Arms crossed, the ghost of tattoos hidden beneath my skin. Waiting to be called upon.

"I think you know, Father," I reply, staring him down. His gaze burns back into mine.

Again, his face splits into that too-smooth smile.

"Well, I was always a lousy liar. Ever since I was born. And ah, what a profession I've found myself in since then."

"Exorcists? Like in those movies? *The Conjuring* and the other retro '80s one?" Stace whistles, long and slow. "Damn, Gamin just keeps getting weirder and weirder."

"I'm afraid I am. Though we aren't as flashy as those ones." Father Way laughs and pockets the envelope in one smooth motion, his hand dipping into the black of his cassock and returning empty. "What do you want to know?"

"What did you do to Indah?" Patty asks.

"Why do you have pixie dust?" Stace questions.

And finally.

"Who are you?" That one's me, and Father Way, though he looks to each of us in turn, stares most intensely at me.

When he draws his hand back, a silver cross in the shape of a dagger rests in the meat of his palm. The blade sits like a patient dog, waiting for blood. "For the whole story," he says, "we should enter the church. I'm afraid you're not the only ones with enemies in Gamin."

And with that, he turns to enter the hallowed halls of St. Benedict. Patty follows and Stace after. Wilbur pauses just long enough to cast a pitiful glance at me, his wings folded sadly up. His dark-brown eyes moping.

Gritting my teeth, I take one step onto the hallowed stones and feel the surge of power from beneath me.

It's like all my weaknesses hit at once. My super strength is gone. My talons retract. My ancient names are hidden deep within my blood, so far gone that not even fear can call them now. *The sacred is kryptonite to us, the profane.*

I'm a knight without her armor. A cat without claws.

Here on holy ground, I'm no longer Lilit. Lilītu. ki-sikil-lil-la-ke. Lamia. The First. The Dark Maid. Maiden of Desolation....

Here, I'm just Lili. And even then, I'm barely that.

Chapter Nineteen

I'm so drunk, I'm sober. Or wait...was it the other way around?

"UH, LILI?" STACE walks to my left. Or are they on my right?

I raise my finger to their face, or where I think their nose is. "You've got pink eyes. Huh, not pink eyes like the eye infection. No, like...like pink lemonade." I giggle at that. "Huh. So pretty. Pretty human. You're cooler than me, you know." I lean in close to whisper. My voice feels funny and tickles my throat. "I want to be *you* when I grow up."

"Okay then!" Patty's voice splits my skull. Every step I take, it smells like old dusty robes and holy water. Holy water is like regular water, but it smells spicy, like it's slick with oil or something at the top of it, some kind of blessing. It also stinks like hell to demons. Or rather, like heaven. "Come on then, Lil!" Patty takes my arm up in hers. Suddenly, I feel I'm balanced enough to walk again.

When did the world go sideways?

"Uh, is she drunk?" Stace wrinkles her nose at me.

Wilbur snorts happily, like he's chattering his teeth at my behavior.

"You!" I point to Wilbur who bares his teeth at me. "You. Bacon!"

"Yup, punch-drunk on blessings. It's kind of like what happens with vampires. Just, Lili's stronger than them. Less shrivel-into-ashes and more like downed a couple too many beers at the frat party. Savvy?" Patty grunts as Stace takes my other side, carrying me through this blasted church. And the hallways go on and on and on. And it smells like old priest. And there are faces in the corners staring at me, clutching their beads and their rosaries. The choir kids snicker at me behind their books, scared eyes rushing out as Father Way, the liar, shoos them out the area.

"All right, set her down on the pews here." Father Way pats a wooden bench stretched out beneath the cool interior of the church. Everywhere, the stones round on us like gray slate. Far above us, light filters down from stained glass. The church feels like being trapped at the bottom of a well. And some guy on a cross stares down at us.

"Him, he doesn't look like he's having fun!" I point again.

Patty pushes my finger down. "Not now, Lili. And no, of course, he's not. That's the point. Would you calm down, babe?"

"No, babe!" I snicker at that. "Ah, Jo would've loved it here. She liked colorful things. Like her blue hair. The stained glass looks like her..." I sniffle again, tears leaking from my eyes.

"Is she crying?" Father Way asks, handing me a tissue. I dab at my eyes, wondering at the hole in my chest. "Maybe we should speak another day."

"No!" I shout so loud, and the resulting echo tells me the church is mostly empty. It's just us here. Us in this place. This place at the bottom of the well where nothing reaches except for the scent of damp and books and old robes folded on chairs. "No, people are in danger. And I...we must solve it. Solve this mystery. So. Tell us your story then, Father." I pause, staring at Stace's and Patty's concerned faces in turn. "Please?"

Father Way places his hands to his face. He turns his eyes up to the ceiling, to the silent, saintly faces also turned upward in supplication. He exhales, long and slow. I can see the hairs on his beard tilt with his breath.

Funny. If you blink twice, it's almost like he's acting. Acting well at being alive. A person in a costume.

Aren't we all?

"In truth, I brought you in here because I suspected who you are. I was testing you, and you passed the first test, Lili. In fact, you all did." Father Way glances nervously at me and Patty. "Nobody could have entered St. Benedict's if they weren't worthy. Not with the exorcist wards on it."

"I'm a non-magical human!" Stace shouts.

Father Way shakes his head. "No, you're too cool. Thought you were an enchanter at least. Had to be safe about it."

Stace harrumphs but is pleased at the compliment from the little quirk at the corner of their lips.

"And what makes someone worthy to enter this

space, Father?" Patty asks, arms crossed, pale eyes focused.

"A soul," Father Way answers. "A good soul, specifically."

Patty, Stace, and the exorcist priest all stare at me in turn. I gape, my jaw feeling suddenly too heavy to hold open with the shock. Everything feels too heavy. My head still swims, and I must blink to stay awake, then remind myself to blink again.

"I'm sorry, I must have wax in my ears." I smack my palm against my ear with a gentle pop. "Did you say I have a soul?"

"Yes, and a clean one at that."

I laugh extra hard at that one. "I'm sorry, Father. I thought priests can't tell a lie. That's the best joke I've ever heard. Have you heard the one about the priest who walked into a bar, oh, I'll tell you!" I get to my feet, only for Patty to try to pull me back down. She could've saved the effort because I fall back down with my butt in the cold pews anyways. "You don't know who I am, Father. I've brought royalty to their knees. I made villages beg for their life. I'm no saint."

"But I know what you are, Lili. Who you try to hide."

And here, Father Way reveals a small silver pendant in his hand. On the front is some inscription, and on the back is a mirrored surface. In it, I see my eyes, glowing bright red.

"Somehow, a higher power took favor on you, Lili. Someone gave you a second chance. Something purified your soul, somehow." He digs into his cassock and pulls out the pixie dust again. It sparkles beneath his hands.

"The exorcists have been distributing this at key spots in the community. It's a truth serum. It reveals who people *really* are." He leans back, the pixie dust gone from his palm in an instant. Or it's just my mind, spinning, playing tricks on me with time lapses. "And we imprison the demons who prove themselves too dangerous to be in society."

"That's bullshit!" Now Patty's enraged, her flush returning, red spreading all the way down her arms. "You used that shit on Indah at the Kraken Club and scrambled her brain. She's not a killer! She had to defend herself against assault. You can take your black-and-white morality and shove it up your—"

The priest interjects. "I'm sorry if we used this on your friend, but I assure you, we mean you no harm. In fact, I think you'll find we're on the same side here, Miss Sweeney. We don't believe in strictly good or strictly bad either. It's more of a gentle nudge." He smiles, and in the next instant, he's frowning. I can't tell. But his eyes, no matter how much my vision swims. His eyes remain constant. Staring, so deeply, into my very core. "With truth serum, you have nothing to fear if you have nothing to hide."

It's like the rest of the world fades away, or perhaps I'm fading. The exorcist wards have their claws sunk deep into me. His voice grows clearer as everything fades. I lean forward until Father Way's face is all I see. The sparkle of pixie dust between his forefinger and thumb.

"We've been waiting for you, Lili." His voice runs through my ears, weaving a single thread there, crystalline. "We've asked questions all through the demonic underbelly of this town, trying to find you. In truth, trying to kill you. But now we know for certain who you are... funnily enough, that Alethea Styx character called you a god. We offered to spring her free from that witch's prison, but she just wanted to look upon your face one more time. Poor, misguided demon."

Alethea's bargain wasn't freedom. She just wanted to see me one more time. Fool.

Father Way keeps talking, his voice a hymn echoing against this stone chamber. "Alethea was right in one thing, demon, or no. You're special, Lili. The demon who found a soul."

Patty holds her arm out to mine. "Lili, get away from him. He admitted it, didn't he? He's drugging monsters to kill them, and he'll do the same to you."

"Nonsense, we imprison demons. Murder's a sin, you know." Father Way's lips thin as he grits his teeth together. "No, you see. We aren't the killers because someone's been attacking our brethren in the middle of the night. We've been targets too." He holds out his hand, as if in blessing, to me. "We need your help, Lili."

A cry from my other side. "Whoa, and now the copycat killer is killing monsters *and* exorcists too. Plot twist! Wilbur, you can't fetch popcorn for this drama, can you?" Stace glances at Wilbur; the battle boar just blinks happily up at them. "No? It was worth a shot."

There's a ringing smash. Shouts of concern as a stone wall topples. Suddenly, the sun rips into the church from a gaping hole in the wall. Debris fallen over twisted pews. Splinters of dust as a giant force crumbles the wall like building blocks.

Silhouettes stand with vines and shields and glowing staves at their sides. Beautiful beings standing at various heights, the shortest at three feet to nine feet at the tallest, with skin like willow bark and emeralds. Flesh in hues of the night sky, deep blues, and violets and brown like the earth. Gold and quartz and beautiful black eyes. Thick arms, soft bellies. Others with long necks and lanky figures. Muscle and softness and soft curves all abound, every beauty imaginable. Instead of limbs, some bear vines. Others float like specks of dust on wings.

My head clears as the sanctity is disturbed, left in rubble and dust. The exorcist wards must weaken as the building does. I stand to face the newcomers head-on.

Father Way gets to his feet beside me, revealing a long, thin silver cross that expands into a lethal-looking blade. "How did you enter here?"

"Simple," the lead-most of the figures answers, their three-inch long nails gleaming in gold as the rest of their body shines like copper in the sun, raven curls falling over one eye, "your little human wards block those with bad souls from entering through the front door. But we didn't enter your space nicely—we smashed our way in." They run their hand into the symbol of a figure-eight. "Loophole, mate." He taps his ears, slender with soft gray fur, like a donkey. He has a tail that whips back and forth beneath the gentle slope of his spine. "And we overheard it all. Following our good friends here. Hope you liked the death threat with the flowers, by the way."

"I actually thought the toxic flowers were quite interesting from a botanist's perspective," Stace replies, just to get glared at by Patty. "What? They were!"

"Anyways." The head fairy levels a revolver at us that's cobbled together from clock gears and fungus and broken crystals from the forest floor. "You killed our leader, Sam Hain. You and your friends are coming with us peacefully now, Father. Or we drag you by your ears. But priests need to be peaceful. That's another loophole, isn't it?"

With a smile, he unfurls his fingers and shows us none other than Bluebell, the *ellyl* sent to murder us back at Wilbur's farm. "Loophole, motherfuckers!"

I should've fed that little shit to Wilbur when I had the chance.

*

How many ways can you kill an ellyl?

No, seriously, I'm asking. I have plans for that little imp.

"LOOK, I'M SORRY for locking you in a soft drink container filled with iron shavings. But, I mean, you escaped anyways! So, we didn't actually *mean* to lock you up." I whine out of the carriage bars, staring at that little, blue-hued, flower-petal flying *ellyl*.

Little shit.

"I escaped with no help from you!" the *ellyl* spits back. "Your werewolf friend's distraction gave me enough time to run. And watching him step on your spine was hilarious!"

We sit in a cart molded like a pumpkin out of Cinderella's stories. However, this carriage has reinforced bars like witch's talons molded from crystals, and it's driven by a large, hopping toad at the front. The fairies have me, Father Way, and Patty bound with cords of pumpkin vines, and Wilbur, the traitor, they charmed to sit up top with some truffles.

The fairies also refused to bind Stace. I think they too are convinced they're a fairy. That, or they were so intimidated by Stace's botanist knowledge they decided better against it.

I tap on the bars again as Bluebell dances a little jig in front of us, relishing the emerald-hued fairy forest air. Past the bars, I see bits of trees. Trees carved with shining faces. Giant creatures that blend with shadows. *We're going further into fairy country.* "Come on, Bluebell, I didn't mean it."

The little shit bites my thumb in answer.

"My name's not Bluebell!" it shrieks. "And I hope you rot."

"Well." I grimace, wrapping my thumb in my jacket sleeves. "What should I call you if not Bluebell?"

The *ellyl* snarls at me, baring its sharpened teeth. Its flower-petal wings whiff pollen into my face. "You won't get my name so easily, immortal."

"Why would your name be so bad?" Father Way asks, recognition sparking in those dark eyes of his.

"A fairy's name allows you to control them," I spit, sitting back into the rocking pumpkin carriage. I rub my wrists against the cords, wincing as they're enchanted to tighten the more you struggle. "They didn't teach you about fairy lore with the whole *vade retro satana* bit?"

Father Way smirks. "Oh, of course! Remind me, was

that chapter before or after the New Testament and pigs flying?"

The carriage lurches to a halt. Only Stace manages to keep from propelling forward. The rest of us, bound as we are, smack into each other like a set of dolls. I hit my forehead against one of the bars.

"I hope you remembered your lessons on exorcist asskicking," I mutter around one of my newly healing teeth, granting me a slight lisp thanks to my battle with Grendel. "You're going to need it considering how much Tinkerbell and company seem to miss Sam Hain. And the fact that you, good Father, provided the drug that killed him."

Father Way winks at me then. "Why would I need to kick ass? You're clearly well-versed in that field, enough to defend the both of us." He points to one of my stillgrowing teeth.

"Oh, the priest has a sense of humor!" The carriage doors open to filtered green light. A carousel of lanterns shifts the luminescence like a disco ball, shadows spinning in a dance of glee. Fairy hands reach inside. Long nails and feathers and wings brush my skin as they tug me out. "I hope that sense of humor gets you through the pearly gates when you perish!"

A nixie smacks her damp palm against my cheek, hissing at me with her gills like decorative feathers around her face. She wears a lace gown that slithers like water beside her. "You killed Sam Hain?" she asks.

"He did." I nod to Father Way who glares at me. "What, you did! Never tell a lie, Father. That's a sin, isn't it?"

"So is putting another man to death!" he snaps back.

"Should've thought of that before spreading your truth serum into Indah and getting us in this mess in the first place," Patty responds, spitting at his feet.

"I was following the exorcist code," he answers. "A demon's a demon."

I roll my eyes at that. "If you believe that, then don't ask the mother of demons for help."

He really is a lousy liar.

In a moment, our arms are taken up by the original leader of the fairies. The man with ears like an ass. He's quite pretty with his curls and winking smile. His tail smacks our legs as we walk, trying to trip us.

Fairy guards line up in armor fashioned of mirrored plates, all standing in front of a giant willow tree that curls upward to oblivion. We're beneath a forest canopy that shifts at angles, revealing glimpses of starry domes in the sky. The air has a quality of violets within it, the scent of lavender woven between vines. The Summerland, the place where the Fae reign. They keep to themselves if you're lucky.

If you aren't, then you're summoned to their violent hedonist court.

Grasses reach up with tiny pixies riding on sheltered leaves. Tiny hands nip at our heels and snag at our feet. They bob near Stace's ear and "ooh" and "aww" softly at Stace's lemonade-pink contacts and dyed purple hair. A nixie and a merman leave their ponds to appreciate the tattoos of vines and a blue moon on Stace's arms.

"Surely you know Gog the Great?" they ask Stace, eyes pleading. "Or perhaps we saw you at court with Lady Fortuna?"

"I'm not a fairy!" Stace yelps in reply. "I'm just a regular person."

"Nonsense!" they reply, whisking Stace away further into the party scene.

The oak has stairs fashioned from the thinnest metal imaginable, wrought metal like air encrusted with gemstones at intervals. Dancing bare feet and painted nails and claws spin around a dance floor covered in floating lanterns. At the top of the stairs, high above the mighty oak, a balcony carries the mighty throne of a king, carved from a boulder the size of Stonehenge. The throne bears the likeness of a figure in violent green hues staring out over his massive court. The creatures with scales and feathers and tails all dance and laugh with glee.

Wilbur is now visibly agitated that the pixies have dragged Stace further away from him. He tries to make a break for it, but one fairy pulls out a flute and serenades the pig. The music lulls him into an unnatural slumber. His wings fold in on himself as he snores soundly.

"*Who enters my court?*" A voice surrounds us, booming in our ears.

The young man, or old man in an eternally young man's body I suppose, the one with donkey ears, kneels before the throne and drags us all down with him.

"Some call me Candlewick," he replies, to some laughter from the court. *It's not his true name, not really.* "I've brought the murderers of Sam Hain here for justice."

"*I see. A moment, Candlewick.*"

A brilliant emerald light flashes from the balcony high above us. From the splendor, a large figure rises. Broad shoulders, a deep-green cape, and a suit made of velvet. His beard trails nearly to the ground, braided in vines and flowers, daisies and sunflowers and roses in bloom. Gemstones like teardrops adorn the corners of his eyes. His skin matches the green of a forest floor, of the energy of the court of Summerland.

"The Green Man…" Patty shakes her head. "I read about him in my parents' bestiary. Lili, he's the Green Man!"

Stace frowns at us. "Who the hell is the Green Man? Is that like the Green Giant who makes you eat your vegetables?"

The Green Man, of course.

It would only make sense that the father of the Green Prince, Sam Hain, would be none other than the Green Man. The figure of old legend who symbolized all that was life and verdancy, all that was sorcery, magic, and all that is and was of the earth itself.

"Silence, mortals! I only want the demon and the murderer to speak."

Patty and Stace's lips seem sewn together by a magical force. No matter how hard they try, they can't open their mouths to speak. Stace crosses their arms while Patty shoots the Green Man the middle finger.

"Much better." The great figure seems to have risen from his granite throne. His fists are large as boulders themselves, and his voice booms with the ancient song. "So, you murdered my son, did you?"

Patty and I glance at Father Way, who stares in silence at the floor.

"Ah." Even from so far away, nothing escapes the giant man's sight. "A priest, how funny. Like the start of a joke. What happens when a priest and a fairy prince enter a bar, is that how it goes?" The court laughs, cackling and crackling with mirth and liquor and glee. The laughter stops when he holds his hand up. "Why bring these fools to your Rí, Candlewick? Do you want riches? Glory?"

"Nothing, great Rí. Only justice." And here, the pretty Candlewick's fist curls until his nails pierce his skin, only for it to heal again. "I want justice for the ones who poisoned that *Kuntilanak* dancer to murder Sam Hain."

He shifts away and his curls draw back from his pointed ears, and on the furred lobes, I see them. Perfect emerald orbs hidden in black glass. Shining brightly, the emeralds move like...

Like eyes.

These eyes, unfortunately, I recognize as the eyes of Sam Hain. And from the pain in Candlewick's expression, the absolute anguish set in the tears that sparkle but refuse to fall...

Our captor, Candlewick, was Sam Hain's lover. No wonder he wants us dead.

"Hey, uh, Mr. Candlewick?" I try to nudge him gently and nearly fall flat on my face, kneeling and bound and all. "I think, personally, you'll do far better now that Sam Hain is gone. You're too good for him."

"I *loved* him as much as any of our kind can." With each word, Candlewick's lower lip trembles in violent fury. His eyes flash like comets from heaven.

"He was a bastard and had no respect for dancers, but fine." I shrug. "To each their own."

Candlewick, feigning innocence, shoves me in my ribs. He knocks the wind out of me and throws me into the mud.

Geez, Lili, pull that charm back or it'll get you losing what teeth you have left.

"I request you kill them all!" Candlewick shouts. Father Adam shifts next to me. He awkwardly crooks his elbow near my arms to help me huff and struggle my way upward.

"You got a plan?" I spit out dirt and it tastes like fairy wine.

"Watch me," Father Way replies.

Leaning back up, I now see that Father Way has, on bended knee, turned to the Rí, the king, above us. "Uh, great Rí!" Father Way cries out. A couple of nymphs are making seductive gestures in his direction, whispering about the charms of mortal men. *Geez, they're just as bad as the bachelorettes back in the hotel.* "Don't kill the others. I worked alone to kill your son, that's true. So, only I should die. I'll even help you do it!"

A hush, then outraged whispers and laughter in the court.

"This human fool wants to help us *kill him?"*

"How stupid."

"A handsome face, but such a fool! All humans are."

The Green Man smirks at that, leaning back in his throne with one green-jeweled hand on his knee while he waves the other dismissively at the priest. Candlewick drags us up, none too gently, to stand. Father Adam sets his jaw tight, locking his knees to keep himself from falling.

"How will you help us, little man?" The Green Man's question booms.

"Simple," Father Way answers, his voice cracking and telling us this is, in no way, the foremost plan he would've preferred to carry out, but it's the one he's stuck with. "I'm a priest, and I committed a crime. A sin. And now, I must help you atone for my horrible act. Only then will my crimes be wiped clean. Call it my redemption."

"Redemption?" asks the Green Man.

"I will tell you *how* to kill me," Adam Way replies.

I crook an eyebrow at that. *I mean, maybe he's into that sort of thing.*

"And how will you die, little man?" But the Green Man is getting into it now. His court has even paused from the dance floor for a bit, watching this handsome human stranger with a redemption complex play out his little scene.

If fairies love anything more than merriment, it's games. And Father Way seems to be pulling off a splendid one called "how to kill a murderer."

Father Way bares his muscular neck, revealing his Adam's apple (ah, puns) tensed on his gentle throat. Around his neck swings a metallic cross. "You may strangle me. Nothing more personal than that, huh?"

The Green Man smirks and waves at Candlewick. "Go on. Do the deed. You were my son's lover, after all. Surely you would love this most."

Candlewick pushes back his sleeves, revealing furred arms and long, golden claws. "With pleasure." He braces himself in front of Father Way, extending his talons all the way.

Stace turns away. Patty peers through her bound hands. Wilbur snuffles sadly.

A moment passes and as Candlewick's fingers brush Father Way's throat, there's a horrid sound. It's a screeching and hissing, like a cat with its tail all twisted. Another moment and I realize the horrid sound is driven from Candlewick's throat. Smoke and fire spits from his hands, leaving behind angry red welts in the shape of half a cross.

"Iron and silver. You tricked us!" he howls. "You *fucking* human."

"Celibate, actually," Father Way replies with a shrug.

The great Rí chuckles a bit, reveling in Candlewick's misfortune. He sulks off to the side of the dance floor. Tables laden with platters of food and fresh fruit and fairy wine fountains line the edges. Candlewick dips his singed palms into a crystal bowl of fairy wine. The smell emanating from it is like burnt strawberries.

Iron crosses. Lucky...

Or not luck at all.

"I tire of this game. Off with his head." The Green Man sighs, leaning back in his throne and already turning his eyes away from us like we're so much trash. Fairy guards come closer to us, their swords at the ready, red with mortal blood, no doubt. Unfortunate mortals who refused to dance for them.

"I have a better idea!" Father Way's regular timbre of a voice comes out more like a desperate squeak. "How about something more violent? How about you rip out my ribs?"

Does this man have a hellbent desire to avoid Hell through this sick redemption? Or, unless I'm mistaken, and I hope I'm not, he has a plan.

The Green Man cocks an eyebrow at that. "Rip out

your ribs?" A slow smile spreads on his bearded, ivy-covered face. "Wait, that could be great fun. We'll send your ribs out to make a fine chandelier for the Unseelie Court." He points to a section of beautiful maidens near the fountains of wine. Their hair, run through with lily flowers, is perpetually damp no matter how long they remain on land, and they are dressed in sheer fabrics like liquid water turned to thread.

"Bring forth a *gwragged annwn* to count his ribs," the great Rí commands. "Let us document how many gifts to give to the Unseelie Court."

One of the maidens comes forth. "The people of the court call me Llyn. I am the great Rí's physician at court." She wears a fabric in dazzling white, like the crest of a wave before it crashes upon the shore. She has spectacles that drip with wires of diamonds and her blue hair is combed back. "We shall count your ribs, mortal murderer."

She runs her hand along Father Way's shoulders. His cassock falls from his shoulders, leaving him in black pants and a belt studded with knives. The guards kick his weapons away. On Father Way's flesh, there's a map of scars and what I recognize as healed bite marks. Werewolf or larger by the look of them, entire chunks of skin turned into valleys or pale moons. There's something odd about his left side too, but I can't place it.

Some of the fairy courtiers titter or bat their eyelashes at him.

"Am I that interesting to look at?" Father Way asks.

I tear my eyes away from his scars, realizing that I've been staring at him for longer than appropriate. "Cool it.

I'm demi and have a girlfriend, buddy."

"If you fell in love with her, I'm sure she's a wonderful person. I'd like to meet her if I survive," he tells me.

If we ever escape at all.

"I'll begin the exam." Llyn runs her hand just above Father Way's skin. He hisses and bends his neck back. Magic folds in angry lines of red beneath his flesh, illuminating his ribs from within, like a human anatomy model gone glow-in-the-dark.

"It feels like bees buzzing." Father Way trembles as Llyn pulls away. His ribs are illuminated from within.

"Fairy magic doesn't know what to do with humans. Trust me when I say it doesn't want to be there either. It's just trying to get out..." Llyn's eyes dart over Father Way's left side, the side that didn't look quite right.

Illuminated from within, I see it then.

A gap where one of his ribs should be.

Father Adam Way's missing one of his ribs, leaving him at a total of twenty-three instead of the usual twenty-four.

Just like...he reminds me of...

After all this time... No, could it be...?

"I'm sorry, milord." Llyn bows her head and lowers her hand. Father Way, panting, bows his head as the fairy magic leaves him. "He's missing a rib. The Unseelie Court wouldn't accept him as a gift."

"*Enough!*" The Green Man's voice shakes the entire court. Llyn bows and returns to her spot with the rest of the *gwragged annwn* at the fountain. "It was a pleasant game, but my son's murder demands satisfaction. You drugged him, mortal, for your own strange ends for your brethren. Summerland does not forget. Take them away. Torture him to death or something."

"Wait!" Father Way, sweating profusely from the physician's fairy magic, shakes condensation from his dark curls. He tries to hold his cassock together with bound hands. Llyn, in an odd moment of kindness, waves her fingers and the cassock rights itself on his shoulders. "I have a gift to give you. One gift to make up for your son's life."

"Then go ahead. Tell me." The great Rí leans back in his throne, his boots on either side of the balcony. His beard draws up into the vines and branches of the oak.

"I um...uh..." Father Way turns this way and that, terrified.

Ah, he had no plan. Just dumb luck. I guess we're alike in some ways.

"Tear him apart!" Rí shouts.

"*Wait!*"

The entirety of the court pauses its chatter. Even Wilbur, in fright, falls onto his belly on the ground, scattering the gifts of truffles the fairy children gave to him.

It takes but a second to realize the sound didn't come from the great Rí or the executioner or anyone else but...

Me.

Am I trying to save this fool's life? Maybe I really have changed for the better.

"I know what gift he can give you." I tilt my head back, let my stance give some indication that I am the one in control here, despite my bindings. *Better to argue than fight if I can help it. I'm still a bit sore from Grendel, after all.*

"What will you give me?" the great Rí groans, rolling his eyes in exasperation.

Good, keep him talking.

"Something no fairy possesses. Not even *you*, oh great Rí."

The court gasps, muttering amongst themselves. Glittering eyes latch on to me, some lips mumbling curses while others whisper curiosities.

"That's right! All of us have it, and you don't." I don't back down, refusing to fall back against the fairies' harsh, hissing chorus. Even Candlewick's disdain can't stop me from rambling on. "Father Way has it. Patty has it, and Stace. Wilbur would...in some areas of thought." I grin even wider. "Some people tell me that, heck, even *I* have one."

"What is it called?" He leans in closer, and it's then the balcony collapses, or rather, grows outward from the great oak. The bejeweled staircase lines a path for the giant Green Man to walk down. The famous father of the infamous Sam Hain. Father to the murdered Green Prince.

And I'm defending the murderer. Immortality turns you into a lawyer, who knew.

"A soul." I wink at Father Way as he stares back, open-mouthed at me.

The Green Man, the great Rí, the king lumbers down from his post up near the heavens of Summerland's canopy. His deep-green cloak and dark eyeliner has him blend in with the tree. His skin reflects the colors of the changing, shimmering forest surrounding him.

"This soul..." the Green Man intones, "what purpose

does it have? Does it spin straw into gold or draw horses from rivers? Does it make swans into princes or allow you to dance for years at a time?" He grins and between his teeth shine bits of jade. "Is a soul for pleasure or does it serve the court of pain?"

"Both. Neither. It makes all of the above seem meaningless because a soul is...is..." The words come heavier now. I glance to my side, see a guard spin a dagger point menacingly in my direction.

"It's intangible." Father Way speaks up then. "But, at the same time, it's realer than real. It's everything at once."

"If it's so important, why do mere humans have it?" The Green Man peers closer at me, staring deep into my eyes. He sniffles and a flock of moths fly from his beard, translucent, papery wings flittering. "How did a demon get one?"

"Mother of demons..." I mutter.

"Not with ease, I'll tell you. In truth, I'm not sure how Lili got one," Father Way continues. "But it makes normal humans what we are. We have nothing else. No amazing strength. No magic. No superpowers. No immortality. No eternal youth. We can't take flight without machines or dance through fire. But souls give our finite lives meaning. In truth, we aren't even entirely sure how we have them, if we do. But whether we call it a soul or something other, every mortal has something that makes us thoroughly and completely *us* that nobody can take away. Not even a fairy."

The Green Man scratches his chin, and a hummingbird wraps like a cuff on his ear. A bumblebee rests wearily in his beard, and a blue jay takes wing from the Green Man's golden nest of a crown. "I see," the Green Man whispers. "This soul, how do I get one?"

And it's then that Adam Way has him. I *know* he has him.

Because he smiles and says, "Great Rí, I need only say a brief sentence or two. A prayer, or incantation, if you will." He clears his throat and tilts his head back, eyes raised to the heavens. A glimmer of light peers down from the canopy above, a sliver of silver moon and orange sun all at once. This strange Summerland light of neither here nor there, a fairy light. "I ask St. Benedict, patron of our church, to deliver our words to on high. May the heavenly host lay blessings at the feet of the great Rí and grant him the gift of a soul."

Here, he pauses, staring upwards with tears falling from his eyes.

What a good actor... Unless he isn't acting at all.

"Grant...grant...I'm sorry. Who shall I grant a soul to?"

The Green Man intones, "Viridios, lord of verdure."

"Grant Viridios a soul," someone in the fairy court screams. But Father Way finishes his prayer, a smirk turning upwards at his lips. "Amen."

"Amen," I whisper, a smile of my own appearing.

The priest got the Green Man's true name. And when you have a fairy's true name, you have them.

"Viridios," I finish for him. "Let Patty and Stace free."

A golden light passes through the glade and, all at

once, surrounds Patty and Stace, melting away their bindings. Stace leaps up at once, drawing Wilbur into trotting dutifully to their side. "Hallelujah! That was the worst round of the quiet game I've ever played."

"Ditto," Patty mutters, massaging her jaw with her fingers. "Damn, fairy magic really does feel like bees. Thank goodness I grew out of that allergy."

"Viridios." I set my shoulders back, staring him down even as he towers above me. "Set us all free."

Viridios pauses a moment, staring down at me and Father Way. He raises one mighty hand, his eyes flashing as dark as a storm set to tear all of Summerland apart. The violence in his fist, in the trembling of his gritted teeth. It aches to witness.

"You..." Viridios growls, raising his hand high.

Father Way closes his eyes, sure he's going to die.

Slowly, Viridios lowers his hand. With his gesture, my and Father Way's bindings melt away, falling apart like dust over our skin. "You are free to go." But Viridios leans in close then, and his voice goes barely above the sound of the wind rustling through leaves. "Lili, mother of demons," he begins, "my fairies aren't the only ones who stalk you in the night. Just because we're gone, your battle is far from over."

"What?" I turn to Viridios, trying to find meaning in his face, and only finding sorrow. "What are you saying?"

"Beware of the one with kind eyes," Viridios tells me. "They hide more than you know." And with that, the Green Man waves his hand and banishes us from Summerland, seemingly forever.

But forever's a very long time for an immortal, and

rarely lasts half as long.

I won't tell you how we got out of Summerland. The fairies like to keep their dwelling very hush-hush, after all.

But I will tell you that I saw the Green Prince, Sam Hain's former lover, Candlewick again. I saw him exiting the riotous court room on the arm of a very handsome dryad decked out in the branches of his tree. The dryad stranger had moody eyes that melted like maple wood and was in the middle of finishing a flower crown to turn Candlewick's frown upside-down.

All's well that ends well, I guess.

Chapter Twenty

The smell of fear

A Google search told me that twenty percent of all accidents happen in parking lots.

Guess where we are now?

"GODDESS, AM I glad to be out of Summerland." Patty shudders, glancing behind her as we walk to her vehicle.

"Thank you, Lili, for helping me get out of there." Father Way bows at the waist, all formal.

"Thank yourself..." I'm about to turn around and leave when something glints in Father Way's outstretched hand.

"Take it," he urges, his hand moving so close to mine that I can nearly touch his fingertips. I make out the glint of a gun in his palm bearing a target like a silver cross on its end. "There's no telling what other threats are out there."

I fold his fingers over the weapon and push it away from me. "Keep it for yourself, Father. Guns aren't really my style."

He smiles, but the smile doesn't reach his eyes. The weapon disappears inside the folds of his torn cassock. "Very well." He works his jaw, fist curling and uncurling as he contemplates, brow pulled down low. "Lili... Before I was an exorcist, a priest, I was a husband. I lost my wife, but I was given a second chance to help others. To save others."

"Save the savior talk for your congregation." I turn around again, and Father Way reaches out to empty air.

"Lili. In truth, I pretend to be a hero because I'm afraid of what the opposite means."

There's something there in his voice now, hiding beneath the bravado. Is that fear I smell? Its sour scent, creeping beneath hair follicles. Trembling between flesh and spirit.

"And what are you afraid of becoming, Father?"

Father Adam Way pauses, staring at his shoes. "If you aren't the one saving," he murmurs, the words dropping from his mouth as rotten truth, "then you're the one being saved."

*

On the road again

"IF YOU AREN'T the one saving...then you're the one being *saved*," Stace mimics, their eyes all mock intensity. Putting so much pain in their voice they could give the iconic Bella Swan in *Twilight* a run for her money. "I didn't realize how many dramatic one-liners are involved in the detective business, Lili."

I shrug. "It's part of the job."

"*It's part of the job.*" Stace snorts as they dodge my halfhearted swipe from the passenger's seat. Wilbur snaps lazily at my fingers from his spot on Stace's lap in the back. "Seriously, it just keeps going! Chill out, Blade Runner. Hey, Patty, are we heading home yet?"

"Not quite." Patty smiles slightly, staring at the road. "We've got one more stop planned."

Something is different about Patty, an air of nervousness. A twinkle of happiness in her eyes. Of hope.

Something we need more of these days.

"Ah, and now there's the cryptic description of the mysterious place we're going." Stace sighs, nestling their neck in the crook of the headrest. "What's next, a scene heading?"

*

Here's your scene heading, Stace

Grid's Griddle

IT SMELLS LIKE French fries served with ketchup, like oil that sticks to your flesh and fresh blood sourced from untraceable sources. The booths are all filmy, sticking to your skin when you sit down in one. But this visit isn't ours, though Stace and I took great pleasure in ordering off Grid's killer menu.

See the pun there? I'm only in it for the puns, and helping people too, I guess.

Stace gets a basket of sea salt chips and I order a helping of heart blood soup, red as tomatoes with a grilled cheese on the side that remains untouched. Grilled cheese. A decorative, lactose sandwich, I guess, unless vampires are into food poisoning. Blood poisoning? Whatever.

Stace's lemonade-pink contacts are currently zeroed in on that grilled cheese. They lick their lips and reveal their tongue ring.

"All right, all right. Take it already." I shove the grilled cheese in their direction. "You just had to ask if you wanted it. Human food isn't really my jam. Get it...jam?"

"Ha-ha, Dad. And I was trying to be sly. All cool and suave like you guys." Stace kicks back, speaking around a big mouthful of melted mozzarella. "Did it work?"

I shush them as I peer over Stace's side of the booth. They swallow their bite of grilled cheese and glance curiously up at me, head tilted to the side. A bat earring swings from their left lobe. "Can you see her?"

"Oh yeah." I catch glimpses of Patty's red locks cascading down her back. She's taken her hair down and done a quick change in the bathroom with a gym bag she keeps "for romantic emergencies". She wears a green peekaboo dress and a leather vest with matching leather cord earrings. And across from her, tensely sitting upright, is none other than her date for this evening.

Indah.

Indah drinks her blood-red milk tea, mashed together with what appear to be cow eyeballs as boba. She wears one of Dr. Weddo's and Erzulie Freda's promotional tees for the shelter, the telltale Rainbow Serpent against a backdrop of black, and a pair of loose-fitting jean shorts tugged over it. She looks like a regular human in the light, albeit one with a metal nail sticking out of the back of her neck, hidden by a choker. But whenever a shadow falls over her from someone passing by, even for a second, I see glimpses of her true form. Blood-red eyes and thick fangs protruding past lips like raw steak split in half.

But the shadow disappears and she's back to her regular self, beautiful like moonlight with dark, gleaming skin and long hair tied off at her shoulder.

No matter what form, Patty just sighs and stares dreamily at her, her eyes darting guiltily to Indah's lips and back again.

"So...are your friends going to join us?" Indah points at me, unapologetically peeking over Stace's booth.

Patty whips around, and her glare sends shivers down my immortal-yet-chicken-shit-right-now spine.

"Stop. Embarrassing. Me. You. Two," Patty grunts.

Stace shoots a peace sign up and pops their head over the booth, halfway blocking my view. "Never."

"I don't mind. This isn't our first date, right?" Indah laughs and Patty laughs harder to compensate.

"First date?" Patty tugs on her leather vest, zipping and unzipping it. "Pfft...no...I mean..."

"I wouldn't mind if it *was*." Indah purrs. "I've never dated a witch before."

Patty opens her mouth and lets out a desperate wheeze.

Indah takes this in stride, saving Patty from her agonizing lovesickness. "I heard some of what you said to Dr.

Weddo over the phone. You brought Sam Hain's killer to justice, so the fairies aren't after me anymore. And now I'm free to go dance in a field of daisies, is that right?"

"Something like that." Patty goes to reach for her drink and Indah does the same to her own drink, cozied up next to Patty's. Their fingers touch for a moment and Patty snaps her hand back, her cheeks aflame. Indah smirks and takes a slow sip. "I mean..." Patty coughs to clear her throat, her voice cracking with nerves. "Yes, your name has been cleared. And the fairies will allow you to return to the Kraken Club if you wish." Patty lowers her voice then. "Your former supervisor..."

"Pelle's dead too." Indah shrugs. "Probably just going to get replaced by another asshole with how the Kraken Club operates. You know anyone hiring sweet-yet-deadly *Kuntilanaks*?"

"I...um...I..." Patty glances up at me, her eyes, once burning, now frozen with first date fear and pleading for help.

"You can help at the Sweeney Inn," I offer.

Patty practically melts in her chair.

Indah pauses, glancing at the backs of her long, long nails. "All right," she drawls, waiting a moment longer and smirking at Patty. "Do I get to work closely with you?"

Patty pauses. Swallows. And looks up. "Yes," she squeaks.

Indah sighs, falling back into her chair with her hands behind her head. "I'm afraid I can't. I don't like dating a coworker."

"Dating a..."

Indah reaches for Patty's hand and brings it close to

her lips to kiss. "What do you say, Detective Sweeney?" Indah grins. "Will you take me on a date?"

Patty beams so widely that the sun couldn't compete. "Yes." She brings Indah in for a hug and a peck on the cheek. "I'd be honored."

Stace starts to applaud. Every head, and headless phantom, in the whole diner turns to look at us. I have to pull them down from their spying place on the booth. Wilbur, meanwhile, is eating Stace's grilled cheese and smelling suspiciously like limburger.

"Let them have their moment," I hiss as Stace tries to pull out their cell phone to snap a picture. "Stace!"

"I'm sorry. They just look like gay happiness personified."

They might've been a bit nosy, but Stace has a point. As Patty stares dotingly into Indah's glimmering eyes, they do look happy together. Indah sidles up to Patty so they are sharing the same end of the booth, sitting shoulder to shoulder and thigh to thigh. They look so peaceful, like nothing in the world can get to them. Well, almost nothing.

Chapter Twenty-One

No name

THERE'S A VIOLENT knocking on my door. I shuffle over and shove my bare feet into unzipped boots to answer. I pull on my peacoat over a pair of boxers and a tee that sticks to my skin.

"Yeah, yeah...I'll get it." I draw the deadbolt and pull the door aside.

The priest, Father Adam Way, all but falls into my room. His momentum takes him forward, his curls dripping wet from the thunderstorm I hear blaring outside. Lightning strikes. Thunder crashes.

It's a good night for something bad to happen.

"Where is she?"

"Where is who? How you get in here?" I help him get to his feet. He wears street clothes. Black sweatpants and some shirt, too faded to make out the symbol. He wears a long jacket, unzipped, and something gleams silver in his right hand. The gun with the cross. "No, seriously, how the hell did you get in here? The front door requires a hotel card at night. You aren't staying here anymore."

"I followed another person in." His eyes are wild, unfocused. He trembles so hard that he nearly drops the gun.

I reach down for his collar and pull him to his feet. "That's enough. We helped you once, but now you're breaking and entering. Probably waking up half the people in this place, and you're *lucky* I don't sleep. Stalking the guests..."

"She wasn't a guest!"

Those words stop me. If I could feel fear the same way mortals do, there'd be a chill running down my spine right about now. Instead, I feel something move inside me. Calling me to run. To hunt. To tear something apart until my bloodlust and anxiety is sated.

"She picked the lock with some form of magic," Adam tells me as he leans in closer. "She's waiting outside this door for you."

I turn to the door, watching how the corners bleed into shadow. How the thunder outside rattles the doorknob, or perhaps something else raps on the wood. The exorcist priest trembles behind me, hair plastered to his head. Fear wild in his eyes.

I move to open the door, and just by pressing my fingertips against the cool metal...

The door swings open.

Phantom impressions of scars and bruises lay like kisses in her skin. Sinewy muscles lie beneath a black tank, sweatpants stuffed into boots. Her azure hair brushes against her collar, the other half of her head shaved. When she turns her head, I see her telltale tattoo. A tattoo of wings to fly away.

To escape, and all too soon, I wish to join her.

Jo Kim...

I thought I'd lost you.

Jo Kim's eyes, black and sparkling like the night sky, stare pleadingly at me. She falls into me. Not a ghost, not exactly flesh. As real as can be for one of the Reanimated, but she's finally *here*. She's in this realm, with me.

Yet her arms are pulled tightly behind her back, bound with thick, silver cuffs. A shining, metal braid is stuffed past her lips, keeping her silent past her screams.

I gasp at the cold silver that digs into my spine. Father Adam Way stands at his full height now. His usual weapon, the holy gun with the cross, burns into my skin.

"Soul or no soul," he whispers, voice hoarse. Fear and something else trapped in his eyes. "You can still lose your life, or whatever you call this. Lili..."

He presses the gun forward, and I hiss as the cross burns foully in my back. My head swims, like a human with one-too-many shots of vodka.

"Move," he orders.

Jo staggers to her feet before me, trying to reach weakly for my hands. Adam presses between us, forcing us apart. I keep trying to whip my head around, to catch glimpses of Jo. To see her eyes. Her lips. Just to run my fingers through her hair again...

But Adam whips the gun across my forehead, and I catch a glimpse of a cross in blood across my temple. I feel it sting, cold blood in my eyes.

"Move," he orders.

And this time, I listen.

For now.

*

MY EYES WHIP back and forth as we go down the hall. The carpeting and warped wood meet our shuffling footsteps. The dimmed nighttime lights are on in the hotel, the lowered lamplight bleeding soft yellow across the rouge carpets.

We shuffle along farther, our muted footsteps so agonizingly slow. Thunder continues to howl outside. Lightning flashes across windowpanes. Rain pelts relentlessly onward, cheering on our grim march.

The lights under Patty's door are out.

She must be out with Indah still. Good for her. Bad for me and Jo.

We go a little further and reach Stace's door. Wilbur lies in front of it, his wings folded in as he snuffles weakly.

I hiss, trying to keep my voice low to avoid another smack to the head. Or worse, Jo getting punished. "You killed him! You mother—"

I grunt as Adam smacks his fist into my belly, knocking my protest out of me.

"He's just sleeping. Same as the other one, with the strange-colored eyes." He reveals a small, golden incense burner that releases a violet-colored smoke. The smoke curls like a sleeping cat, weaving past Wilbur's nostrils. Slipping beneath the door.

I hear Stace, fortunately for them, snoring behind the door.

"The incense lulls them to immediate slumber." Adam chuckles at that. "Blessings from St. Benedict that this is a relatively painless extraction."

Extraction, like rotting teeth.

"Move," Adam repeats, digging the barrel of the gun into my back again. Jo rattles along, her dark eyes flicking to meet mine on occasion.

I run my thumb against her knuckles, and that brief contact almost makes it all seem worth it. Just to feel her near me again. *We're getting out of this. Or at least Jo will.* "There's no way I'll lose you again..." I whisper, but she doesn't look my way.

*

HE PUTS A blindfold on both of us as we get to the parking lot. Gamin, true to its small-town nature, is devoid of much traffic. Add a storm to the mix, and the odds that anyone is out here drop to nil.

I hear the sliding of a rusty van door. The cloth smells like mothballs as it rests over my nose, pulling tight against my eyelids. Wicking the rain from my forehead.

The car rumbles along then, but I feel Jo's palm pressing into my knee. The chains and cuffs drag along too. But it's her hand. Her flesh. *She's alive. Alive as any of our kind can be. She's here. With me.*

And even now, kidnapped by a manic exorcist convinced that his version of right is the rightest anyone in the world will ever be. Kidnapped by an exorcist probably high-fiving himself for snagging the Mother of all Demons...

Even now...

My love.

I feel Jo beside me. I take her hand in mine, cupping

her fingers. Running my thumb along hers. When I squeeze her hand, she squeezes mine back.

I'm here, Jo. Finally.

Here.

*

THE BLINDFOLDS ARE torn from our eyes. Water streams down our skin. Wind howls in our ears in a rage.

I stare into the eyes of Father Adam Way as his ankles sink into the mud beneath us. Slick brown leaves gone gray with age and worms crawling onto the concrete of the road beyond us. I hear the river Lethe before I see it, angry waters swirling. I hear the water calling to the winds, the winds calling to the rains to crash upon the earth.

"You got us," I mutter, testing my jaw, gritting my teeth.

Adam grins. "What a catch. Mother of Demons. And her lover. Oh, to save your souls. I'd be the greatest exorcist alive then, eh?"

Jo, her gag and blindfold removed, spits at his feet.

"Why are you so angry, dear?" He shakes his head. "You were the one who...argh." He sniffs, hard, but it's too late. I see the blood trickle from his nose, dripping down to his cupid's bow on his lips, mingling with the sweat and the stress and the rain.

Dig and don't stop. Dig where a living mortal's nose bleeds and that's where the Crossroads will find you.

"You took us to the Crossroads." I swipe my fingers against my cheek, wiping away the rain, tossing flecks of it into the river Lethe. "Maybe you want Baron Samedi's help. If you bury a corpse at the Baron's Crossroads, it won't come back again as a zombie. Is that what you want, Father Way? To kill us and keep us from coming back again?"

"Superstition. I only came here because my brethren struck a deal with the demonic being here. What's done here, remains here. Our little secret." Adam Way shakes his head, coming toward me quick. I stumble back, my hands bound, but he catches my wrists in his hands. When lightning cracks, the shadows only deepen beneath his otherwise golden eyes. Pretty, golden eyes that only look possessed now. "I had a dream. Like how I lost my last wife. I couldn't save her, but I can save you..."

I try to shake him off me, but his grip only tightens. The silver cuffs, the smack to my forehead with that holy gun. They all make me too weak. "There it is again. I'm getting sick of your savior talk."

The priest trembles like the weight of his head's too heavy upon his shoulders. "No, please. Listen. The church of St. Benedict. We were called here because we heard a demon was here. We thought it was you until we realized what you really are...And to meet you. Oh, to meet you. I'm in awe." He laughs then, the smile not reaching his eyes. Teeth flashing too bright.

The headlights of a gray van shine on us, parked halfway in the forest. Tire tracks in mud, leading us out to these Crossroads. The place where a mortal's nose bleeds.

I'm sure that'd show up easy on a GPS.

"I'm in awe," Father Way says, "because the story comes together, doesn't it? My mother's family, in Zahlé, they looked at me and said I'd be Adam."

"You're not Adam though, not my...my first..." My eyes flicker down to where his missing rib was revealed before. "Back in Summerland..."

"No. I'm not *the* Adam. Not the first Adam." He smiles at me then. "Just a coincidence. Nor was my late wife's name's Eve. It was Alia." He holds out his hand to me. "But you're the real thing, aren't you? I'm just a sad imitator. A wannabe. But you're real. The *real* Lilith, created from the same clay as Adam."

He raises the gun again and points it at Jo. I step between them, and Jo reaches out to me. She wraps her arms around my waist and pulls me in tight.

Don't let go, baby. Her lips murmur against the back of my neck.

"Why are you doing this to us?" I snarl, glancing down to see my skin bubbling. Power surfacing as ink comes to light. My true form hidden beneath. Morphing. Reshaping my flesh like clay. My nails extend, stretching my fingers into claws. Farther. Sharper.

Ready to wipe this twisted exorcist from the face of the earth.

"There's good in you, Lili," Adam says. The rest of his body trembles with nervous adrenaline, but the hand that holds the gun remains eerily steady. Jo buries her nose into the back of my shoulder blades, slumping over behind me. "You saved me back in Summerland when you could've let me suffer. The only reason you'd even be able to enter St. Benedict's was proof enough... God." He tilts his head back a little, lips hanging open in supplication. "You have a *soul*, Lili. A demon with a soul. I've seen it. In dreams, in visions. But you have to make the choice."

He turns the gun around then, rain pouring in sheets around us. Our ankles deep in cold mud, mud that seeps past my unzipped boots and gets stuck in metal teeth. My jacket clings to my skin, trying its best to keep my gray boxers and shirt from being deluged in their entirety.

The gun's handle almost floats between us, a choice. *He's giving up his weapon for what?*

"You scared the shit out of me for what? To just give me a choice?" The words drop like lead past my lips. It sounds even crazier when I voice it.

"I'm just the humble messenger. Lili, please..." He takes in a deep breath, blinking rapidly, trying to focus his weak mortal eyes on mine. "When the visions, the angels' visions... When they showed me who did this, who did all this, they told me the only one who could defeat this... They told me it was you. But you wouldn't go willingly." He laughs, the noise half-strangled in his throat. "I'm sorry, Lili. Rarely do the chosen ever *wish* to be chosen, am I right? Not even me. No, not even me."

I slowly take the gun from his grasp. "You're mad. Something they did to you in Summerland. Did you drink the fairy wine?"

"No, Lili. The devil is a liar, please..."

And then, he just stops.

He stops speaking altogether as Jo stands over him, heaving. Holding a large stone between her cuffed hands. She spits again, spluttering out from between rainwater rivulets.

"Finally. I thought he'd never shut—"

And she falls to her knees besides the unconscious priest.

Chapter Twenty-Two

The devil is a liar. I'm not the devil, unless I'm lying

SHE CRUMPLES INTO my chest as I hold her. I run my fingers through her silver-blue hair, feeling how the shorter strands give way to those of unruly length. I'm careful, so careful. She isn't as sunken as when I saw her before. She isn't...

"You're back," I whisper, as her black eyes blink slowly at me. We embrace over the unconscious exorcist, holding each other against the rain. Against the world.

"I never left," she whimpers. "I mean, I never wanted to."

I run my hands over her arms, her bony elbows. They all feel solid, not a phantom of my imagination. Not a dream.

Not a bad dream, anyways.

"But how are you awake and walking around? How did Adam find you?"

"I...I can't recall." She smiles, sleepily pressing her nose into my neck. "I missed you."

"Jo." There's something she's holding back. She can

never hold my gaze for too long. *Almost as if she's avoiding it.* "Jo, if he hurt you—"

"No, no. Nothing like that."

"Then what?"

She sighs, taking a step back. Her entire face rests all at once. Her eyebrows, her trembling lips. Everything smoothed out, as easy as switching a mask. It's unnerving, like seeing blood wash away in a river.

Too clean.

"I wish you weren't so curious, Lili. Why can't you just be happy I'm back?"

I hold my hands out at the rain, releasing her entirely. I move my feet a little, shaking off the excess mud, feeling it drip into hollow places. "Jo, because you don't have to be a detective to realize that none of this makes sense. Because I—"

A gasp then. Adam rises, spasming really. An involuntary muscle reaction.

But, just in case it isn't, I fall upon him. It's instinct really, from spending all those years hunting my prey. All those centuries chasing them down; I've turned into more animal than anything. If one could ever claim I resembled a person at all...

"Ple...th...lis...." Adam gasps. His jaw isn't working right, not after being struck by Jo. I'm surprised the mortal's conscious at all.

Perhaps a great being really is on his side.

I lean in close, pressing my ear to his chapped lips.

"She...here...kidnapped..."

"She brought me...against my..."

And finally, the words that draw a chill down my

spine.

"I...was...the...one who was...kidnapped."

I look up and draw back quickly, accidentally kicking Father Adam Way's head in the process. He slumps back into the mud. I barely turn his face out of it in time.

Jo's staring directly at me with that same, stony expression. She's half-crouched over Adam, but her entire torso is twisted toward me. Her eyes are so blank. There's a tattoo outline on her forehead.

The parchment sealing spell of the *gangshi*.

Why didn't I notice that before?

It's like staring into a void.

Jo grins, but the rest of her face doesn't follow suit. Her voice remains monotone. False placation. "You don't believe him, do you?"

I stare back at her, wondering how someone I love so much, have yearned for so much, could turn into this creature. How this moment that brought me such joy can quickly spiral into something so terrifying. If my heart could beat faster in my chest, it would. But not out of love.

"What did he mean by that, Jo?"

Jo shrugs, getting up. She nudges him with her worn sneaker, staring down at him with her lips drawn back, like watching roadkill lying out in the sun. A disgusting thing.

I walk backward, slowly. My hands at my sides, talons still growing. My teeth peek out past my lips, slipping into fangs.

My blood calls to me: fight or flight.

"What did he mean, Jo?" My voice is different now. Desperate. I don't want to be desperate. But this sickening feeling, it gnaws on my insides. A dark, impish beast gripping at my organs. That the one who owns my loving devotion…

That Jo is the bad one here.

"What did he mean, Jo?"

Her face tears as her voice erupts, rage and aggression and sorrow ripping out from her throat. Rain like tears down her face, even as she fights to keep it emotionless.

"Why couldn't you just be happy for me?"

My chest is heaving now, my arms wrapped around Jo's thin shoulders. I'm gripping her so hard that my talons dig in, but she's gripping back. Her fingers leave bruises on my skin.

My tattoos swirl. My names, my *real* names in ink within my blood. *Lili. Lilit. Lilītu.*

"I made a deal with Baron Samedi. They needed someone to collect souls…who better than a *gangshi*?"

ki-sikil-lil-la-ke

"Baron Samedi told me to collect some souls, then I'd be able to leave the Crossroads. Each soul I collected, I got stronger. Soon, I could leave."

Lamia. The First.

"But then they asked me to collect a soul, an impossible soul. You remember, Lili. You remember how you died? They told me Alethea killed you. I cried and raged in the Crossroads. But Baron Samedi told me it'd be fine."

"Because you came back."

The Dark Maid.

"Iam gave you a new soul, the shiny soul. The one Father Adam Way loved so much, the one that convinced them you were worthy."

"But I'm a *gangshi*. I'm a soul collector. I'm not picky, right?"

"You have to understand. I did it for you."

The Maiden of Desolation.

"I took in your old soul, my love. The soul that had mercilessly killed and hunted and murdered. The soul of a murderer. The soul of a monster…"

"I did this for you. I collected the soul of the old-you that died, so the new-you could live. Do you understand?"

"I did this for us. So that we could be together."

"I struck a bargain with Baron Samedi, but even they couldn't know…" Jo's eyes, the whites of them go entirely black now. Her skin bubbles, frothing, like water boiling over on a stove. Her head jerks back.

Her fingers grow longer. Half a foot. A foot. Talons and teeth sharpen.

Mother of Anathema.

"Even they couldn't know what devouring your old soul would do to me."

Her voice shifts now. Her body stretches to tower over me.

My own change comes slower.

Come on, fight.

Fight.

A crack and the world beneath me falls away. My old names come to me. Aramaic. Hebrew. Greek. Latin. Indigenous tongues. Names the world spat out before it became the world. The ground starts to rush away as the change comes on.

I stretch and grow. My muscles tensing. My true form

breaking free. Skin and flesh fashioned of the same clay of the earth that made me. A face that yawns into a gaping mouth with two rows of teeth...

But Jo grows too. Into a titan. Her eyes burn black. Beautiful and terrifying. Her form bubbles, spewing obsidian fluid from her ears and eyes.

A false god.

"I know the worst parts of you now, Lili. The parts you tried to hide. To pretend that they never existed. I took them inside me. I made them mine. I made you mine."

The ground rushes away from us both now. I stare into my lover's eyes, or what's left of my lover after the change. *After what my old, monstrous soul turned her into.* Her eyes, black. Mine, reflecting the souls trapped in Jo's belly. The soul-collector.

The devourer.

Her smile matches mine, two rows of teeth.

"After I collected your maladapted, ancient soul, I started working overtime for Baron Samedi. Collecting souls that weren't even on their list. Ending the bad lives early and taking their souls before they could do more harm. First, I started by saving that *Kuntilanak* from that noxious fairy boy. Then I figured I'd make life easier for you by targeting those who hurt you. Then there was that irritating elf who put his hands on you at the nightclub. I tried doing your old enemy Alethea in with pixie dust, but Alethea just gave it away to that troll instead..."

Sam Hain. Pelle. Grendel.

"Why pixie dust?" My voice rings deeper now. A hardened battle warrior, drawing power from the earth. The vessel of the Mother of Demons. Nails grown into machete blades. My dark hair drawn back into coils like serpents, worn like a cloak of steel upon my scarred back.

Jo grins.

"Pixie dust helps you see the true monsters hiding underneath. Makes the collecting faster. And truthfully, Lili." A growl comes from deep within Jo. Or the titan resembling Jo, as we stand easily above most of the buildings of Gamin now. "Ever since devouring your soul, I find that I'm *always* hungry now."

"I did this to you. The old me, my old, rotten soul...I thought that part of me was long gone. Dead." Rain drips down my face, but it feels hot. It tastes salty. "Shit, I'm so sorry, Jo. I didn't know..."

I take one, large step toward her. The river breaks with the flooding rain now, curling around my legs. I hold my arms out to her.

"Why do we have to fight, Jo?" I reach for her, retracting my talons with a soft hiss. "Please, just come back to me. We'll fix this together. We can turn you back to normal, give Baron Samedi another soul to replace it."

Something flickers in her eyes. The old Jo. Dark eyes so soft. So kind. Then they harden. And I see my own eyes staring back at me. Staring into the old me, the one who never knew love. The one who only knew war and blood and power. The one who didn't know who they were. Who I was. Who I am.

I am...

"Jo..."

Pain erupts, fire-hot, in my stomach. I look down and see nails trailing back, going up into Jo's giant arm. I see blood dripping down her wrist, blood like gold and ink and fired clay all mixed up in one.

And a familiar sparkle.

Pixie dust.

She drugged me with pixie dust.

A deep surge of anger comes from deep within my chest. From the hidden places I've tried so long to hide.

Hold it together, Lil.

"I'm sorry," she tells me. "I'm barely Jo anymore. I'm...I'm *you*. The old you." She removes her talons from my chest with a soft burble. Staring in wonder at the blood, my blood, as it mingles with the rain. She runs her tongue along it, closing her eyes. "I'm a new me too."

Hold it...

I stare at my blood, dripping down her wrist.

...together.

She goes for my throat, and I go low, ducking down as I ram my whole body into the center of her chest. She falls backward into the rushing river Lethe, the trees beside us dampening down with wind and wet.

The waters beneath us seem to expand with the floods, mud and blood dragging Jo's head down into the river. I move my hands, slippery, up to her collar. She snarls and tries to bite at my hand, I readjust. Sloppy. My talons sink into her shoulder, pushing her back down beneath the water. My head swims. I feel unhinged. Floating. The pixie dust calls to the old rage within me. But something breaks through. A soul if you can call it that.

"I don't want to do this, Jo!" I let go, just enough for her to lift her head.

As the water and swirling mud streams from her

silvery hair, her face comes into light.

No, not her face.

I stare directly into my own eyes. Gray eyes, a sharp, arched nose. Lips that are blood-red, as though drenched in the blood of my fallen enemies.

My face sits atop hers like a mask upon a child at All Hallows Eve. But it's unmistakably mine. But more twisted. Eyes that hold the screams of my past victims.

I loosen my grip again, and that's all it takes for Jo to get the upper hand. She pounces on me, pushing me back with her knees, snapping at my neck with her teeth. I push her jaws back with my fingers, my thumb sinking into her fangs. The waters disperse beneath us. A log cracks under my massive weight. We stand as titans now. When we clash, thunder masks the sounds of our battle. Lightning whips across the sky and reveals the terror and the rage in Jo's eyes.

"I did this…" The mask nearly sits perfectly atop Jo's face now. The last of her silvery hair slipping away to mine, to raven locks that were never hers. Ghosts of my tattoos stand out at her skin. Flesh like clay clambers over hers, trying to submerge her. Jo gasps as her lips give way beneath the mask, as the clay solidifies, "Even if the real me dies. I did this for *us*, Lili. To see you again. To be a part of you, even the cruelest parts of you. Forev—"

The mask finally seals, and her words get swallowed up by the clay.

I scream, hurling us back, lifting the titan's weight with my legs and pinning it once more beneath the water. I draw my arms and legs tighter around its chest, pulling inward. Wanting to drown it beneath the mud.

But the lower half of its face refuses to fall under. It's laughing. Laughing.

Its mouth...*my* mouth. It bends back and smiles, revealing the rows of sharpened teeth. Broken stones sitting at the foot of a cave drenched in blood.

"Hello, me," it whispers, in a voice that's a rotting, echoing parody of my own. "Call me Nakheyr, one of our first tongues."

Nakheyr, Farsi for "no."

"No. You want me to call you 'no'?" But I barely choke the words out. The rain feels so heavy on my tongue. Perhaps it's the drugs.

"Yes." The demon titan smiles. "Call me *No*." My grip slips again, and I feel weaker. I can't tense my stomach muscles after Jo's first assault. Her early talons had drawn a tendon there. Nakheyr's shoulder wounds, the blood fades away as new clay pours over its flesh, making it whole again. I stare into my own dead, gray eyes as the creature mocks me. "Call me Nakheyr. I am all that is wrong with you. The sins you tried to hide. Trying to forget. If you are whole and good, then I am the opposite. I am Nakheyr. The No to your Yes. I am the negative space."

It draws its knee up and slams it into my stomach wound. I choke on the rain, throwing my head back. This is enough for Nakheyr to rise from the water and buck me off.

I give up my hold on it and leap up, one hand clutching my wound. In the other, I hold my talons out to my side, the sword of the destroyer of empires. Devourer of all who disobeyed me. Or at least...

Try to remember who you were. Try to fight like

your old ways. Only your old, vile self might save you now.

Nakheyr wipes the mud from its face, the clay rising over all its wounds. Patching up my old, tainted soul with shadow and clay. A golem. My old soul has taken the form of some golem, a nebulous creature of clay. A shell encasing Jo...

Jo.

I did this for us.

"Let her go, Nakheyr. It's just me you want. You want to take over my place, is that it? To kill me for trying to drown you in the river Lethe."

I spread my arms to my side, wincing as my stomach wound slowly, oh-so-slowly, tries to heal itself. *It'd go faster if I devoured mortal flesh.*

But no. You aren't that creature anymore.

And that creature, Nakheyr, surveys me like a cruel circus master forcing a lion through flaming hoops. Wondering why the lion doesn't just rise and kill it. Wondering why I'm so cowed. Tamed.

"But you didn't drown me, Lili. Didn't kill me." Nakheyr speaks with a voice that's hollow. A metal spoon scraping the bottom of an empty glass. "You abandoned me at the riverbank. The *loa*, Baron Samedi. They knew it was impossible even for a *gangshi* to collect me. Not such a rotted, twisted soul. Even the *loa* couldn't hold me for long." Its mouth twists down into a sick imitation of a petulant child. "You abandoned me, Lili." It raises its arm, the clay solidifying into solid muscle. Making the titan whole again.

"I thought you were gone forever," I repeat.

It rushes forward, faster than I can track. It digs its talons into my stomach again, its fingers stretching out. Poking, prodding me. Pain erupts everywhere. I'm staring once more at the sky, wondering if I can gather myself enough to think about anything...anything else.

If I was born into this world as lightning instead, what bliss. A roar of power. A crash. Light. And then, nothingness. Not pain like this.

"You knew I wasn't gone," Nakheyr hisses. "I was your mistake, Lili. Millennia of endless mistakes. I don't just *disappear,* Lili. Sins don't vanish."

Nakheyr twists its talon again. This time, it throws its other hand into my stomach. My screams are drowned out by the storm. But not to my ears, they just keep going. And going. And...

"Old sins remain," Nakheyr says with a smile.

I grit my teeth and do the unthinkable.

I pull Nakheyr in closer, screaming at the pain. Nakheyr's talons are trapped within me now. It can't use them as a weapon.

I grip my hands around Nakheyr's throat and sink my talons into it. It gurgles and the clay froths and streams over my hands, but my grip only tightens.

"Is this what you wanted? We're one again, Nakheyr. Isn't this what you wanted?"

Pixie dust. Pixie dust. Pixie dust. Keep control.

But the pain's driven me too far now. I stare into Nakheyr's eyes. The mask is cracked along its cheek, clay flaking away. A cup shattered on the floor.

"We're one."

Nakheyr gurgles again, trying desperately to speak.

I squeeze harder. Harder...

I lean in so close I could almost taste Nakheyr's fear if I wanted.

But then another rumble in the earth. And Nakheyr's visage cracks.

A piece of clay flakes away to reveal golden skin beneath. Half of a face with black eyes and soft lips. A single strand of blue-silver hair.

Jo...

I release my grip enough for Nakheyr to relax. They fall back and crack their head against a tree. A big oak, slumping into the riverbank with determined, ancient roots.

Their legs twist at an unnatural angle, following the tree roots.

I sacrifice my own body to keep Nakheyr pinned in place, its hands trapped.

"Jo." Rain drops from my face onto the golem's. The rain tastes like blood. It feels warm. "Jo. Give me Jo back."

"Never," Nakheyr croaks. "Can't you see? I'm the embodiment of all your evils. You can't get rid of me, Lili. Not unless..." It looks to my hands. "You have to end me now. Wipe the slate clean. Pretend I never existed, and enjoy your shiny, new soul."

The pixie dust pounds in my ears, reveling in my bloodlust. I lean my weight forward, watching as Nakheyr gasps and sputters.

But no, as I stare into Jo's eyes... *She's dying too.*

I let go and stagger to my feet. Nakheyr's talons exit with a soft, damp sound. I get up, only to fall again. On my knees at the base of the oak, staring at a clay creature that's half broken. Pottery shattered on the floor. Rain streaming down its face. Jo's eye, trapped, staring back at me with Nakheyr's gray eye on the other side.

I cup my mouth, releasing a silent scream. Shuddering as the rain drips into my wounds. Trying to wash out the evil that, surely, resides inside me no matter what.

"You can't run from your sins, زيبا. Ziba. Beautiful." Nakheyr looks off into the river, staring at the waters, rising steadily over us. "Remember, when the earth was very young. A little girl ran off after some sheep…"

"No," I moan. "No, no, no…"

"And her big brother ran off, looking after her. He was taken by your beauty. Weren't they all? And you were picking your teeth with her bones. You took his sight just for looking at you and sent him running back to his family." Nakheyr smiles. "And remember, a few centuries ago. You knew the secret of a powdered, diamond-wearing queen who preferred the company of women over men. And you'd take bits of her flesh every night in return for keeping her secret. Not in the seductive way, of course. You weren't much for seduction. Even if you give tender kisses to this *gangshi* now…"

Nakheyr draws itself up onto its elbows, staring at me. Half its gaze damning. Half is terrified, unbelieving. "You know what you are, Lili. What you did. Nothing more than a hungry beast pretending it has a soul. Pretending I never existed."

"No…" I try to find my voice, hidden as it is by the storm raging both outside and within me. "No, I won't deny it. I won't deny you."

Nakheyr's smile disappears. "What?"

"I did wrong in the past. I did evil. I'd do even more evil to deny it." I take Nakheyr's hand in mine, staring into both their faces. My old, vile soul. At Jo, who now knows just a fraction of what I was.

"What about the young laborers off the coast? You stuck their corpses outside the homes of their mamas and laughed on the shore…"

I run my fingers along Nakheyr's arm. They flinch at my touch. Jo's eye doesn't leave me. "Nakheyr. Jo. If I'm to do anything good with my power. I must accept the evil I did. I have to acknowledge it."

"Or when…" Nakheyr mutters, losing its ability to speak. The mask slips. "Or remember the fire you set at that town that forgot to pay your tithe on time? You were cooking them, you said… Like they were nothing but…"

I lift its hand and press it softly to my lips. "I won't ask you to forgive me. Only those I hurt can forgive me. In whatever *after* there is, they will judge me, I'm sure." Jo's eye, water falls from it. Soft. Tasting sweet. "I will not deny the sins of my past to build a future where I learn from my wrongs. I promise you that."

I place my hand on Nakheyr's face. The mask gives way with little force, no reluctance. I take it and stare at it. The clay melts, slowly, into my skin.

Never forget. Nakheyr whispers to me. *Never forget your promise.*

I blink my eyes, and it's just Jo and me again. At our normal heights. Covered in mud. Our clothes from before hopelessly shredded. I draw her, trembling, to me.

"I'm sorry you had to bear the bad for me, Jo. That

holding all my bad parts for me...that you turned into something you weren't," I whisper. "I meant what I said. I'll use my power for good from now on. I promise."

Jo turns up to face me.

She draws me closer.

The flood waters keep rising...rising.

"Lili, if we don't leave. We'll get submerged. And I...I can't..."

I stare at Jo's injured legs, trying to pull her to me. But my stomach wound only reopens again, a deep gouge slicing open at my abdomen. Innards peeking through. I groan, holding in my pain.

"I... Jo, I'm so sorry..."

We watch the flood waters rise, holding each other tight.

Then, in the distance, a crack of bright energy. I catch a glimpse of bright-red hair whipping in the wind. Patty Sweeney and the *Kuntilanak* Indah at her side, holding Patty's high heels at the side of the road. Indah holds on to Patty's hand, her eyes shut. Focused.

Giving Patty her monstrous vision to see through the dark.

Patty holds out her hands, guiding the worst of the storm winds and rain away from us, the symbol of the Eye burning brightly in red in the center of her forehead.

Stace follows the makeshift cavalry. They're astride Wilbur's back, the battle boar sprinting toward us over the floods.

"Hyah!" Stace shouts and the boar takes flight, wings expanding, a dramatic shadow and shield against the sky.

Pigs flying. Just end me. This is too ridiculous a way

to get saved.

Stace fights through the flood and heaves at Jo, the muscles in their strong arms tensing. I struggle to help ease Jo over Wilbur's back. Then it's my turn.

Airlifted on the back of a flying battle boar. Glad I didn't turn you into bacon, Wilbur. You're a good friend after all.

Wilbur and Stace lift us gently to the higher road, where Patty and Indah are still guiding the storm. Patty lowers her hands, the symbol of the Eye in her forehead still burning bright, matching the unnatural, ruby color of her eyes with the magic flowing through her.

"I told you not to leave us behind," Patty whispers, clutching me tight. "Thank Goddess you made it."

I hold her tighter. "Thank everything you came for me, friend." I look to everyone. Stace stroking Wilbur's side. Indah wiping us off with blankets from the trunk. *"Friends."*

We hold each other until the storm subsides and the flood waters draw back.

"Who...who brought you here?"

Patty glances back. "He ran all through the storm to get us."

Father Adam Way stumbles up from behind Patty's car. I quite forgot our titanic battle had shredded our clothes until that moment. When you've lived as long as I have, you forget the little things.

Averting his eyes respectfully, Father Adam Way holds a familiar peacoat out to me. And he tosses an overcoat to Jo.

"You dropped this," he mutters. Then, with a smile as

we all limp, slowly, to Patty's car, "You did good, Lili."

I shake my head, staring past the priest, at the shadow that lingers behind him. Beautiful, terrible, bearing a shovel and shades. A full black skirt, a blazer, and top hat, which they take off and tip teasingly at me.

Baron Samedi.

"What I did," I tell them both, "was just the start."

Konprann?

Chapter Twenty-Three

Fin

"I'M SO FUCKING happy to get out of Gamin." Patty lugs her giant pink trunk out of her room, wearing a bright-red woolen jacket and tall, beige boots. Indah slinks out behind her in black fishnets and an oversized sweater embellished with a cutesy skull.

"Me too." Indah plants a gentle kiss on Patty's cheek and Patty goes even redder. But, determined, she turns back to kiss Indah more firmly.

"Ugh, enough, lovebirds. It's bad enough just seeing you two off to the airport." Byron floats in then, trailing after Erik. Erik presses a mechanism on what, at first glance, appears like a regular set of car keys. Except the fob has a glowing purple vial connected to it. And when the car ignition growls in the distance, it sounds like a werewolf.

"We aren't lovebirds?" Erik teases, his brows raised at the ghost.

"We're the *best* lovebirds," Byron shoots back with a kiss and a wink.

We hurry quickly down the halls of the inn, and I help Patty load her and Indah's packages into the back of Erik's flashy hearse-turned-sports-car. Shockingly, there's plenty of room. And the interior glows a faint, futuristic blue.

"It also has Wi-Fi," Erik tells me with a wink.

The trunk opens to reveal black leather seats and a disco ball in the ceiling. The gearshift at the front is a dial fashioned, yet again, of bone.

I turn to Patty, taking a break from loading luggage. "Be careful in New York. I think there's a *garuda* in Queens who owes me some money. Especially Jason. I just *know* that he would get all his money stolen. Damn card shark."

"Card *sharp*, Lili." Patty smirks.

"Yeah, that's what I said...ow..." I try to bend over to lift Patty's pink suitcase, but my stomach wound tears again.

"Someone call for a big, strong botanist?" Stace winks, easily picking the pink suitcase up with only one hand.

Sigh. They're still so cool.

"It's okay darling." Jo wheels up behind me. "You'll be your old, crotchety, buff self soon enough."

I crouch down to hold her tight. She smells like morning coffee and an everything bagel.

Heavens above, I don't think bagels could ever smell better.

Jo and I have been eating only animal products for a while. As a *gangshi*, Jo technically sustains on souls and not flesh, but a good sheep heart does its job well enough.

Sure, we aren't in the prime of our monstrous ability, but we also aren't the old monsters we were.

We even source from the local farm we got Wilbur from. But don't tell Wilbur we said that.

"Grid's bringing over some, ahem, *unique* steak from her grill. For helping solve who drugged Toothpick and all. Turning me back to normal," Jo whispers in my ear. "We can share it."

Unique steak, eh? Maybe a mortal necromancer donated their body for the monstrous cause...

Again, it's a start.

"Grid and Toothpick, I saw them picking out a pothos plant together." Byron cackles. "You know what that means." He pauses, tilting his transparent head. "What would a werewolf-giant-human baby even look like?"

Stace shakes their head at that. They bend down, showing the coin around their neck bearing Sam Hain's image. Apparently, the fairies took a shine to Stace, still probably under the assumption they are secretly a fairy. Fairy amulets. It grants Stace a supernatural eye into our world.

They can be one of us.

"And now, for my suitcase."

Stace bends down and heaves a duffel bag up and into the trunk. The vine tattoos on their arms pulsate with the movement.

I bite my lower lip.

Don't cry. They won't be gone forever. Don't cry... Don't...

"Oh, come here, Lil."

Stace pulls me into a bear hug. And when Patty and

Indah spy them hugging me, they join in right away.

Soon, we're all enveloped in a big, magical, monstrous version of a hug.

Sure, my stomach wound hurts a bit at the pressure, but it'd hurt more to not say goodbye. To watch my friends as they head to New York...to...to...

"I meant it about that card shark *garuda*..." I whimper.

"We know, Lil." Patty pulls back from the hug with a laugh. "We know."

I look into Patty's soft eyes, like honey. Indah's watchful gaze, her dark hair past her shoulders. I watch Stace, the newest of friends, bend down to kiss a saddened, slumping Wilbur's nose.

"I don't say goodbyes," I tell them all, holding Jo's hand in mine for comfort. "How about just... How about..."

"We love you, Lil," Patty tells me. Stace and Indah echo the sentiment.

"I love you too." But the words barely croak past my lips. They hurt as much as they heal.

I watch as they all get into the car, one by one. Erik gets into the driver's seat, setting the GPS for the airport. Soon the flashy car drives away, the exhaust belching out shimmering, unnatural air behind it. It leaves, in its wake, only one ridiculous, floating phantom in Byron. A silver-haired, bagel-eating *gangshi* with her black eyes glimmering with tears. And one, endless immortal.

I stare after them, watching their car disappear in the distance.

"We'll be inside," Jo whispers, kissing my neck softly.

"My love," she calls.

"My heart," I reply, squeezing her hand before she goes.

They all re-enter the Sweeney Inn, leaving me staring into the rising sun. I imagine I can hear all of Gamin, magical, monstrous, unique. I swear I hear the river Lethe, crashing and dragging secrets down to its depths. I smell Detective Ikiaq making his trademark hot cocoa. I imagine that I hear a voice calling to me, whispering my name.

Lili.

Lili. Hear us.

I turn to my side and find Detective Ikiaq leaning down and helping Wilbur perk up by offering the battle boar a little bit of butternut squash soup. In his other hand, he holds a giant, metal flask.

"You never solve a mystery without sustaining horrible injuries, do you, Lili?"

The boar topples over the cup of soup, slurping up bits of mud with its lips.

"It hurts," I tell the detective. He glances at the bandages around my ribs. "No, not just that."

"I know, kid." Detective Ikiaq sighs, staring down at his hands. He takes out a flask of hot cocoa and two cups and pours some melted, gooey chocolate for me.

I take a sip and rest my head on his shoulder.

"Not goodbye," he says, as we watch Gamin wake up, rearing its sleepy, messy, blood-stained head in the distance.

I sigh, staring up at the sun, still shining through the sky. No matter how cloudy.

"Not goodbye," I reply, a secret hidden in my voice.

"Not if we remember."

*

Dreams

WHEN I DREAM, I walk in the Crossroads.

On my one side is emptiness. A vast expanse of nothing.

On my other side, a familiar figure with a full skirt, a top hat, and a cane. They walk by my side, refusing to leave me alone.

"Let me rest," I tell them.

Why? They ask me. *Why give up?*

"I'm not giving up. My adventures are over. You and the *loas* are safe. My work here is done."

Laughter in those eyes. Sparkling. New.

Your work is never done, Lili. Guard your people here in Gamin. Guard the wonderful. The magical. The strange.

"Why should I?"

Why not?

I stare into the expanse as, slowly, things come into view. Faces of my friends, some still living, others gone beyond. Others gone entirely to worlds where even I can't follow.

I stare into the expanse and feel my power coursing through me. Calling to me.

A new soul.

A new beginning.

I clench my fist, and beneath my skin, howling in my

blood, lies the power of my names. Lilit. Lilītu. ki-sikil-lil-la-ke. Lamia. The First. The Dark Maid. Maiden of Desolation. Mother of Anathema...and...

Lili.

Acknowledgements

To the NSP team for being there for me throughout the entire process, especially Elizabeth Coldwell who took a chance on my series of immortals still finding a way to "grow up" despite being ancient.

To the teachers who took a chance on me and my craft, including Mrs. Lori Rogalski, David Kornfeld, and David Strauss. Thank you for believing in my magical stories.

About the Author

Sophie Whittemore is a Dartmouth Film/Digital Arts major with a mom from Indonesia and a dad from Minnesota. They're known for their *Gamin Immortals* series (*Catch Lili Too*) and *Legends of Rahasia* series, specifically, the viral publication *Priestess for the Blind God*. Their writing career kicked off with the whimsical *Impetus Rising* collection, published at age seventeen.

They grew up in Chicago and live a life of thoroughly unexpected adventures and a dash of mayhem: whether that's making video games or short films, scripting for a webcomic, or writing about all the punk-rock antiheroes we should give another chance (and subsequently blogging about them).

Sophie's been featured as a Standout in the *Daily Herald* and makes animated-live-action films on the side. Their queer-gamer film *IRL—In Real Life* won in the Freedom & Unity Young Filmmaker Contest (JAMIE KANZLER AWARDS Second Prize; ADULT: Personal Stories, Third Prize) and was a Semifinalist at the NYC Rainbow Cinema Film Festival.

Their prior works include *A Clock's Work* in a Handersen Publishing magazine, *Blind Man's Bluff* in Parallel Ink, a Staff Writer for AsAm News (covering the comic book convention was a dream), and numerous articles as an HXCampus Dartmouth Correspondent. Ultimately, Sophie lives life with these ideas: 1) live your truth unapologetically and 2) don't make bets with supernatural creatures.

Email

authorsophiawhittemore@gmail.com

Facebook

www.facebook.com/thesophiewhit

Twitter

@thesophiewhit

Website

www.sophiawhittemore.com

Other NSP books by author:

Gamin Immortals series
Catch Lili Too

Connect with NineStar Press

www.ninestarpress.com

www.facebook.com/ninestarpress

www.facebook.com/groups/NineStarNiche

www.twitter.com/ninestarpress

www.ingramcontent.com/pod-product-compliance
Lightning Source LLC
Chambersburg PA
CBHW060226100726

47907CB00003B/526